THE SILVER LINING

The Silver Lining

Rory C. Ford

Rory C. Ford

ACKNOWLEDGEMENTS

TO MY PARENTS, WHO TAUGHT ME TO NEVER DOUBT OR BE AFRAID.

I OWE YOU THE COURAGE TO GET OUT OF MY COMFORT ZONE TIME AND TIME AGAIN.

1

ENNUI

"Ryan ran his hand along my jaw and cupped my chin," Ann said into the microphone. "He leaned closer, ghosting his lips over mine."

"I want to kiss you," I read, my voice husky.

"I moaned and stepped on tiptoes to press my lips on his. He tilted my head and deepened the kiss. My heart was—"

"Cut." Danny's voice suddenly boomed through our headphones, interrupting us. In that short word only, I could hear his annoyance. "I'm sorry, guys, but the computer crashed again, and we lost that last part. Can you start over?"

Ann threw her hands in the air.

I removed the headphones and pushed my glasses to rest on top of my head, before turning to the window separating us from the technical room where Danny was. "Seriously?"

"Yeah, I'm sorry. I don't know what's wrong here."

We had been working on the same chapter of Danny's audiobook for what seemed like hours. But the computer in the recording studio kept switching off at odd times, and we always had to start over. It was getting ridiculous.

"Danny, it's almost five already, and I think Ann and I are both exhausted. Can we call it a day?"

Danny heaved a heavy sigh and ran a hand over his buzzed hair. "Yeah, okay."

Ann whispered a "Thank you" when she walked past me. We left the recording booth and joined Danny and the technician in the computer room.

"Can you come for a few hours tomorrow morning?" Danny asked, sounding apologetic. "I know it's Saturday, but if we can finish this chapter, at least we'll be able to stick to the schedule."

"I'll have to be done by midday," Ann replied a bit curtly. "So, make sure the computer's working so we can wrap it up quickly."

"We'll make it work," Danny assured her. "Let's meet here at nine."

We grabbed our stuff, said goodbye to the team, and left. Outside the studio, Danny suggested going for a drink.

"I can't," Ann replied. "I have to pick up the kids from my in-laws. I'll see you tomorrow."

Danny turned to me. "Steve?"

"Hotel bar?"

"Sure."

Danny and I both lived in San Francisco. We were staying in a hotel in New York for a few days while we were recording Danny's latest novel.

Danny Mitchell was a renowned writer—and incidentally one of my best friends. Five years ago, he had contacted me to record an audiobook for him, and we had bonded very quickly. We had been close ever since. He had been there for me when my ex-wife and I had separated, and I had supported him when he had gone through a severe writer's block last year.

Danny and I shared a taxi to the hotel and went straight to the bar. It was still early, and the place was quiet; a few patrons occupied a table in the corner and were watching reruns of a football game on the large TV screen, and soft rock music was playing in the background. We sat at the counter and ordered two beers.

"What time does Sam land tomorrow?" I asked.

"At two. I'll pick her up after we're done in the studio."

"And how is it, living with her?"

Danny and Sam had moved in together a few months ago, and I hadn't had the chance to see their place since.

Danny smiled. "It's great, mate. Well, her stuff is everywhere, and you know how I am with the mess."

Boy, did I know it. Danny was a control freak, and very house-proud. He had an unbending no-shoes-in-the-house rule, which I had broken a few times, to his indignation.

"You haven't kicked her out yet, so it can't be that bad."

He grinned, his gleaming white teeth contrasting with his dark skin. "Well, there are also a lot of benefits. She's a great cook, she's funny, and she wants to have sex every morning. What more could I ask for?"

"Jeez, I don't need to know about that!" I covered my ears in mock horror, and Danny burst out laughing. "I'm happy for you, Danny. You guys are good together."

"I know, mate." His eyes crinkled. "She's changed my life."

"Oh, that's too cute," I said in a mushy voice.

He shoved me. "Shut up."

I chuckled. It was true, though. Since they had met about a year ago, Danny had been a completely different man. He kept telling me I was the one who cured him of his block, but I was pretty sure Sam had a lot more to do with it than I did.

Sometimes, seeing Danny and Sam together gave me a pang of longing. I was happy for them, of course. I knew Danny had gone through some bad relationships in the past, and he deserved all the good Sam was giving him. But seeing how his eyes brightened whenever he talked about her reminded me that I used to have that with my ex-wife before she showed her true colors.

"There's something I've been meaning to tell you about Sam." Danny's voice wavered, and he stopped talking, looking down at his beer.

I elbowed him gently. "What is it?"

He lifted his head, looked at me for a second, then fished in his coat pocket. He took out a small, red velvet box, opened it, and showed me the diamond ring it contained. I looked from the ring to Danny, then back at the ring.

"So, what do you think?" Danny asked.

I put a hand on my chest. "I love you too, man, and I'm flattered, but I really can't accept."

Danny rolled his eyes.

I grinned. "You're really going to propose?"

"I booked a table at the Bernardin for next Friday."

"That's great, Danny."

Danny's brows knitted. "You don't think it's too soon?"

I shrugged. "You know her better than I do. If you think it's the right time, it must be."

I looked back at the ring. The white gold band held six small sapphires, three on each side of a small, but absolutely gorgeous, diamond. I knew Sam would love it.

"That ring is gorgeous," I said. "If she refuses, can I have it?"

Danny threw his coaster at me, and I caught it, laughing.

"So, the ring and the Bernardin? That has to cost an arm or two, doesn't it?"

"She's worth it." Danny was smiling again. He put the ring back in his coat, then turned to me, his serious face in place. "What about you? Did you hear from Nicole recently?"

A heavy weight dropped in my stomach, as it did every time I heard my ex-wife's name. Danny knew that, but he never shied away from talking about her. He knew me too well and knew I tended to bury all negative thoughts until they caught up with me.

That's what I had done two years ago, after I had found Nicole in our bed with one of her college students. I had moved out of our flat in Seattle, come back to San Francisco, filed for divorce, and hadn't talked about it to anyone. After a few months spent watching me sink into depression, Danny had forced the truth out of me; and only then had I started to recover from the pain.

So now, he always pushed for me to open up and talk. I might act peeved about it, but I was secretly thankful.

"Not since the divorce was finalized," I answered.

"That was what, five months ago?"

"Yeah, pretty much."

"Kind of a record for her, isn't it?"

Yes, it was. Ever since I had filed for divorce, Nicole had been calling or texting me at least once a month, sometimes to try and make me change my mind about the divorce, sometimes to apologize, but mostly to put the blame on me.

She seemed to have had a thousand reasons to cheat on me. She said she had been feeling lonely at that time since I had been traveling a lot for work, or that I hadn't satisfied her sexually. Sometimes she blamed her mid-life crisis—she had been thirty-four at the time. She even once mentioned that my not wanting children had weighed heavily on her and she had needed some release from the stress of it.

I had never answered any of her messages. After a while, I even stopped reading or listening to them.

"And how have you been?" Danny asked.

I shrugged. "Fine."

"Dating anyone?"

"No," I said in a flat voice.

"Have you even tried to meet anyone since Nicole?"

"No," I repeated.

A line appeared between Danny's eyebrows.

I shrugged his concern off. "I'm fine, Danny, I've just been busy, moving back to San Francisco and all. And I've had a lot of work, too." Danny opened his mouth to speak, but I didn't let him and continued, sarcastically, "Oh, and don't forget about my annoying best friend who constantly sends me stuff to proofread."

Danny rolled his eyes. "Don't push it, mate."

"Did you watch the game last night?"

That was a lame attempt at moving away from the topic of dating, and Danny wasn't fooled. He watched me for a few seconds and must have seen the plea in my eyes, because he dropped the subject. It didn't completely leave my mind, though.

***

The following morning, Danny and I arrived at the studio shortly before nine. Ann was still in a mood, but thankfully we had no more technical problems and managed to catch up with the schedule faster than we expected. After we left, Danny met with Sam, and I found myself wandering around the city on my own.

The streets were busy, as they always were in New York City. People were walking briskly, bumping into each other and not apologizing for it. It always surprised me how I could be surrounded by so many people, and yet feel so lonely—like we were all living in separate bubbles, never truly connecting. It was drizzling and a bitterly cold wind was blowing. My damp jeans were sticking uncomfortably to my skin.

The weather perfectly suited my mood because, since last night's conversation with Danny, I had been stuck inside my own head. My thoughts kept drifting back to all the things Nicole had said to me during our divorce. I had sacrificed a lot for her. Three years ago, I had left San Francisco, where I had lived all my life, to move to Seattle when Nicole had found a job at the university there. I had left behind my family, my friends, and the house I had inherited from my aunt. I had even given my cat, Colonel Mustard, to my friend Jeffrey before the move. That had been the hardest thing to do. But Nicole had claimed to have developed an allergy to cat hair, and since we were going to live in an apartment, I had thought that living at Jeffrey's house would be better for Colonel. Also, I was stupidly in love with Nicole at the time, and would have done anything for her.

The only thing I had refused to give up was my job as a voice actor. Nicole had always resented it. She didn't mind it when I was working on documentaries or commercials, or even video games. But when I got into narration, she started to look down on my work—especially when I worked on spicy romance novels. She had insisted I used a pseudonym for that aspect of my job. But over the years, Saul had become more popular than Steve Randall, and I always had the feeling that Nicole was jealous of my fans. It seemed ludicrous to me, since no one—to my knowledge, at least—had ever connected my pseudonym to my real name. But, still, she wanted me to find a *real* job, one that would not shame her.

Sometimes, I couldn't understand why I had stayed with her for so long. But then I remembered how kind and supportive she had been for the first two years of our relationship. She used to encourage me, and my parents had loved her from the start. Her love for me had dimmed down after our marriage and had turned to disinterest after we had moved to Seattle. And I never knew why.

Gosh, I need to stop thinking about her.

My left eye had started twitching, and I pressed my hand to it. In an attempt to take my mind off Nicole, I took out my phone and called my mother.

"Hi, honey," she said when she picked up. "How's New York?"

"Cold and rainy. How's San Francisco?"

"Nice and sunny."

I groaned. "I can't wait to come back. How's the little monster?"

"Don't call your cat that," she chided. "He's a sweet-heart."

I heard a muffled voice in the background. "What was that?" I asked.

My mother chuckled. "Your dad says he's not, but that's just because Colonel peed in his shoes again."

I cringed. I had gotten Colonel back when I had moved back to San Francisco after the divorce. I hadn't planned to take him back, but when I had visited Jeffrey, Colonel had jumped in my arms, letting out heart-wrenching meows. One year apart, and he hadn't forgotten me. For now, he was at my parents' so they could take care of him while I was in New York.

The problem with Colonel was that he was a moody creature. Among other weird things, he had the disgusting habit of peeing in the shoes of the people he disliked. Not that he hated my father per se. But I had always thought he was jealous of him, given that he was very fond of my mother. I had hoped that having him neutered would solve the issue, but it hadn't. My vet concluded that Colonel was just spoiled rotten. Seeing how my mother always cuddled him and gave him treats, the vet was probably right.

"I'm sorry," I said.

"That's fine, honey, I'm used to it by now, I know how to get rid of the smell." I could hear the smile in my mother's voice. "It's your dad's fault, anyway. I keep telling him not to leave his shoes in the living room, but he always does."

I heard my father grumble again, and chuckled. "Thanks again for catsitting him."

"It's no problem, honey, you know I love him."

I did know that. My mother was a real sucker for my cat. Nicole, on the other hand, had never cared for him. I could still remember the day Colonel had peed on one of Nicole's Louboutin shoes. She had thrown a tantrum, tried to kick him, and almost thrown him out of the house. I should have known then that she wasn't a good person. And yet, I stuck with her and punished Colonel instead. I could be such an idiot sometimes.

I closed my eyes and groaned. "I've got to go, mom. I'll be back on Friday to pick him up. Say hi to Dad and tell him to put his shoes away."

"I will, honey. Love you."

We hung up, and I ran a hand through my hair. Fuck. Even on the phone with my mother, my thoughts kept circling back to Nicole.

It occurred to me then that I was becoming bitter. I had to admit it to myself... I was lonely. But the idea of dating anyone scared the hell out of me. I used to love going out and meeting new people, but since the divorce, the idea of chatting up strangers was terrifying. I supposed Nicole had done a fantastic job of crushing my self-esteem.

"And I'm back to that again," I muttered under my breath, kicking myself inwardly.

If I was going to wallow in self-pity, I might as well go back to my hotel room and get drunk. I dragged my feet back to the hotel, feeling sorry for myself, and hating it.

When I arrived at the hotel, there was cheering and laughing coming from the bar. It was packed with people watching a baseball game on TV, and I remembered that the Giants were playing tonight. I might come back downstairs and watch the game after I showered.

As I walked to the elevator, I caught up with a young woman. She was huffing and puffing, struggling to drag a suitcase while keeping her backpack and shoulder bag in place. When she tried to press the button for the elevator, she dropped her room key and sighed. I hurried to pick it up and handed it to her.

"Thanks," she said without looking at me.

"No problem. Do you want some help with your luggage?"

She turned and stared at me for a few seconds, and I fell into the depths of her wide eyes. They were the lightest gray I had ever seen. Her lips curled into a small, lopsided smile and her eyes sparkled with an expression I couldn't read.

She turned back to the elevator. "I'm fine, thanks."

The elevator dinged, and we went in. "Which floor?" I asked.

"Fifteenth."

"We're going in the same direction."

She chuckled. I mentally smacked my forehead at my lame comment. I'd better shut up instead of making a fool of myself.

The doors closed. I leaned my back against the side-wall so I could look at her inconspicuously. She was gorgeous. Her dark hair was cut into a short, boyish style that looked all messy. In the fluorescent light of the elevator, her light gray eyes were almost transparent. She was barely shorter than I was, and her baggy blue jeans and large coat did nothing to hide her slim frame. I looked down at myself, feeling scrubby in my drenched, worn-out jeans and jacket.

She must have felt me staring because she turned to me, raising an eyebrow in question. Trying to ignore the flush creeping up my neck, I asked, "Going on vacation or moving out?"

"Vacation."

I looked down at her bags. "I'm guessing you're not going on a weekend trip?"

She threw me a cheeky smile. "Why would you think that? Too many bags for one weekend?"

"Well..." I dragged the word, feigning thinking about it.

She laughed. "I'm staying for a few months."

"Here in New York?"

"No, I'm only in New York for the weekend. I'm leaving on Monday morning."

There was an unusual rhythm in the way she spoke, almost as though English wasn't her first language.

"How long have you been here?"

She looked at her watch. "Thirty-six hours. I've just arrived from France."

"Oh, you're French?" So, that was it. "Your English is excellent."

"Thanks." She turned to me. "I'm Ally, by the way."

"Steve."

"Steve Randall, right?"

I gaped at her. "Um... Yes? Have we met before?"

I was sure I would have remembered her if we'd had.

Ally smiled a bit sheepishly and turned back towards the doors. "No, we haven't." She shrugged one shoulder. "I recognized your voice."

"You recognized my voice?" I repeated.

She shrugged. "I listen to a lot of audiobooks. It's almost an addiction, really. And you are among my favorite narrators."

Warmth spread through my chest and crept up my face. The elevator felt very small and warm all of a sudden. I hoped I wasn't blushing too violently.

"You always give wonderful performances," she continued. "And you have a beautiful voice."

I had to swallow the ball of emotions that had formed in my throat.

"Thank you," I said quietly, afraid that my voice would shake. I coughed to clear my throat, and trying to keep my voice steady, I asked, "What genre do you listen to?"

"A bit of everything. I tend to go for psychological thrillers, but I also read fantasy novels and comedies, and the occasional non-fiction book."

"No romance?" I asked casually.

"Not anymore, but I used to listen to quite a lot of romance." She threw me a sideway glance. "I know your pseudonym, in case you're wondering."

Well, shit.

"I knew you as Saul," she continued. "Then I listened to a book you narrated under your real name, *Beyond the Sea* I think it was, and I connected the dots."

"You did?"

She chuckled. "It took me about five seconds, to be honest. You have a very specific voice. It has this raspy quality that sets you apart from other male narrators."

I was stunned. I didn't know what to say. I had never been recognized before, and I had to admit it felt validating. I didn't realize I was actually puffing out my chest. It was a good thing that the elevator stopped at that moment, or I would have started preening. We walked down the corridor and Ally stopped in front of room 1512.

"This is me," she said, tipping her head towards the door.

I pointed my thumb toward the elevator and said, "I'm three rooms down."

We looked at each other for a few seconds. I shuffled my feet, not knowing what to say. I didn't want to let her go yet, but couldn't figure out how to tell her. As it turned out, I didn't have to.

"I don't know about you, but I'd love to continue this conversation," she said.

"Me too," I answered without hesitation.

"Do you want to grab something to eat later?"

My heart skipped a beat. "Good idea."

2

PASSION

Ally and I agreed to meet in the corridor at six, and I bounced to my room. My heart was leaping in my chest. I couldn't believe I had asked someone out! Well, technically, Ally had done the asking. But still, I was going out with a beautiful woman for the first time in years! I had a date!

It made me giddy, like a star-struck teenager. And at the same time, I couldn't help but feel like a fool. Ally was exuding so much confidence, it unsettled me. I knew I would have to up my game if I didn't want to pass for an utter idiot tonight. I was trying not to expect anything of the evening. After all, I had no idea if Ally meant for us to go on a date, or just to spend time in someone else's company. Or maybe just wanting to know someone she was a fan of? She did say she liked my work, didn't she?

Also, I hadn't dated anyone in a long time—not since I had met Nicole five years ago. I wasn't sure I remembered the etiquette of dating, and I couldn't help but freak out a bit.

Back in my room, I showered, put on a fresh set of clothes, and tried without success to do my hair. Despite my best effort, the dark strands behind my ears were curling ridiculously. I wished I'd had it cut before coming to New York. Sighing, I hung my glasses on the neck of my sweater, just in case I needed them to read the menu, and gave up trying to look nice.

I got out of my room just in time to see Ally walk out of hers. She had changed into baggy jeans and a blue crew-neck sweater. Her short hair was still a bit wet from the shower, and even messier than it had been before. She had a coat hanging on her arm and a yellow scarf around her neck.

She smiled at me, and again, I was entranced. Her smile was a genuine one, one that lit up her whole face, as though someone had turned on the lights in a dark room.

"Ready?" I asked.

"Starving," she answered.

We walked to an Italian place not too far from the hotel in an awkward silence. I had no clue what to say or how to start a conversation. The streets were still as busy as usual, and cars splashed water on the sidewalk.

We managed to get a table at the restaurant and sat facing each other. The uncomfortable silence stretched for a few minutes, and I was considering going to the restrooms just to escape the situation when Ally started talking.

"So, what are you doing in New York?" she asked.

"I'm recording an audiobook with a colleague."

"So, you don't live here?"

"No, I live in San Francisco."

She tilted her head, looking puzzled. "I don't get it. Aren't there any recording studios in San Francisco?"

I chuckled. "There are. I mostly work from my home studio, but occasionally I have to travel, either here or to Los Angeles. We're doing a duet narration on this book, and my colleague and I wanted to be in the same place to record. She couldn't travel to San Francisco, so we decided to come here."

"We?"

"Me and Danny Mitchell. We're working on his latest novel."

She perked up. "Oh, I know of him. I've read many of his books." Her eyes were gleaming with wonder. "He's quite good. It's been a while since he published any-thing, though, hasn't it?"

I nodded. "He went through a rough patch last year, but he's back on track." As she looked at me with sur-prise, I added, "He and I are close friends."

"Really?" Her smile grew bigger. "What's he like?"

I laughed.

Ally crinkled her nose. "Sorry, I don't mean to pry or sound like a groupie." She waved her hand. "Just ignore me. You don't have to answer."

I grinned. "He's a great guy. He's my best mate, actually. He's staying at the same hotel as us, maybe you'll get to meet him."

"Oh, that would be so cool. How long are you staying here?" she asked.

"Ten days. We started recording on Wednesday. We have another four days of work, then Danny and I fly back to San Francisco."

"What's San Francisco like?"

"It's very different from New York." I shrugged. "I don't really know how to describe the city. I've lived there my whole life, and I don't think I'll ever leave the city again. All my family's there, and I've got a house, and a cat. San Francisco is home to me, I guess."

"You're a cat person, huh?" Ally's face softened. "What's its name?"

"Colonel Mustard."

Ally snorted. "Really? Why? Did he kill a mouse in the library, or something?"

I barked out a laugh. "He's never killed anything in his life, except shoes, I guess. Just today, he peed in my dad's shoes, for about the hundredth time."

"Oh my god! Did he really?"

"Yeah, it's a disgusting habit he has. I don't know why he does that. It's his way of punishing people."

"Has he peed in your shoes?"

"No, he only shreds my underwear."

Ally laughed.

"What about you?" I asked. "You said you're only staying for the weekend?"

She nodded. "I found a cheap car on the Internet, and the seller promised to have it ready for me on Monday. He was kind enough to take care of the DMV for me."

"Where are you going?"

She shrugged. "I'm not sure yet. I'm just going with the wind." She looked out the window for a second. "I think I'll start with the southern states during the winter and early spring, to avoid the cold, then I'll travel north during the summer."

"That's not a short trip," I said. "How long are you planning to stay in the country?"

"I've got a tourist visa for six months."

Six months? She was going to spend six months in a foreign country, all by herself? "I'm sorry if it's none of my business, but don't you have a job?"

She nodded. "I took an unpaid leave of absence."

"And what prompted you to leave for so long?"

Ally shrugged. "Just needed a change of scenery."

"Won't your family miss you? Or a boyfriend?"

She looked down and her shoulders hunched slightly. "No," she said simply.

There was something more to that, I could see it. Her gray eyes had tightened, and her posture had closed up. I didn't push, though, and changed the subject. "So, do you have any plans for tomorrow?"

Ally lifted her head to look at me. "No, I'll just walk around the city."

"I can show you around if you want," I offered before I could second-guess myself.

"Don't you have to work?"

I shook my head. "Not tomorrow. I have nothing to do, and I don't feel like staying in my hotel room all day."

"I'd love to have some company, if you're offering."

I shrugged, trying for nonchalant. "Sure." I stretched out my hand to take my glass of wine, and Ally grabbed the bottle of water at the same time. Our fingers brushed, making my heart leap in my chest. I cleared my throat, trying to hide my reaction. "Is there anything in particular you want to see?"

"Why don't you show me your favorite places?"

"Um, okay," I answered hesitantly. What could I show her? Times Square? The Statue of Liberty? The Empire State Building? That was too run-of-the-mill. Ally seemed like the type of person who wanted unique experiences. My hands started prickling with nerves, and I breathed deeply to try and calm down.

Ally must have felt my rising panic, because she put her hand on mine and said, "Don't overthink it. Anything you show me will be great."

We went back to the hotel late that night. In front of her room, Ally stepped on her tiptoes and kissed me on the cheek, before backing into her room and closing the door quietly.

***

The following day, I woke up before my alarm went off. I bounced out of bed, full of energy, and jumped in the shower. At some point during the night, I had decided that today would be a great day, and for that to happen, I had to be bolder. I used to be a lot of fun when I was younger. I even was a bit over-confident, if not cocky. But I had lost all of that with my marriage and the divorce. I wanted to find that part of me again. I wanted to be myself again.

Ally and I had decided to meet at ten in the morning. But when I arrived at the hotel restaurant for breakfast, she was already sitting at a table, sipping coffee, a notebook in hand. I watched her for a few seconds, not sure whether I should disturb her or not.

Ally must have felt my gaze on her, because she lifted her head. When she saw me, she smiled and waved for me to join her.

"Hey, handsome," she said when I approached her table.

My mouth went dry, and I swallowed thickly. "Good morning," I said in a strained voice.

I could feel my cheeks go red again. What was that about? I had never been a blusher before.

Be bold, Steve.

"Sit with me," Ally said.

"Let me get something to eat first. Do you need anything?"

"Some coffee would be great."

"Black?"

"A lot of milk, no sugar."

I went to the buffet, loaded a tray with breakfast and two cups of coffee, and went back to Ally's table. I sat down and handed her a cup.

"Thanks."

"Hi, mate," said a voice next to me.

I turned my head to find Danny and Sam standing behind me.

"Hi." I stood up and bumped fists with Danny, then hugged Sam. "It's great to see you again, Sam." I turned to the table. "Guys, this is Ally. Ally, this is Samantha—"

"Sam," Sam corrected.

"Sorry, Sam. And this is Danny Mitchell."

Ally's cheeks grew pink. "Hi. It's nice to meet you."

That color was lovely on her cheeks. Sure, she was blushing for my best friend, but I wasn't about to be jealous of Danny.

I turned to Danny. "Ally is one of your biggest fans."

Ally's blush deepened. "Thanks for that, Steve." She turned to Danny. "It's true, though. I love your work. When Steve told me you were both working here at the moment, I got a bit over-excited."

Sam's bark of laughter startled us. "Girl, you and I would get along swimmingly."

Ally chuckled. "I can't wait to listen to your next book."

Danny looked surprised. "Thanks, that means a lot." He smirked, pointing his thumb toward me. "I hope this moron isn't boring you to death."

"Okay, you need to leave now," I said, pushing him away.

Ally chuckled.

Sam took Danny's hand and pulled him away from our table. "Come on, babe, let's leave the lovebirds alone, I'm starving."

Lovebirds? Really?

And there it was, that fucking blush on my face again. I needed to get my emotions under control.

"Ally, it was great meeting you," Danny said. "Steve, see you tomorrow."

"Sure. Bye, guys."

When they had left, I sat back down and looked at Ally. She was still grinning, looking amused.

"He seems like a nice guy," she smirked.

"He's a jerk," I said. "Unfortunately, he's also my best friend."

"And Sam seems really sweet."

I nodded. "She is."

"How long have they been together?"

"About a year. She's been really good for him." I leaned forward and gestured for Ally to do the same, then whispered, "He's going to propose to her in a few days."

Ally's eyes opened wide and her smile grew bigger. "Really?" she whispered back. "That's great. Good for them."

We both leaned back, grinning.

I picked at my yogurt in silence. Out of the corner of my eye, I could see Danny and Sam throwing us glances and laughing. They were sitting at the opposite end of the restaurant, but it was clear they were talking about us. Damn them. I needed to find some new friends.

Ally broke the silence that had settled between us. "What about you?"

I jumped slightly. "What about me?"

"Is there anyone in your life?"

I shook my head and looked down. "I got divorced last year." The words escaped me before I could stop them and I winced.

"Oh, I'm sorry."

I brushed it off with an uncomfortable shrug. I didn't feel like telling her that my ex-wife had cheated on me. I knew that was stupid, but I thought it reflected badly on me. Fortunately, Ally wasn't the prying type.

"And you? Anyone back home?" I asked.

"No."

Somehow, I knew that was all I was going to get. Her shoulders hunched, as if the weight of that simple question was too heavy to carry. I was determined to respect her privacy, the same way she respected mine. But I couldn't help wondering why all the secrets. Why wouldn't she talk about herself? Did something happen to her? I didn't ask, though, and we finished our breakfast in comfortable silence.

We spent the whole day discovering the city together. I showed her some of the unusual places I had found the few times I'd come here, and we ate hot dogs in Central

Park. When my eyes grew tired and I had to put on my glasses, Ally made fun of me.

"You really rock the professor look. It's like your IQ went up a few points."

"Haha," I said dryly. "Don't make fun, I hate having to wear glasses."

"Is it a new thing?"

"Yeah. The perks of getting old."

"Come on, you're not that old."

"I'm getting close to forty."

She snorted. "Well, you don't need to worry. Those glasses make you look really hot."

And I was blushing again. For Pete's sake. "And how not old are you?" I asked.

"Thirty-four."

The same age Nicole was when she cheated on me.

No, don't go there. There's no room for her today.

As the day progressed, I grew more and more comfortable with Ally. We took a few selfies at the Cherry Hill fountain, laughing hard as we sang the theme song of *Friends*, and reenacted the opening credits of the show. I had never met anyone like Ally. She was wild, open, funny, and smart. Her confidence helped me find mine, and I managed to keep the promise I had made to myself that morning. I also took a lot of pride in making her laugh. Every time she smiled, it was as though the sun was breaking through the heavy curtain of clouds. But there was also some darkness in her gray eyes. When we weren't talking and she thought I wasn't looking, her face grew serious and her eyes became heavy with sorrow. I wished she would tell me about her past, but she kept dodging my questions, so I stopped asking.

When it was getting dark, it started drizzling and a chilly wind began to blow, so we decided to go back to the hotel and have a drink at the bar. All the tables were occupied—it was jazz night at the hotel, so most guests had come down to listen to the band. We sat at the counter and ordered two gin and tonics.

And we started talking again. I was amazed at how much Ally and I had to share. Not once today had there been an awkward moment between us. Since the bar was crowded, we had to lean close so we could hear each other over the music and the chatter. The feel of her warm breath on my neck sent shivers down my body.

After our third drink, I was nicely buzzed and completely relaxed. We were sitting facing each other, her left knee between my thighs. With every touch of her leg against my thigh or our hands brushing against each other, my body heated a bit more and my heart thumped a bit faster. My eyes focused on her lips, and I found myself leaning forward unconsciously.

"This book you're working on," Ally said, shaking me out of my trance. "I'm guessing it's a romance novel since Danny Mitchell wrote it?"

I mentally slapped myself and tried to focus on the conversation. "Not really. It's a psychological thriller. Danny wanted to try something new. But he's still Danny, so there's romance in it too."

"Is it hot?" she asked with a cheeky smile.

I snorted. "Like I said, it's still Danny, so of course it's hot. The whole book is a lot darker than what he usually writes, but I think it's great. And yes, there are some really hot scenes."

"I've often wondered, isn't it weird to record a sex scene? Especially when you're in a studio with other actors?"

I chuckled. "I was a bit uncomfortable when I started working on romance novels, but I quickly got used to it."

"Are there words you don't like saying?"

I shook my head. "I don't think of the words when I narrate, I see the story and the characters in it." I leaned closer to her and whispered in her ear, "I like saying 'Fuck', though."

Ally shivered. "And you say it so well," she responded in a low voice.

I leaned back to look at her. "I do?"

She nodded. "I don't usually like hearing swear words in audiobooks, but with that voice of yours, the word is very sexy." She looked contemplative for a second and lowered her eyes, before adding, "A lot of things sound hot when you say them."

Warmth spread through my body. The buzz from the alcohol dimmed, giving room to a different, more sensual kind of buzz.

Ally cleared her throat and took a sip of her drink. "I have to admit," she said, "that if I'd known you were staying in this hotel, I would've stayed somewhere else."

Well, that hurt.

"Really? Why?"

"I didn't want to risk associating a face with the voice. I prefer picturing the characters, instead of the narrator, and I didn't want that to change." Her eyes locked onto mine, her gaze so intense I couldn't look away. "I'm glad I met you, though. You're much hotter than I could ever have imagined."

My brain misfired at her words. I sat there, staring at her, unable to think of a response. I might have groaned.

I stood up, threw a fifty on the counter—not caring that I had already paid for our drinks—took Ally's hand, and dragged her to the elevator. She pushed on the fifteenth-floor button, and as soon as the door closed, I was on her.

I cradled her face in my hands and kissed her as I had never kissed anyone before. I devoured her. Her hands slid down to my waist, and she pulled me against her. I lifted her, pressing her against the wall of the elevator, and she locked her legs behind my back. I let my mouth slide down her jaw and kissed her neck, making her moan.

When the elevator stopped at our floor, I carried her out.

"Your room or mine?" I asked in a hoarse voice.

"Yours is closer," she breathed out.

I put Ally down in front of my door. I fumbled with the key as she slid her hands under my shirt and caressed my back, making me shiver.

Once the door opened, I pushed her inside and against the wall again, letting the door close behind us. She started to undo my shirt as I kissed my way down her neck, her throat, her shoulders. Her soft skin felt like silk under my lips, and I couldn't get enough of her. I reluctantly pulled away so I could take off her sweater, then burrowed my face in her neck again, inhaling her faint, earthy scent that reminded me of spring.

I continued my way down and took off her jeans. I stopped, kneeling in front of her, and looked up at her. The sight was...

"You're beautiful," I whispered.

Ally was without a doubt the most gorgeous woman I had ever been with. She was very fit, all tone and lean muscles. I ran my hand over her long legs, from the ankle to the top of her thighs, and looked up at her.

She was still leaning heavily against the wall, watching me with clouded eyes. Her breath grew heavier and heavier as I kissed her stomach, gently biting her soft skin, and took off her underwear. I lifted one of her legs and rested it on my shoulder. I kissed between her thighs and, slowly, started pleasuring her. Her leg got heavier on my shoulder as I was caressing her. Ally didn't say my name or whimper, but her breathing became more and more labored, until she let out a guttural, wild groan.

I tried not to look too proud of myself when I looked up at her. Her head was resting against the wall, her eyes closed, her chest lifting with her heavy breathing.

I stood. She opened her eyes and looked at me. "You're really good at that," she said in a low voice.

I wasn't. In fact, I was having a hard time believing this was real. I couldn't remember my ex-wife ever having such a reaction to my touch.

I was so surprised that I blurted out, "Did you fake it?"

She snorted. "What? Why would I do that?"

I stood up and shrugged. "I don't know." Because Nicole had.

Ally took my face in her hands and looked me straight in the eyes. "I never fake. About anything. If I tell you that you need to fuck me hard, right now, then it's true."

Heat spread in my body, and I leaned down to kiss her.

"Please tell me you've got a condom," Ally whispered.

"I bought a box yesterday," I whispered back.

She leaned back and smirked. "Um, confident-much?"

I snorted. "Shut up, I was just being hopeful."

I switched off the lights when she started undressing me. I hadn't been comfortable with my body in a long time—sure, I worked out, went running every week, and occasionally played volleyball with Danny—but I wasn't ripped. My soft belly didn't show any abs, and my biceps had been MIA for a few years.

But Ally turned the bedside lights on again. "I want to look at you," she said softly.

"Why?" I said, feeling uneasy.

"Because you're beautiful too."

I laughed, embarrassed. She didn't. Instead, she let her hand roam over my body. And the way she was looking at me, I couldn't help but believe her.

That night, we had sex, talked a bit, had sex again, talked a bit more, and had some more sex. As we talked and loved the night away, she made me feel sexy, smart, funny. She made me feel better than I had felt in a long time. Certainly better than I had ever felt with Nicole in our five years together. Every caress, every compliment, every smile sent a warm wave of comfort through my body, nibbling away my insecurities.

We finally fell asleep in the wee hours of the morning. When I woke up a few hours later, Ally wasn't in bed. I called for her, thinking she might be in the bathroom, but she didn't answer. I sat up and looked around. On the pillow was a flash drive with a Post-it note stuck on it. Two words were written in loopy handwriting. "Watch me".

A feeling of foreboding crept over me. With shaking hands, I switched on my computer and plugged in the flash drive. There was only one video file on it.

"Hey, handsome." Ally's serious, unsmiling face filled the screen. Behind her, I could see the shower curtain of the hotel bathroom. I stopped breathing. "You must be wondering where I am right now. I'm really sorry, but I had to go"

My stomach dropped. She had to go? Did she leave without saying goodbye?

"I'm sorry I left this way. I know this is shitty. The time we spent together was perfect. You gave me everything I needed—comfort, confidence, sweetness..." Her eyes softened, but she still didn't smile. "You know I'm picking up the car and leaving today, and I didn't want things to be weird this morning. I don't usually have casual flings—I'm not even sure that's what this was, to be honest, because it felt anything but casual."

To me either, Ally.

"Anyway, I didn't know how to say goodbye. Actually, I didn't want to say goodbye. So, I just left. I hope you won't be angry for too long. I'll always think very fondly of this weekend with you, and I hope one day, when you stop hating me, you will too. I'll be on the lookout for your next audiobook. Be proud of who you are, Steve, because you're wonderful."

The video cut. With shaking hands, I unplugged the flash drive and closed my laptop. I bowed my head and pressed a hand to my aching heart. I couldn't believe it. She was gone. My heart broke a little.

Maybe more than a little.

I didn't even know her last name.

3

LONGING

Almost two months had gone by since that wonderful weekend in New York, and I still couldn't get Ally out of my mind. I had done everything I could think of to try and find her. I had called the hotel, but they had told me they couldn't disclose customers' personal information. I had searched her name online and on social media, but with only her first name, obviously nothing came up. I had even posted messages on my Twitter and Instagram accounts, asking her to get in touch. A lot of people had commented, but Ally hadn't replied.

The day after Ally had left, when I arrived in the studio, Danny started questioning me about her, but he saw on my face that something must have gone wrong and dropped the subject.

Since then, I had slid back into my old habits, burying myself in work, and not talking about Ally to anyone. It didn't stop me from thinking about her, though. Pretty much all the time.

I had just come back from my morning run on Saturday morning when someone knocked on the door. I opened and found myself face-to-face with a grinning Danny.

"Hey." We bumped fists, and I stepped back to let him in.

Danny hung his coat in the cupboard and took off his shoes.

"What are you doing here?" I asked.

"I need to ask you something. Can we talk?"

I led him into the living room, feeling a bit wary, and sat on the armchair. Danny took a seat on the couch.

"So, what's up?" I asked him.

"You know that Sam agreed to marry me," he said.

"I do recall you mentioning it once or twice, yes. Or maybe a hundred times, I'm not sure," I said, smirking.

"I know, I can't help it," he said, bobbing his head and smiling broadly. "I still can't believe she said yes."

"Yeah, me neither."

He snorted. "Anyway, I need you to be my best man."

I froze, my glass of water halfway to my mouth. "What?" I asked, my voice going ridiculously high.

"You have to be my best man at the wedding."

I put the glass down on the coffee table. "Are you asking or telling?"

His smile grew so big it looked as if his ears would fall off. "What do you think?"

My lips curved into a smile. "Are you serious?"

"Of course. You're my best mate, Steve, I want you by my side."

Warmth spread through my body. I ran a hand through my hair. "I'd be honored."

We looked at each other in a silence heavy with emotions.

I cleared my throat. "Who's going to be maid of honor?"

"Sam's cousin, Jill. I don't know if you remember her, she was at our party on New Year's Eve."

"The tall woman with long red hair?"

He nodded. "She's like a sister to Sam."

"Do you have a date?"

"Not yet. We want to get married in the spring next year, but we don't have a date yet."

We talked for a while about their wedding plans, then Danny's face grew serious.

"Are you ever going to tell me what's wrong?" he asked, taking me by surprise.

The warm feeling left my body in a rush.

"Nothing's wrong," I answered after a second.

"Don't give me that bullshit, Steve, I know there's something going on with you."

I lifted my chin and crossed my arms. "I don't know what you're talking about."

"Yes, you do." His tone was caustic. "You're acting the same way as when Nicole cheated on you."

That made me pause. Was I? I didn't think it was as bad as it had been then, but maybe I didn't have the best perspective.

"I know something happened in New York," Danny continued. "With that girl you met. What was her name again? Anne?"

"Ally," I corrected without thinking.

Danny smirked, and I knew I had given myself away.

My shoulders sagged. "Fuck."

I leaned forward, resting my elbows on my knees, and put my head in my hands. And I told Danny everything. He listened, never interrupting. He kept watching me, his index finger going over his lips. When I stopped talking, he stayed quiet for a while.

"I've tried to find her," I said. "But everything I've done was a dead end. I mean, I don't have much to go on, all I know about her is that she's from France. I don't even know her last name, just Ally."

"And that might not even be her real name," Danny said.

I froze and stared at him. I hadn't even thought of that. I leaned back on the couch and let my head fall back, feeling defeated.

"There might be something you can try…" Danny said slowly. "She said she would listen to your next audiobook. That would be the one we recorded in New York?"

I nodded.

"The book's ready for release now, but if you hurry, you can record a message for her and I'll have the team add it in the final credits."

I stared at Danny for a second. "Would you really add it to your book?"

Danny's eyes softened. "Of course, mate."

"But how would that work?"

Danny ran a hand over his short hair. "Maybe you can ask her to get in touch with you or something."

I kept staring in silence.

"I know it's a long shot," Danny continued. "But who knows, maybe she'll hear it and get in touch with you."

"How would she do that?"

"I don't know." He shrugged. "Twitter?"

"I tried contacting her on Twitter, but she never replied."

"Instagram?"

"Same. Facebook, too. I'm starting to think she doesn't have any social media account. Or she just doesn't follow me."

Danny scratched his head, thinking. "Well, then, maybe you can leave a phone number in the message?"

"And receive calls from fans for the rest of my life?"

"An email address, then."

I shook my head. "I'll be bombarded with emails. You should have seen the number of private messages I got on Twitter when I posted about her."

"Well, don't give your personal email address. You can create one specifically for that, and when you're done, you delete the account."

"I really don't think it's a good idea, Danny." I sighed.

Danny threw his hands in the air. "Stop being a drag, Steve," he said in a clipped voice. "Do you want to see her again, or not?"

I nodded.

"Then quit making excuses and get your head out of your ass."

I stayed silent. I hated it when Danny was right.

Danny sighed. "Think about it, okay?" he said in a softer voice. "What do you have to lose? As I said, it's a long shot, but at least you'll have tried everything."

I still didn't answer. Danny sighed and stood up.

"I've got to go, mate, I'm having lunch at Sam's parents."

I followed him to the door.

Just before leaving, Danny turned to me and said, "You look terrible, Steve. You really scare me when you do that, shutting yourself up. I worry about you." His voice sounded pained. "I wish you trusted me enough to talk to me."

His pinched look made me feel guilty.

"I know, man." I sighed and ran a hand down my face. "I'm really sorry. I do trust you. It's just hard for me to open up since... well, you know."

"Yeah, I do."

"You don't need to worry about me. I'm fine."

"That's the main problem, isn't it? You're just fine. But what will happen when fine isn't good enough?" Danny gave me a bear hug. "Think about what I said." He leaned back. "And call me if you need to talk."

When he was gone, I fell back onto the couch. My cat came out of the laundry room, where he spent most of his days, and joined me in the living room.

Colonel Mustard was a yellowish Maine Coon. He wasn't a beauty—one of his ears was missing the tip, and he had crossed eyes and bowed legs. I had found him about six years ago at the corner of the street, hiding under a garbage can. He had been a scrawny thing with a bloody ear, almost starved to death and covered with fleas. It had been a long struggle to bring him back to life, but he had turned into a huge ball of fur. He wasn't always great company, since he was still scared of almost everything and spent a lot of time hiding in the laundry room or under my bed. But still, he was a presence in the house, and occasionally proved to be very cuddly, especially when I was feeling blue.

In a move that was surprisingly graceful considering his size and weight, Colonel jumped on the couch and settled in my lap, purring. I scratched him behind the ears. Danny's last words kept reeling in my head.

That's the problem, you're just fine.

Was it a problem? I mean, I truly was fine. I had a job I loved, a comfortable house that was all paid for, a loving family, and the best of all best friends. What else could I ask for?

What will happen when fine isn't good enough?

If I was being honest, my life had been on standby since the divorce. I didn't go out much, let alone date anyone. My life was routine, predictable—even slightly boring, I guessed. That uncomfortable feeling I'd had in New York came back to me. I really was lonely and bitter. Maybe Danny was right. It might be time to shake things up a bit.

I looked down at my cat. "What do you think, buddy? Should I try it?"

Colonel purred louder.

"Yes? You think it will work?"

Even more purring.

"You want to meet her, don't you?"

He meowed and started kneading my knees. I took that as a yes. That settled it. I had to give it a try.

It took me a whole day and a forest worth of paper to come up with a message that didn't sound pathetic, or whiny, or angry. But when I started recording, I realized it wouldn't work. It didn't sound like me—like the Steve Ally knew. I had tried to be more spontaneous with her, and this message, that I had spent hours writing, was anything but. So, I ended up not using it and just winging it.

"We met in an elevator on March 3. On March 4, I showed you a side of me that very few people get to see. On March 5, you were gone. I didn't get to say goodbye. I'd love to get to see you again and tell you how much that time meant to me. If you want to get in touch, meet up for coffee with too much milk, or simply get your flash drive back, you can contact me at saul@romance-narration.com."

When the file was ready, I sent it to Danny, asking for his opinion. He called me right away.

"It's good, mate. Honest and straight to the point," he said.

"Do you think she'll like it?" I asked.

"I don't know, I only spoke to her for five minutes. I guess you know her better than I do."

I shook my head. "I really don't know her. And I'm still not convinced this is a good idea."

"I do, Steve. Trust me. Have I ever let you down?"

"No," I answered begrudgingly.

"Exactly. So, can I send it to the team?"

I scratched my head and thought about it for one last second, then said, "Yeah, okay. Let's do it."

I had just hung up when my phone rang again. I looked at the screen and saw Nicole's name. *Fuck.*

I hadn't heard from her in almost eight months. Immediately, my mind came up with a hundred reasons why she would call me after such a long time. It couldn't be about the divorce again, could it? Maybe something had happened to her father? She knew he and I had been close.

I plumped myself on the sofa, took a deep breath, and answered the call.

"What do you want?"

"Hello, Stevie." Nicole's affected voice, although cheerful enough, immediately stirred unpleasant memories in my mind. "I haven't heard from you in a while. How are you? Are you still in Seattle?"

I sighed heavily. "You know I'm not."

"Oh, that's right, you've just moved back to San Francisco, haven't you?"

"Yes." Almost two years ago, but whatever.

"Are you all settled then?" She sounded chirpy, which annoyed me even more.

I tried to tamp down my irritation before answering, "Yes."

"Did you move back to your aunt's house?"

"Yes."

Was I being a jerk? Yes. Did I care? Absolutely not. Not at all. She had made me go through enough in the last two years, I had no more patience for her. Colonel Mustard curled into my lap again, and I plunged my free hand into his thick fur, trying to calm myself down.

"And how is work?" she asked, apparently trying to pry more than one-word answers out of me.

I had to stifle a growl of irritation. I closed my eyes, forcing myself to breathe deeply.

"What do you want, Nicole?" I asked again, my voice crisp.

"There is no need to be aggressive, Stevie, I—"

"Really?" I interrupted. "No need to be aggressive. You cheated on me, forced me to move out of our apartment, ripped me off of everything I owned, and made my life a living hell during our divorce. And you still expect me to be nice?"

"I have apologized several times already, Stevie. It is time you get over it, don't you think?"

Bullshit. Nicole had never apologized. She had never admitted to being the reason we got divorced. Anger welled up in my chest, and I knew I was about to explode. I stood up abruptly, forgetting about my cat still curled in my lap. Colonel jumped on the floor and let out an irritated meow. I breathed slowly, trying to contain all the rage I'd been nurturing against Nicole, and answered in a shaky voice.

"We're divorced now, Nicole, so I guess I'm over it, but it seems you aren't. Why else would you still be calling me?"

"Stevie, I—"

"And I've told you a thousand times, stop calling me Stevie, I hate that." I almost shouted the last words. This call had better end quickly, or I wouldn't be able to control myself.

"I'm sorry," she said softly.

I heard some shuffling on the line, and I suddenly had an image of Nicole walking around in her living room. I remembered that she would always do that when she was on the phone. God, why couldn't I forget about the life we had shared? I closed my eyes, trying to get rid of the image.

"Look, Steve, I've been thinking about you a lot recently, and I—Well, I want to see you."

"Why?"

"I miss you."

I stayed silent.

"I suppose you're right," she continued, her voice shaking lightly. "I haven't had closure yet. I think seeing you will help me. We used to be friends, didn't we?" She paused, as if waiting for an answer—she didn't get one—then continued. "I have to go to Berkeley for a seminar next month. I can stop by your place before I go back to Seattle. What do you think?"

"It's not a good idea," I clipped.

"Can you at least consider it?"

"I've got to go," I said dismissively.

"I'll see you soon, Steve."

I hung up without saying goodbye. I threw my phone on the couch so forcefully that it bounced back and fell on the ground, right next to Colonel, who hissed and ran into the laundry room.

"Great," I muttered. "Thanks a lot, Nicole."

I went after Colonel to try and calm him down before he destroyed all my underwear in revenge. Yep, that had happened before.

4

AGGRAVATION

June

Dear Saul,

I remember the time we spent together. It meant a lot to me too. I'd love to see you again. Here's my number. Call me or text me, any time you want. I can't wait to hear from you.

Xoxo, Ally.

Saul,

Hearing that message from you made me want to be Ally. I can be Ally if that's who you need. Call me and I'll prove to you I can be anyone you want.

Dear Saul,

Loved your message. It was so sweet. I hope you find the person you're looking for. Best of luck,

Maddie.

Leave Ally alone. If she hasn't contacted you yet, maybe it's time you get the message and stop harassing her. Piss off. You don't deserve her.

In the weeks that followed the release of the audiobook, I received a shit-load of emails. Most of them supposedly were from Ally, but they were all very generic so I couldn't be sure—although I would have bet my cat that not one of them was really from her. For one thing, they didn't sound like her. I knew I hadn't spent much time with her, but I thought I would be able to recognize an email from her right away. Also, Ally had never called me by my pseudonym, and yet none of the messages I had received so far were addressed to Steve.

Since it had been Danny's idea to put a message at the end of the book, I had spitefully forwarded all the emails to him, and he had called me a few times, laughing to tears at the absurdity of what was written in some of them. He had particularly loved the insulting emails telling me to shut up and leave Ally alone.

***

Life went on. I recorded books and did some voice-over, I went running twice a week and I started working out a bit more regularly. I spent my evenings sitting on the couch with Colonel, screening through emails from all the fake Allys in the world.

49

And before I knew it, summer had arrived. One evening, I received a text that got me out of my routine.

Nicole: <In SF for the weekend. When can we meet?>

I had forgotten about that. A flash of irritation shot through my chest. Not a *Can we meet*, but *when?* As though she already knew I would cave.

Who was I kidding? Of course, I would cave. I always did when it came to Nicole. I'd never been able to tell her no. For Pete's sake, I'd abandoned my cat for her.

I switched off my phone without answering and went running.

When I turned on my phone again the next day, I had ten text messages and two missed calls from Nicole. By the sound of her voice on my voicemail, she was getting both angry and desperate to talk to me. Despite my frustration with her, I couldn't stop myself from feeling curious about what she had to say.

Before I realized what I was doing, I texted back.

Steve: <Come at five on Saturday. I'll give you one hour.>

I hesitated for one second before sending the message, wondering whether it would be better to meet in a coffee shop instead. But I figured that meeting at my place would give me the upper hand, and the right to kick her out any time I wanted.

And right on time on Saturday, there was a sharp knock on my door. I opened and, for the first time in almost a year, I set eyes on Nicole. I was immediately reminded of why I had loved her all those years ago. She was as beautiful as she had ever been. Petite, curvy, with long blond hair and blue eyes, and that sweet smile that had made me fall over heels for her. Damn it, I still felt a pang of sadness and longing at her sight.

I turned around without saying a word and walked into the living room. I sat in the armchair, and let her find her way to the couch. And I waited. She sat down and started picking lint from her cashmere jumper, her foot jiggling on the floor. I almost felt bad at how nervous she was. But she had asked to see me, so she could make the effort. I wasn't about to make things easy for her. I didn't even look at her.

After a while, Nicole said, "You look well, Steve."

I sighed heavily. "I only have one hour before I have to go. Skip the polite small talk and get straight to the point. What do you want?"

To my total disbelief, Nicole burst into tears. "I'm so sorry, Steve. I've been so stupid. I keep thinking about you, and how good you were to me. I can't believe I made such a mess of everything. I miss you so much." Her voice broke.

I was stunned. Nicole kept on talking for a while, giving me teary apologies. It was the first time she admitted to being in the wrong. She wasn't trying to justify what she had done—she completely owned up to it. And that, more than anything, had me give in.

Against my will, I could feel my armor start to crack a little, and I found myself sitting next to her and putting an arm around her shoulder in an attempt to comfort her. When she leaned into me, my arms went around her on their own accord, and I hugged her. Her touch was both familiar and foreign at the same time. We had been together for five years after all, but she was now part of another life for me.

After a while, she leaned back and wiped her face. A soft meow at our feet made us both look down at my cat.

"Is that Colonel Mustard?" Nicole asked.

"Yes, I got him back when I moved here."

She looked at me, brows knitting. "Wouldn't it have been better to leave him with Jeffrey? I mean, he lived there for a year, he must have had his habits there."

I looked at her, slightly surprised that she cared about Colonel's well-being. She never used to give a damn.

"I visited Jeffrey when I came back to San Francisco," I said. "Colonel jumped on me when he saw me. With the way he was purring, trying to knead my chest and climb me at the same time, I think he was happy to see me. He wouldn't leave my arms, so I didn't have a choice but to take him back." I looked down at Colonel, who was still staring at us from the carpet, his eyes slightly crossed. "He's a lot more confident and cuddly than before, so I think he's fine."

Colonel jumped on the sofa, trying to get close to Nicole. He didn't like it when people cried and considered it his duty to comfort them. But Nicole shooed him away.

"Can't you lock him in another room while I'm here? You know I am allergic to cats."

Oh, that's right. I had forgotten how selfish Nicole could be. Those cracks in my armor? They vanished in a flash. She didn't care at all, did she? The concern I had seen in her eyes wasn't about Colonel's happiness, but about getting long yellow hair on her fancy clothes. She just didn't want him close to her. Because Nicole had never been allergic to cats—she just didn't like them. I had been a fool to think she had changed.

I took Colonel in my arms and went back to sit in the armchair.

"I'm not going to lock him anywhere," I said through gritted teeth. "This is his house, not yours. You can leave any time you want."

Nicole's face closed up. "I still have to talk to you." Her words were clipped, and I understood that her pretend truce was over.

"Then talk."

I kept Colonel in my arms, scratching his lopsided ears. He started kneading my chest with his gigantic front paws. His purrs vibrated in my chest, keeping me centered.

"I need your help, Steve. You know that—that guy, two years ago, the one I—"

"You mean the student you fucked behind my back?" I interrupted.

She grimaced. "You don't need to be so harsh, Steve. You know I don't like it when you curse."

I shrugged. "Just calling a cat a cat."

She glared at me, then cast her eyes down. "Anyway, so—we—"

Hearing Nicole struggle through her words put me even more on edge. I had never heard her be so inarticulate.

She cleared her throat. "We broke up a few months ago. It didn't end very well."

"I'm surprised you stayed with him that long," I bit. "You couldn't find another toy boy to replace him before?"

Nicole's look of shock mixed with contempt made me gloat inside. It was petty, but I felt sort of proud of myself.

"And now," Nicole continued, raising her voice. "He's failing my class, and he decided to blackmail me. He is threatening to tell the faculty about us if I don't give him money."

Despite my feelings—or lack thereof—for Nicole, I had to admit, this was fucked up.

Against my better judgment, I asked her, "And that would be a big deal why, exactly?"

Her face contracted. "I will lose my job."

"But why would they believe him?" I asked.

She winced, keeping her eyes on her hands. She answered so quietly I almost didn't hear her. "He has a video of us."

A video? A *video*? Did I hear that right?

I stayed silent. What could I say to that, really? When she had been with me, Nicole had never wanted to keep the lights on. No matter how often I told her she was beautiful, she never believed me. And yet, she had been comfortable enough with that guy to film herself having sex with him? I shook my head in disbelief.

"That was stupid of me," she said, scrunching up her face.

I let out a humorless snort. "No kidding."

I looked at her. Her face was pink, her eyes red-rimmed, and she was still looking at her hands clasped tightly on her lap.

"I thought you were smart, Nicole. How could you do something so utterly idiotic?"

"I don't know." She started crying again. "I trusted him. We were just having fun, and I never thought he would keep the video, let alone use it to blackmail me."

"How much is he asking for?"

She took in a shaky breath. "Twenty thousand. He says he wants to pay back his student loan."

I gaped at Nicole. Twenty thousand. That was an awful lot of money.

"I still don't know what I have to do with this," I said.

She finally looked up at me. "I don't have that much money, Steve."

It took a few seconds for my brain to catch up, and when it did, it almost imploded with rage. "I'm not giving you money," I scoffed.

"Please, Steve. I could lose my job and my reputation."

"I don't care." I shook my head in disbelief. "We settled the finances when we finalized the divorce. You got more than your share, so deal with it yourself."

"I'll pay you back, I promise." Nicole's voice rose and her eyes grew bigger and shinier.

I rubbed my face. It had been a mistake to see her. I had nothing to give her anymore. She was out of my life and could stay there. And I definitely didn't want to know about the guy she had cheated on me with. My arms were starting to shake, and my vision narrowed. I hadn't felt that furious since the shit-storm that our divorce had been. This meeting had to end before I did something I might regret.

"You know what, I don't need to hear this," I said. "I'm finally getting my life back on track and I don't want you to drag me down again." I stood up and put Colonel back down on the armchair. "You need to go."

"Steve, please. I don't know what else to do." And the waterworks turned on again.

"Asking your ex-husband for money to deal with the mess you created definitely isn't your best idea." I grabbed her by the arm and pulled her up. "Out."

I all but dragged her to the door, and almost pushed her out of the house. I caught a last glimpse of her devastated face before I closed the door behind her. I went straight to the kitchen, poured myself an unhealthy dose of gin, and gulped it down. My hands were still shaking. Was it rage? Disbelief? Indignation? I couldn't tell. But it wasn't sympathy for Nicole.

I needed to go out. I texted Danny.

Me: <Need to get drunk. Want to join me?>

He replied right away.

Danny: <Pick you up in 30.>

Danny really was the best of friends. No questions, only actions. And since he was picking me up, I could drink as much as I wanted to. Precisely the silver lining I needed tonight.

5

OBSESSION

I didn't hear a word from Nicole over the next five weeks. Nor from Ally. The flow of emails was starting to ebb a little. On my Twitter account, on the other hand, the comments kept coming in, to the point where I had to delete my tweet about Ally.

I had plans to celebrate Independence Day at Danny's and Sam's place with a group of friends. I usually didn't go out on a weekday, because going out, drinking, eating too much, or even talking a lot, put a strain on my voice, and it could be hard to record the next day. But celebrating the Fourth of July together was a ritual. And I needed to get out of my house, anyway.

I had promised to help Danny and Sam set everything up before the guests arrived, so I showed up at their house in Bayview in the late afternoon. They lived in a beautiful semi-detached house Danny had bought a few years ago. The house had been in terrible condition, but he had put in a lot of work himself and had managed to transform it into a comfortable family home.

Sam opened the door when I knocked. "Steve!" She hugged me tightly.

Sam might be small and cute, but she was a firecracker. Her long auburn hair was always flying around her face like flames, and her blue eyes were often wide open in excitement. She didn't seem to need to blink as often as most people, which gave her an over-excited look.

"Danny isn't here yet," she said. "He's making groceries. Where y'at?"

I grinned. Since Danny and Sam had gotten together, I had had plenty of time to get used to her Louisiana dialect, but I still couldn't fight a smile every time I heard her talk. She knew it, and she would sometimes overdo it just to make me laugh. In return, I rejoiced in trying to mimic her speech.

I walked into the entry hall and took off my shoes before padding on the hardwood floor of the living room. I still remembered the state it had been in when Danny had bought the house, and the many hours I had spent helping him sand it. Even now, I was still careful not to damage it.

I followed Sam to the kitchen, where she instructed me on what to do and handed me ingredients to make enough canapés to feed an army. I settled on the dining table, while Sam stood in the open-plan kitchen across from me, making a salad and chatting almost non-stop.

After ten minutes of endless babble, she asked out of the blue, "Have you had any news from Ally yet?"

I jumped and dropped a canapé in surprise. It fell face down, spreading hummus on the wooden table. I didn't dare lift my eyes to look at Sam.

"I should have known Danny would tell you about it," I muttered.

She chuckled. "What did you expect? You know how much I love drama."

I rolled my eyes. "Yes, I do."

"So? D'you hear from her?"

I shook my head.

"I'm sorry," Sam said.

I shrugged. "It was a long shot, anyway."

Sam mused. "It's only been two months, she probably hasn't listened to the book yet."

"Yeah, maybe."

I still couldn't look at her, but I could see from the corner of my eyes that she was watching me. Her piercing blue eyes were burning a hole in my skull. I looked up and pointed the spoon I was holding at her.

"That salad isn't going to make itself, you know," I said, trying for jest.

She ignored me. "I invited a few girlfriends tonight. Two of them are single."

I cringed inwardly. I had enough of Danny and my mother meddling in my love life, I didn't need Sam to do it too. "Don't take this the wrong way, Sam, but I don't want to be set up."

I got up, went into the kitchen area, and grabbed everything I needed in the fridge to make guacamole.

"I'm not setting you up. I know you have a lot going on. I'm just saying, it would be understandable if you wanted to take your mind off things and, I don't know, release some pressure." She said the last words making quotation marks with her fingers.

I snorted. "Release some pressure? That's nicely put." I shook my head. "You know I'm not a hookup kind of guy."

She tilted her head. "Isn't that what you had with Ally?"

I stared at Sam, unable to answer. Had it been just a hookup?

I sighed. "I'm not sure. I guess it was a one-night stand, but it didn't feel like it." I looked down at the avocados I had put on the counter and started mashing them. "I don't know. It makes no sense. I should already have gotten over it, shouldn't I?"

Sam shrugged. "It takes time to get over a crush."

My heart skipped a beat at her words, and I looked up. "I don't have a crush," I said.

"Of course you do," Sam replied, sounding way too overjoyed.

"But I don't even know her."

"That doesn't mean you're not allowed to feel something for her." After a few beats of silence, she added, very quietly, "I would know."

I watched her face go pink and felt a smile stretch my lips. "Oh, there's a story there. Tell me."

Sam shook her head. "Okay, but you have to promise you'll never tell Danny about it."

I didn't like the sound of that. "Is it bad?" I asked.

She snorted. "Not really. I don't want Danny to know how bad of a nerd I was, that's all. I don't want to scare him off."

I barked out a laugh. "That's never going to happen."

"Wait until you hear the story." Sam put down her cutlery and turned to me, leaning against the counter. "You know how crazy I can get sometimes."

I huffed, amused. "Crazy's not a strong enough word to describe you."

Sam shoved me, chuckling. "Jerk. Believe me or not, I used to be a lot worse. Danny thinks we met two years ago, but in fact, we met long before that. He published his first book at twenty-four. I was fifteen at the time. A friend gave me a copy for my birthday, and I became obsessed. I started stalking Danny on the Internet. I read all his short stories on Wattpad, watched all his interviews on YouTube, went to all his public readings I could afford to go to."

Sam was now talking very animatedly, waving her hands around. She knocked the bottle of vinegar on the counter and set it right before continuing.

"I even got his autograph one day."

She chuckled, and my smile grew bigger. I was beginning to enjoy her story.

"I was eighteen, then," she said. "I remember being so love struck that I was unable to say a word when I saw him. He asked me my name, and I mumbled something. I still went by Samantha at that time. I spoke so low that he must have heard wrong because he signed *For Samona*."

I burst out laughing.

"I spent all my free time reading his books again and again, and when that wasn't enough anymore, I started writing fanfictions about us."

I burst out laughing. "You did not!"

She chuckled, blushed a little, and lifted a hand to her cheek.

"I did. I think I still have a few of them somewhere."

"Can I read them?"

"My God, no!"

We laughed harder. "I can't believe you're a stalker!"

Sam slapped my arm. "Shut up, I'm not! I wasn't stalking him. I just read his book, and liked it so much that I had to read everything he wrote, and follow him around, and daydream about him, like any normal person would."

I snorted. "There's nothing normal about that, nor about you." I shook my head. "Are you ever going to tell Danny about it?"

"Sure, after the wedding, when he's stuck with me forever." She wiped her eyes. "Anyway, I grew out of my obsession when I was at university. I had so much to do for classes, it distracted me. I didn't take the time to read his books anymore. And I started dating. But when I saw Danny again two years ago, I realized that I had never stopped loving him."

I stiffened at the L word. "You loved him?" I could feel my eyes bulging and my cheeks heating. "How could you? I mean—" I shook my head. "You didn't know him."

Sam shook her head. "I know that. I didn't really love him, but I loved the idea of him. I had made up the perfect man in my head, with all the snippets of information I had gathered, and that was the man I had fallen in love with." She shrugged. "But see, Danny is profoundly honest. You know that better than I do. Danny Mitchell the author, Danny my fiancé, and Danny your friend all are the same person. He's never playing any role."

I nodded. She was right. Danny was the most upstanding person I knew.

"So, he turned out to be exactly as I had imagined," Sam finished.

We stayed silent for a few heartbeats before Sam spoke again. "Maybe that's what you feel for Ally, too. Maybe you only like the idea of her. Maybe if you see her again, you'll realize that she's nothing like you think she is—or that she really is this perfect person you became obsessed with. But you won't know that unless you see her again. Or you could just decide to move on like I did when I was at university."

I stayed silent, not knowing what to say. We heard the front door open and Danny marched in, calling, "Honey, I'm home."

Sam giggled. Danny joined us, put his grocery bags on the kitchen counter, and kissed Sam. Then he turned to me and we bumped fists. "How are you, mate?"

My head was still spinning from Sam's story, so I didn't answer. Danny took two beers from the fridge, cracked them open, and handed me one.

"Thanks for helping us," he said, clapping me on the shoulder.

"Sure."

"I'll get the grill ready." Danny went to the garden through the sliding glass door. Sam gave me a soft smile and followed him. And I went back to making the guacamole, lost in thought.

When the first guests arrived an hour later, everything was ready. Soon, the living room was packed—I couldn't help but cringe when I saw the dirty prints of shoes on the hardwood floor of the living room.

I spent some time catching up with a few friends.

"How's Colonel?" Jeffrey asked.

"Good. Still the same, afraid of everything and hiding in the laundry room."

Jeffrey chuckled. "I have to say, I miss his grumpy face sometimes."

I winced. "I'm sorry I took him from you."

"No need. I would have felt guilty keeping him away from him. I think he's happier with you." He shrugged.

"I've got my own ball of fluff now, anyway, so everything's good."

"You got a cat?"

He shook his head. "Dog. I got a Chow Chow from a shelter."

I snorted. "That must be a big change."

He smirked. "Not so much. He also spends a lot of time sleeping on my dirty laundry."

When one of Jeffrey's friends joined us, I went to the kitchen to grab two beers and went outside. The garden was quieter than the living room. Only a few people had meandered into the garden to smoke or get a whiff of the grilling meat.

I joined Danny at the grill and handed him a beer. "How was your meeting with your agent yesterday?"

"Good." We clinked our bottles and took a sip. "She landed me a contract with a new publishing house," Danny said.

I frowned. "You want to work with a different publisher?"

He poked at the steaks with the tongs and made a face. "My usual publisher won't take my next book."

"Oh right, the young-adult fantasy novel."

I tried hard to sound convinced by the idea, but I didn't quite manage. Danny grinned and punched my shoulder.

"I know you think I should stick to romance. But wait until you read it. It's good, if I may say so myself."

"I never said you should stick to romance. Your thriller was a hit." I pointed at the sizzling meat. "I think they're ready to be flipped."

Danny did so, then took a mouthful of beer.

"So, when will you send it to me?" I asked.

"The book? In a few days, I think. It's almost ready."

"When's the deadline?"

"September."

I winced. "That's going to be tight."

"Why?"

"I have a voice-acting gig for a new cartoon in a few weeks. I have to go to Los Angeles at the end of the month to record." I scratched my head. "It's a bit short-noticed, and I have a few books to record before—"

I was interrupted by someone calling my name. I turned and saw Sam standing next to another woman, gesturing for me to join them in the dining room.

"Oh, for Pete's sake," I groaned.

Danny turned and looked, then laughed. "She told me she would play match-makers tonight."

I grimaced. "I told her I don't want that."

Danny shook his head. "Sorry, mate. Nothing I can do to stop her, you know how she is." We watched Sam gesturing more and more frantically, and Danny patted my shoulder. "You'd better hurry, or she'll come and get you."

I sighed heavily. "Wish me luck."

I put my bottle of beer on the table next to the grill and dragged my feet to the dining room. *This is Sam's friend*, I told myself, *so don't be rude*. I didn't have to go along with her matchmaking scheme, but that didn't mean I had to be an ass. I could at least try and make a good impression. Who knew what could happen, right?

The closer I got to Sam, the more familiar the other woman looked. She was small—even smaller than Sam—with long, strawberry-blond hair, a small button nose, and a heart-shaped mouth. She was looking at me with a hint of recognition. I squinted, trying to place her. It clicked when I saw all the freckles on her fairy-like face and her warm, light brown eyes.

"Maisy?" I asked, astounded.

The woman smiled warmly. "Hi, Steve. It's been too long." Her voice was as high-pitched and girlish as I remembered, as though she hadn't grown out of childhood.

"Wow." I ran a hand through my hair. "How long has it been?"

"I don't know, fifteen years?"

Sam's eyes were moving from me to Maisy, and back. "Do you know each other?" she asked.

I nodded. "We were at Stanford Art together. We and two other friends were roommates during our last year." I gestured between Sam and Maisy. "How come you two know each other?"

"I went back to college ten years ago," Maisy answered. "We had a few classes together."

"So, you gave up Broadway?" I asked her.

She shrugged. "Yes, I grew tired of it. That life is not for me."

"What do you do now?"

"I'm a journalist at the San Francisco Chronicles."

"That's great," I said, smiling.

"Yes, I like it a lot." She put her hand on my forearm. "What about you? I hear you're still acting?"

I nodded. "Voice acting. I mainly do audiobook narration, but I sometimes do some voice-over too."

Maisy gave my forearm a slight squeeze. "You always liked voice acting, even at university."

I got a glimpse of Sam's smug smile before she turned around and went outside. I didn't mind, though. Maisy and I had a lot to catch up on.

We used to be good friends at university. We had most of our classes together and often teamed up to work on projects. During our last year, we even shared an apartment with two other students, Tyron and Chloe. We lost touch shortly after graduation when she went to New York to try and make it on Broadway.

"Do you want a drink?" I offered.

"Sure. Is there wine?"

We went to the kitchen, and I poured a glass of red wine for Maisy, and took another beer from the fridge for me.

"Have you heard from Ty and Chloe recently?" I asked.

"Not much. I know they're still together, living on the East Coast, I think, but that's all."

I leaned against the kitchen counter, facing Maisy. "So, journalism?"

She smiled. "Yeah."

"Do you like it?"

"A lot. More than theater, that's for sure. It's more varied, too. I mostly work in the office, but sometimes I have to travel for a story. It's a bit unpredictable, but also very stable in a way."

Maisy and I spent most of the evening talking together. She was exactly as I remembered—open, easy to talk to, funny.

Around nine o'clock, some of us walked up Bayview Hill to get a glimpse of the fireworks being launched over the Bay. When we came back, Maisy and I sat on the swing bench in the garden. Sam opened some champagne and poured glasses for everyone. I had already drunk a few beers, and the champagne immediately went to my head. I lost all inhibitions and started talking nonstop. I told Maisy all about Ally, her mesmerizing eyes, her bright smile, but also the way she left. Then I talked about Nicole and the divorce.

"I don't get it," Maisy said. "Is Nicole allergic to cats or not?"

I scoffed. "Of course, she isn't."

"So why did you believe her?"

I shrugged. "I was stupid, in love, and very gullible."

"That's sad," Maisy said with a frown. "Poor Colonel."

"Oh, don't worry, he got his revenge. He ruined Nicole's best pair of Louboutin shoes, and he destroyed my favorite underwear."

Maisy giggled. "Good boy. Do you have pictures of him?"

I took out my phone. Maisy snuggled closer, making the bench swing a little, and leaned her head on my shoulder to look at the photos. "He's a cutie."

"Yeah. Not the most gorgeous cat, but I love him to death. I should have realized sooner, you know. When Nicole asked me to give him up, I should have known then what kind of person she was. Instead, I let her lead me around by the nose. I can be so stupid sometimes."

Maisy pressed a finger over my lips. "No, you're not stupid. You're passionate and loving, and maybe a bit blind to people's true colors, but you're not stupid."

That made me pause. Was I blind? Had I been with Ally? Did I draw an idealistic picture of her?

Maisy's hand brushing my cheek took me out of my musings. "Don't belittle yourself, Steve. You're a very sweet person. You always were."

She pressed her small body against me and gently pressed her lips to mine. I leaned back and looked at her with wide eyes, my mouth opening and closing, like a fish out of water. I was lost for words.

Maisy giggled at my expression, then leaned against me and kissed me again. Her lips were soft and warm against mine. The kiss was dizzying—or maybe it was the champagne—and I got caught up in the moment. My hand went to Maisy's hair, and I tilted her head slightly, deepening the kiss.

She doesn't kiss like Ally.

I froze. Why was I thinking of Ally when I was kissing this beautiful woman?

Because she's not who you crave.

I broke the kiss and gently pushed Maisy back. Her brows knitted together, and I cringed. "I'm sorry."

"What's wrong?"

I scooched further from Maisy and wiped my clammy hands on my jeans. I shook my head. "I'm not in a good place right now. I've got a lot on my mind at the moment, with Ally, Nicole and work, and I don't—"

She smiled softly. "You're allowed to have a good time, you know."

I sighed.

Maisy leaned closer and pressed her small body against mine, her hands roaming over my chest. "I'm not looking for anything serious," she said. Her eyes were on my lips. "I just want to spend some time with you."

I sat back, putting some distance between us, and ran a hand over my face. "Can we just be friends for now?" Could I sound any more like a fourteen-year old girl? I wanted to kick myself in the nuts.

I was certain that Maisy would get angry and leave, but she surprised me. She waved a hand and sat up, smiling. "Of course we can. I've missed you as a friend."

I puffed out my cheeks. Maisy started chatting again as if nothing had happened, but my head wasn't in the conversation anymore. I looked around the garden. Most people had left after the fireworks, so it didn't take me long to find Danny. I caught his eyes and sent him a silent plea for help. My skin felt too tight, and I needed a reason to get away. Danny gave a small nod of understanding and walked toward us.

"Sorry to interrupt," he said when he reached us. "Steve, can you help me put the grill in the shed?"

I almost sighed in relief. "Sure." I stood up and turned to Maisy. "I hope you don't mind?"

She waved her hand in a casual gesture. "Go ahead."

I followed Danny to the grill, and together we lifted it and carried it to the shed. When we were done putting it away, Danny turned to me.

"What was that about? You seemed to be having a good time with Maisy. What happened?"

"Nothing." I shook my head. "Does Sam need help with cleaning up?" I started walking toward the door.

Unfortunately, Danny wouldn't let me wriggle out of it so easily. He grabbed my arm to stop me and forced me to turn around. "Talk to me. What happened?"

I groaned. "We kissed, okay? Well, Maisy kissed me."

"And?"

"And nothing."

A line appeared between Danny's eyebrows. "What do you mean, 'nothing'?"

"Nothing. I told her it wouldn't happen."

Danny's brows furrowed even more. "Why?"

"I don't know," I almost shouted. I rubbed my face with my hands and took a deep breath. "I don't know," I repeated in a calmer voice. "It didn't feel right."

"Are you okay, Steve?" Danny asked. I could see the concern in his chocolate eyes.

"Yeah. I'm tired, and I had too much to drink. I'm going to head home. I've got a lot of work to do tomorrow."

"Okay, mate." He squeezed my shoulder and let me go. "You didn't ride your scooter, I hope?"

I shook my head. "I took an Uber."

"Don't forget our next volleyball game," Danny reminded me.

Every few weeks, Danny, Sam and I met with a few friends to play volleyball and have a barbecue on the beach.

"When is it again?" I asked.

"In two weeks."

I shook my head. "I don't think I'll have the time, that will be right before I leave for Los Angeles."

"Well, make the time, I need to win this one. I can't stand Jeffrey's smug face whenever he wins. I need to kick his ass."

I chuckled. "I'll try."

"Text me when you get home?"

"Sure."

We hugged, slapping each other's back as we always did, then left the shed. I said goodbye to Sam and Maisy, and called an Uber. On the drive home, I kept revisiting the kiss Maisy and I had shared. I couldn't understand my reaction. Why had I kissed her back? And why, *why* had I pushed her away? My head was a clusterfuck of emotions that I couldn't process right now.

All I knew, was that the image of Ally had popped into my head during that kiss, and that definitely wasn't right. No matter what I did, or who I met, Ally was always at the back of my mind. I hated how obsessed I had become with her. Ally was in my every thought. That had to change, hadn't it? It couldn't be healthy. But I wasn't ready to let her go yet.

6

WORRY

"Will you shut up, please?" I said, looking down at the carrier I was holding. I was trying to talk to Jamie, the vet assistant at the clinic, and we couldn't hear each other over Colonel's meows. He was acting as though we were ripping off his claws.

"Sorry," I said, turning to Jamie. "He's a real drama queen."

He smiled gently. "He still doesn't like coming here, does he?"

Jamie and Dr. Swanson, the vet at the clinic, knew my cat very well. When I had found Colonel in the streets six years ago, I had come here with him, and both of them had helped me bring him back to life. Since then, I often came for check-ups, and it was always the same circus—Colonel would cry and meow non-stop, he would try and escape, scratching Jamie's hands in the process, then we would go back home, and he would refuse to come out of the laundry room for three days.

"So, what's wrong with him?" Jamie asked. "You said on the phone that he's not eating enough?"

"Yeah, he hasn't eaten since last night."

I told Jamie how I had found Colonel this morning, curled up in the laundry basket, looking miserable. When he had seen me, he had barely lifted his head and had let out a pitiful meow.

"Hey, buddy, what's wrong?" I'd asked.

All I got as an answer was another plaintive sound. I knelt to scratch his favorite spot under his chin, but he hissed and pulled away. Locking him securely in my arms never was an easy feat, considering his size and strength, but I managed, and gently rubbed my fingers under his chin. And I felt it. There was a lump near his jaw, the size of a small nut. When I tried to look at it, Colonel hissed again and wriggled out of my arms, so I let him go.

I tried to feed him blueberries, his favorite treat, but he turned his nose up at them and my chest tightened with panic.

So I had called the clinic and explained the symptoms, and they had given me an appointment right away— which was not reassuring in the least since they usually didn't have any openings for a few days.

"Dr. Swanson is waiting for you," Jamie said.

When we were in the surgery, it took Jamie and me to get Colonel out of his carrier and to maintain him in place, so Dr. Swanson could examine him. She didn't say anything while she examined his chin, listening to me telling the whole story again.

"I'm going to take a sample," she said after a few minutes. "Can you hold him still?"

Jamie and I once again wrestled with my cat, locking his head so he wouldn't move during the biopsy. The vet took time examining the sample in the microscope. When she sat up and turned to me, her brows were furrowed in worry.

"I can't say for certain what it is without further analysis. It's not an abscess, but it could be a small tumor or a fibrosarcoma."

My heart sank into my shoes. I knew my face had gone pale, because Dr. Swanson smiled gently.

"I know it sounds worrying, and I'm not going to lie, it can be. A fibrosarcoma can be very serious. But I don't think that's what we have here. It might only be a mast cell tumor, which is benign."

I swallowed the lump in my throat and asked, "How can we be sure?"

"He'll need surgery, so we can remove the lump, and I'll send it to the lab for further analysis, so we know for certain what we're facing."

I nodded. Colonel meowed miserably on the table. "What happens then?"

"If it's a fibrosarcoma, he might need radiotherapy. But we'll cross that bridge when the time comes. For now, let's focus on getting rid of the lump, so he can start eating again." The vet looked at me sternly. "The surgery and the lab analysis are quite expensive, so you might want to think about it."

I looked down at my cat. My big, fluffy buddy. His cross-eyed stare was fixated on me, with that heart-wrenching look he often had. Colonel had mastered the art of looking both affectionate and sorrowful at the same time. My heart squeezed painfully. I had already let him down once when I had moved to Seattle for Nicole. I wasn't about to do that again.

I looked up at Dr. Swanson. "I don't need to think about it. We'll do what we have to do."

The vet went to her computer. "Okay, let's see when we can plan the surgery. I'd say the sooner, the better, considering that he's not eating much. Would next Monday work for you?"

I shook my head. "I'll be away all week for work."

Dr. Swanson mused and scrolled down her screen for a moment. "I can squeeze him in tomorrow morning. I'll have to do it very early, though, so it might be best if he stays here for the night. Would that work?"

"Sure." My fingers tensed in Colonel's fur. I hated the idea of going home without him, but I had no choice. "When can I get him back?"

"He should be fit to go home in the afternoon. Call me in the morning and we'll see how he's doing."

I left the clinic feeling guilty, my ears still ringing with the heart-breaking cries Colonel had made when I left him behind.

When I got back home, the place felt terribly empty. No meow to welcome me, no flash of yellow fur toward the laundry room. The blueberries I had tried to coax into him were still in his bowl, getting all shriveled up.

I sighed. I didn't want to stay here tonight.

I took out my phone and texted Danny.

Me: <Is the game still on tonight?>

Danny: <Yep. Want to join us?>

Tonight was our monthly volleyball game. I hadn't planned to go, but maybe a night out would do me some good.

Me: <Sure. Ocean Beach?>

Danny: <Be there at 6.>

Ocean Beach wasn't too far from my house, so I decided to walk there. There was a game on already. I looked around and spotted Sam near the fire. Maisy was there too, sitting next to her. I almost backed away, afraid things would be weird with Maisy. We hadn't talked since July 4. But before I could turn around, Sam saw me and waved. I sighed and joined them.

I hugged Sam, then turned to Maisy and smiled. "Maisy, it's good to see you again."

She smiled and hugged me.

"How come you decided to join us?" Sam asked. "Danny couldn't believe you agreed to come. It's been so long since you came to play."

I shrugged. I took a beer from the cooler on the picnic table and sat down next to Sam. "I needed to go out."

Sam looked at me shrewdly. "Is everything okay?"

I looked at the game for a while before answering. "Colonel is spending the night at the vet clinic. He's having surgery tomorrow morning." I gulped down half of my beer before telling Sam and Maisy about the appointment at the vet. "I can't figure out what I'm going to do with him next week," I said. "He's going to need care, but I have to go to Los Angeles, and my parents are on vacation."

"Can't you take him with you?" Maisy asked.

I shook my head. "The hotel doesn't allow pets. And he hates flying, anyway. Stressing him so soon after surgery wouldn't be good."

"What about Jeffrey?" Sam suggested. "He knows him well, I'm sure he would agree to keep him for a week."

"Jeffrey has a dog now, so that won't work. You know how Colonel is with other animals." I scrubbed my face. "I don't know what to do."

Sam looked at me sadly. "I'm sorry we can't take him in."

I shook my head. I knew that Sam was allergic to cats. Every time she came by my house, she had to take some antihistamine or her eyes would get all red and puffy.

"I can help if you want," Maisy piped up.

I turned to her. "You would do that?"

"Of course." She shrugged. "I love cats. I used to have one when I was a teen."

"But I have to warn you, he can be bad-tempered, and he destroys things."

"And he pees in people's shoes, I remember," Maisy said. "Don't worry, I'll keep my shoes in the closet, and an eye on him."

I chuckled as a wave of relief swept over me. "Thank you."

Maisy and I agreed that I would drop Colonel off at her place on Sunday evening, as I had to leave early on Monday.

The volleyball game ended, and Danny waved for me to join him for the next game. Playing ball in the sand— and the few beers I drank—helped me relax, and I even managed to have fun. I spent the rest of the evening chatting with Maisy. I shouldn't have worried that she would resent me after the disastrous night on Independence Day. She was as cheerful as always.

On my way home later that night, I realized that, for the first time in a long while, I hadn't thought of Ally at all. My cat's health scare had managed to take me back to the present for a while. And that felt good. Maybe I should just come to terms with the idea of never seeing Ally again. The audiobook had been released for three months, and I still hadn't heard from her. So perhaps it was time for me to move on.

***

I called the clinic during my morning break the following day. Colonel had already woken up from surgery and seemed to be doing fine, so I could go and get him in the late afternoon. A knot untied in my chest at the thought of having my cat back home today.

Time couldn't go fast enough. At four o'clock, I went to the clinic. I could hear Colonel yowling his head off even before I opened the door. Jamie sighed in relief when he saw me.

"He hasn't shut up since he woke up," he said with a grimace.

I cringed. "I'm sorry, he's a real crybaby sometimes."

Jamie snorted. "Yeah, we noticed. I'll need a bubble bath and a bottle of wine to unwind tonight."

I laughed and Jamie took me to my cat. As soon as Colonel saw me, he stopped crying and started purring loudly, making me melt on the spot.

"Everything went fine," Dr. Swanson said. She showed me how to clean the stitches on his chin and gave me some painkillers for the next few days. "You'll need to come back with him for a check-up in ten days. Call me if there's any problem in the meantime."

Back home, I opened the carrier, and Colonel dashed to the kitchen and started moving his bowl around.

"Well, someone's feeling a lot better." I chuckled.

I gave him some biscuits and a few blueberries, and sat with him while he emptied his bowl. Then I picked him up and hugged him tightly.

"I missed you, buddy."

We spent the night together on the couch watching TV like an old couple. Danny often teased me about that—why would I need a girlfriend, when I had a cat? Maybe he had a point. Colonel and I were doing fine together. Weren't we? After all, Colonel's purrs were the best comfort ever.

7

DISILLUSION

Dropping Colonel off at Maisy's apartment wasn't easy. With the look he gave me, I could almost hear him whine, "How can you leave me?" He had a knack for making me feel guilty. He didn't give me that look anymore when I left him with my parents—he knew he would be spoiled rotten by my mother. But leaving him with a stranger? How dare I?

I couldn't help but feel anxious, both about his health and his behavior. What if he wrecked Maisy's place? Or gave her shoes the same treatment he gave my dad's? He was a very moody creature, after all. Well, maybe everything would be fine. At least, that was what Maisy kept telling me.

on Monday evening, I left the recording studio in Los Angeles at five, and immediately texted Maisy to check up on Colonel. I had just finished my first day of work, and I was spent. I loved voice-acting, and it was a nice change from narration, but it was taxing. One of the aspects I loved the most about book narration and working alone from home was handling my own schedule.

Back in my hotel room, I kicked off my shoes, ordered room service, and took a shower. When I came out of the bathroom, Maisy had texted back.

Maisy: <Colonel is fine, stitches are clean, and he's eating like a horse.>

I smiled and sat on the bed. My phone pinged again. I opened the message to see a picture of Maisy sitting on the floor, next to her laundry basket, where Colonel was curled up with his favorite mouse toy between his paws. My heart pinched. I shook my head. It was ridiculous how much I missed my stupid cat.

My heart pinched a bit more at the look on Maisy's face. She seemed so happy to have him with her. I was sure she was taking good care of him. Not everyone understood my cat—let alone loved him—but I could see that she did. And that made me miss her too.

I froze when that thought crossed my mind. Where did that come from? I didn't miss Maisy. Did I? Sure, she was nice, gorgeous, and really sweet to take care of my cat, but she was just being a good friend. On the other hand, she had kissed me before, hadn't she?

Yes, and that made you think of Ally, didn't it?

I dropped my phone on the bedspread and lay down on the bed groaning, my hands on my face. I was too tired to make any sense of my confusing feelings.

Room service arrived shortly after. I ate, then powered up my computer to check my emails and do some work, but I was too exhausted and couldn't focus. Instead, I opened my Ally inbox. I hadn't checked it in a while, and there were a good dozen unread emails. I opened them all, one after the other, deleting them quickly since it was clear they were not from Ally. When I opened the last one, though, my heart skipped a beat.

Hi Steve,

I heard your message in Danny's book. It was a surprise, but to be honest, I was thrilled. I have thought about you a lot lately. I hate the way I left you in New York. I wish I had woken you up to say goodbye. I really want to see you again and make it up to you. Please text me.

Ally.

My stomach flip-flopped. I read the email a few times, reading between the lines, trying to find clues as to whether it really was Ally or just another prank. I couldn't be sure. With shaking hands, I picked up my phone and texted the number in the email.

Me: <Hi Ally. Just read your email. I'm glad to hear from you. I hope you're well. Steve.>

And I sat there, staring at my phone, during the ten minutes it took maybe-Ally to text back. My heart was beating so fast that I thought it would leap out of my chest and start bouncing around the room. But when my phone pinged, it fell in my stomach.

Maybe-Ally: <I'm great. In the Everglades at the moment, it's beautiful.>

And my heart just stopped beating altogether. The Everglades? That didn't make sense. Ally had told me she would spend the summer months in the northern states, to avoid the heat. I asked her about it.

Maybe-Ally: <Change of plans, I enjoy the sun too much.>

That made sense, didn't it?

Me: <I've never been to the Everglades. Do you have a picture?>

She sent me a photo of her bare feet on an airboat, with the wilderness as a background. Not conclusive proof it was her—was I supposed to remember what her feet looked like? Was it another prankster? I still didn't understand why some people would do that. Who would have so much spare time that they would get a kick out of pretending to be someone else? It was both stupid and cruel.

Anyway, until I was sure, I would keep texting. And I would stay cautious. One never knows, right?

Me: <Seen any alligator yet?>

Maybe-Ally: <I hope I won't! That would be way too scary.>

Me: <Watch out for pythons, too.>

She sent a smiling face emoji.

***

The rest of the week in Los Angeles passed in a blur of recordings, business dinners and contract negotiations. Maisy sent me daily news of Colonel. We even FaceTimed once, so I could speak to my cat. When Maisy had suggested it, I had thought it was stupid. But when Colonel's long, thick whiskers brushed the camera of the phone, my chest hurt, I missed him so much.

I also texted Ally every day. From what I gathered, it seemed she was traveling west, but she wouldn't be anywhere near San Francisco for a long time. That didn't matter; just being in touch with her again was thrilling— if it was her, I kept reminding myself. She did know a lot about our time in New York, but the downer Dan in me couldn't stop doubting. Still, the short texts we exchanged were the highlights of my days.

I flew back to San Francisco on Friday evening and went straight to Maisy's apartment. No sooner had I walked into her living room that Colonel came running toward me and crashed into my legs. I leaned down and picked him up, hugging and kissing him.

"Hey, buddy," I cooed.

Purr.

"Yeah, I missed you too."

Purr.

"Have you been a good boy?"

Maisy chuckled. "He's been great."

"Really?"

Colonel meowed in agreement.

I turned to Maisy. "I can't thank you enough for taking care of him."

"Anytime."

I smiled.

"I mean it," Maisy said, putting a hand on my arm. "I'll babysit him anytime you need. I'm here for you if you need help. Especially if it involves this big guy." She patted Colonel's head. "I miss having a cat in the house."

"I'd like to take you out to dinner, as a thank you for catsitting."

Maisy smiled. "That's fair. Give me five minutes to get ready."

I let Colonel go and walked around the room, looking at Maisy's pictures on the bookcase. There were a lot of photos of herself with her family and her friends. I stopped at the far end of the bookcase when I realized I was looking at my own face. There was a large picture of Maisy and me with Chloe and Tyron, our roommates during our last year at university.

I picked up the frame and looked at the photo closely. The four of us were huddled together on the tiny, dingy couch we used to have. Chloe and Tyron—who were now married, as far as I knew—were holding hands and smiling at the camera. I had my arm around Maisy's shoulders, and Maisy was looking up at me, laughing.

I could still remember the day that photo had been taken. It had been shortly before graduation, and we had celebrated ahead of time. We'd had a lot of fun trying to set the timer on the camera, and it had taken a good dozen tries before we had gotten a good picture. I smiled fondly at the memory.

"I found that picture in a box when I moved back here," Maisy said behind me, making me jump in surprise.

I turned around. I had been lost in the memory and hadn't noticed she was standing next to me. I put the frame back on the shelf.

"I can't believe you kept that."

"Of course, I did. That year was one of the best of my life."

I smiled. "Yeah, we had a lot of fun." I turned to her. "Where do you want to go?"

"What about Japanese?" she said. "I'm craving sushi."

I didn't like sushi that much, but this dinner was for her, so I didn't say anything. We walked to a Japanese restaurant close to Maisy's place. It was a modern and casual place. The waiter took us to a table near the open kitchen.

"You look good, Steve," Maisy said when we were seated. "You seem more relaxed. I gather things went well in Los Angeles?"

I nodded. "They did. I've already signed a contract for next season."

"That's fantastic!" She studied my face and mused. "But that's not it, there's something else, I can tell."

My face heated, and I looked down at the menu.

"Oh my god! You heard from Ally, didn't you?"

I cringed. "Yeah."

"That's great, Steve! And about time, too. How is she?"

I waved a hand. "We don't need to talk about it."

Maisy put her hand on my arm. "Please, I want to know."

I looked up and studied Maisy's face. She seemed genuinely glad for me.

"Ally seems fine," I said. "We've been texting for a few days. She's just left Florida and is going to Louisiana."

"Are you going to see her again?" Maisy asked.

I shrugged. "I don't know. I'd love to. We had a great time in New York, and I'd love to see how things would be after all this time. But I'm not sure she'll want to."

"I'm glad for you."

"What about you?" I asked. "Is there anyone special in your life?"

Maisy hummed pensively. "Not really, I don't think."

I grinned and gave her arm a nudge. "I feel like there's a story there. Tell me."

Maisy cast her eyes down again and her cheeks grew pink. "It's nothing. Just an old friend I bumped into recently. But he's not interested."

My smile faded and my stomach dropped to my knees. Well, I had put my foot in it again, now, hadn't I? I could be a real jerk sometimes. Maisy was sweet, and I didn't want to hurt her.

"I'm sorry," I said in a low voice. I put my hand on hers. "I'm just really confused right now. I'm glad we can be friends again, though."

Maisy looked up, smiling. "Me too, Steve." She squeezed my hand before pulling away and leaning back. Her soft smile turned into a cheeky grin. "At least your cat loves me."

I chuckled and picked up the menu again to try and hide my discomfort.

After dinner, we went back to Maisy's apartment. I started gathering Colonel's toys when Maisy asked, "Do you want to stay and watch a film?"

I hesitated, worried that things would get weird again.

"I have popcorn," she added with a smile. "We can snuggle on the couch and stuff ourselves."

Just like we used to do at university.

"You know, for old times' sake," she added.

I smiled back and agreed.

We sat on the couch, the bowl of popcorn between us, and cold beers on the coffee table. Colonel crawled out from under the bookcase and snuggled next to me. Maisy browsed the new additions on Netflix, and we settled on a psychological thriller.

Halfway through the film, Maisy took the almost empty bowl of popcorn and put it on the coffee table. Then she tucked her feet under her thighs and leaned against me. She put her head on my shoulder.

I sat frozen for a while, lost as to what to say or do. There used to be a time when I wouldn't have thought twice about it, and would have tucked her even closer. When we were roommates, we often snuggled together on the couch. It was clear between us that it never meant anything—just two friends spending time together and criticizing films. We used to joke that it was the best kind of homework, us being drama students. But things were different now, more complicated. I didn't want to give Maisy false hopes, but at the same time, I craved human touch and the closeness between us.

Taking a deep breath, I slid my arm around Maisy's waist. Her hand moved up my thigh, along my hip, and under my t-shirt. Her touch sent a shiver through my body, and I squirmed.

Maisy giggled and lifted her head. "That's right, I remember, you're very ticklish."

I hummed. Yes, I was ticklish. But also, her warm hand felt nice on my bare stomach. I couldn't tell her that, though, so I stayed silent. We didn't move until the film ended.

***

Over the next few days, I continued texting Ally regularly—I couldn't help myself from calling her Ally in my head, since I was more and more convinced it was her. I had asked to talk on the phone, but she had refused, arguing that she preferred waiting until we were face-to-face to talk. I couldn't deny that I was disappointed. First, because I wanted to be one hundred percent certain it was Ally. But also, I was dying to hear her voice again— or even see her face, if she had agreed to FaceTime.

I didn't make too much of it though, because Ally had valued her privacy during our weekend in New York, and I respected that about her. I was more than willing to do that for her.

I went back to the clinic on Monday with Colonel, and Dr. Swanson removed the stitches. The scar was clean, the fur had already started growing back.

"I received the lab results," the vet said.

My heart skipped a beat.

"It's good news." She smiled. "It was a mast cell tumor, so now that it's been removed, there's nothing to worry about. Colonel will be fine. He might get other tumors, so make sure you give him a complete check-up from time to time, but that's all you need to worry about."

The knot that had taken place in my stomach since Colonel's surgery came untied at her words. Things were finally brightening up. When I arrived home, I texted Maisy.

Me: <Back from the vet. Colonel will be fine.>

Maisy: <Yay!>

Maisy: <Any news from Ally?>

Me: <We're still texting.>

She replied with a happy face emoji.

I felt cheerful the entire week, chatting with Ally and Maisy, getting back to my regular work schedule, having drinks with Danny, and cuddling with Colonel every night on the couch.

Things started crumbling down about two weeks later.

I knew that Ally had arrived in New Orleans two days earlier. I had visited the city a few times when I was at university—I had mainly been there for Mardi Gras— and I had loved it. And last summer, I had accompanied Danny and Sam when they were visiting Sam's family near Baton Rouge. I had seen wonderful places, and the people were lovely. I was looking forward to going back there. So of course, I wanted to know what Ally thought of the place.

Me: <Hi. How's Louisiana treating you?>

Maybe-Ally: <Hey. I'm moving on soon, I hate this place.>

I frowned. It wasn't like her to be so blunt. Had something gone wrong?

Me: <What happened?>

Maybe-Ally: <Nothing, it's just not a place for me.>

Another text came in.

Maybe-Ally: <There are parties everywhere and people are drunk all the time. Also, I can't understand what people are saying. What's up with that dialect? And the accent? They can hear I'm not from here, but they're not even trying to speak normally.>

My eyes grew wider. I couldn't believe what I was reading. I had never pegged Ally as intolerant, but that text was so full of prejudice that I had to read it twice to make sure I wasn't misunderstanding. My knee started bouncing.

Me: <I'm sorry you don't like it. I think it's a great place.>

I didn't want to sour things between us, so I changed the topic.

Me: <I never asked, what did you think of Danny's book?>

Maybe-Ally: <Not his best work.>

My brows lifted in disbelief. Not his best work? It was Danny's first try at a thriller, and already it was on the New York Times best-seller list.

I stood up and started pacing the room.

Me: <Why?>

Maybe-Ally: <He should stick to romance. Thrillers are more complex to write than romance, and I don't think he's up to it.>

Jesus, was I really reading this? Who had swapped my lovely Ally with this obnoxious person?

Maybe-Ally: <It's lucky you narrated it, you managed to bring some value to the story.>

I clenched my jaw so hard it popped. My phone pinged again.

Maybe-Ally: <I'm sorry I'm being blunt, but you asked.>

Sure, I did ask, but I didn't expect her to say all that. Danny was a fantastic writer. Also, he was my best friend. I didn't hesitate to criticize his work when it needed improving, but I knew for a fact that his last novel was a hit.

Me: <Sorry you didn't like it.>

We exchanged a few other mundane texts after that, but they felt off. Everything she had said that day—her prejudice against Louisiana and, more specifically, her haughty comments about Danny's work—had put a dent in our casual conversations. I had a hard time believing that the shining woman who had helped me build up my self-esteem and who had gushed over Danny's work over breakfast, would look down on things that way.

My mind went back to the conversation I'd had with Sam on July 4, and with Maisy the last time we saw each other. Could it be that I had been wrong about her? That I had idealized her in my mind?

I needed to talk it out with someone. I called Danny, but he didn't pick up. He texted me soon afterward, telling me he was eating out with Sam and that he would call me back the next day. So I went out instead and walked around the city, lost in the memories of Ally and New York.

When I came back to myself, I looked up and realized I was in front of Maisy's building. As I stood there trying to understand why I had come here without even knowing it, a window on the second floor opened, and Maisy's head popped out, smiling at me.

"Hey, you," she said.

I watched her in silence.

Maisy's smile faltered. "Are you okay, Steve?"

I shook my head. "I don't know why I'm here, to be honest."

Maisy frowned. "Do you want to come up?"

I hesitated only one second, then I moved forward and went in. Inside her apartment, she had me sit on the couch and I sank into the mountain of fluffy cushions. Maisy joined me and handed me a beer.

"Talk," Maisy said. "What happened to you?"

Instead of talking, I showed her all the texts Ally and I had exchanged that day.

"I don't understand what's going on here." I sighed. "This doesn't feel like her. She was always joyful and optimistic. How can she be so disrespectful?"

Maisy handed me my phone and looked at me with soft brown eyes.

"Maybe she's having a bad day?"

I shook my head. "That's no excuse. You read what she said. She has no right to be such an asshole."

Maisy chuckled softly. "Just because you never are an asshole, doesn't mean everyone is the same. I know that when *you* are in a bad place, you take it out on yourself, not on other people. But not everyone is as kind as you are."

My stomach jolted. I would have blushed at the compliment if I hadn't been so distressed.

"I just don't get it," I said in a strained voice. I plucked at the label on my bottle. "I never thought she would say such things. She seemed so open-hearted."

Maisy made a soft noise, and I turned to her. She seemed hesitant, but then said, "But you don't know her, do you?" Maisy answered. "I mean, you only spent a few days with her, didn't you?"

I nodded.

Maisy shrugged. "Maybe she was showing you her good side then, and now her true colors are peaking through."

I stared at Maisy. She had a point there. Ally might have been pretending in New York. Maybe it was time I stopped lying to myself. I didn't know her. And honestly, the way she left without saying goodbye, had been a horrible thing to do. Maybe that was the real Ally. Not the cheerful, funny, smart woman I had spent time with, but the cowardly one that had sneaked out of my hotel room and disappeared on me.

"Yeah, you're probably right," I reluctantly agreed.

Maisy put a hand on my arm. "I'm sorry, Steve, I know how much you want to see her again."

"I don't know if I still do."

My chest hurt at the idea of letting Ally go. She had been in the corner of my mind at all times for the last five months. I was afraid of the void she would leave behind if I let her go now. But seeing her again and realizing she was a horrible person would be even worse.

I sighed. "I guess I'll wait and see how she is in the next couple of days. As you said, maybe she's having a bad day and it will pass."

I left Maisy's place an hour later, feeling somewhat better. When I woke up the following morning, I had a new text from Ally.

Maybe-Ally: <Out of the swamp state and moving on to the next. Let's hope Texas treats me better.>

Annoyance flared in my chest again, and I decided not to reply.

8

HOPE

Ally's last text dated a week ago and I still hadn't figured out how to reply—or if I even wanted to reply at all. I kept thinking about everything we had shared and said to each other. I was trying my best to reconcile my memories from New York with the person I was now in touch with. But the more time passed, the harder it was to believe they were the same person. I was starting to wonder whether the whole thing was just a hoax.

On the eve of my thirty-eighth birthday, Danny asked me to meet him at our favorite Irish pub for a birthday drink. I expected it to be just us, maybe Sam too, but when I arrived at the pub, I was immediately assaulted by a chorus of very loud *Happy Birthdays* coming from the corner of the pub. My parents, Danny, Sam, Maisy and Jeffrey were waving at me, with huge grins on their faces and their glasses raised in a toast.

I walked to their table, running a hand through my hair.

"I wasn't expecting this," I said in an unsteady voice.

I hugged my parents, then kissed Maisy and Sam on the cheek, and bumped fists with Jeffrey and Danny.

I sat down next to Maisy. Danny had already gotten me a beer, so I clinked glasses with everyone and took a sip. Then, my so-called best friend asked for a speech, and everyone started clapping and chanting until I caved and stood up.

"Alright, fine. I'll make it short: thank you. Thank you for being here tonight, or basically all the time. Especially you, Danny. You're like a huge bedbug, very persistent, hard to ignore, and impossible to get rid of."

Danny frowned, and Sam chuckled. "Accurate description," she said.

"Thank you, Sam," I continued, turning to her. "Thank you for being here for Danny and keeping him busy so I can have some peace from him."

"It's my pleasure," she said.

"Jeffrey and Maisy, thank you for cheering me up when I need it. And for taking such good care of my monster."

"Don't call Colonel that," my mother chastised me. "He's a sweetheart."

"He's not," my father said in a gruff voice.

I turned to my parents and chuckled. "Mum, Dad, thank you both for putting up with me and all my crap for this long." I opened my arms wide as if I wanted to hug everyone at once. "I couldn't ask for a better family than the one that's here tonight. You're all weird and crazy, and I love you." My mother's eyes started shining suspiciously. I raised my glass and finished my speech. "Now, drink up." And I did, emptying my beer in three gulps.

Everyone cheered, clapped, and drank.

We all ate together at the pub, then my parents went back to their home in Fairmont. The rest of us stayed longer, drinking, joking around, and listening to the band playing live music.

We left together around midnight. Jeffrey, Danny and Sam shared an Uber, and I walked Maisy back to her apartment.

"Big day, tomorrow, isn't it?" Maisy said.

I grimaced. "Yeah, not really. It's a bit depressing, getting close to forty."

She giggled. "Yeah, I always thought I'd be married with kids by the time I'm forty, and I'm nowhere near that."

I snorted. "I hear you."

"Do you have any birthday plans for tomorrow?" she asked me. "We could have lunch, if you're free."

"I'm sorry, I can't, I'm going to my parents'."

Maisy waved a hand. "That's fine. Maybe we can do something later next week?"

"Sure. We're playing beach volleyball on Thursday, you should come."

Maisy made a face. "I'm not sure I'll be able to. I have to check my work schedule, but I think I'm out of town at the end of the week."

We arrived at her front door and stopped, facing each other. I shoved my hands in my pockets and looked around. Maisy stepped closer to me. Her chest was brushing against my stomach. She was so petite that I had to crane my neck down to look her in the eyes.

"I really want to spend more time with you, Steve," she said in a hushed voice.

My stomach somersaulted. I swallowed thickly, my mouth suddenly dry. I was torn between the longing to step closer, and the need to run away. Maisy stepped up on her tiptoes, ghosting her lips over mine, barely touching me. I closed my eyes for a second. Then I bent down and crushed my mouth over hers. I wrapped my arms around her waist, pulling her closer, and deepening the kiss.

When we broke apart, we were both panting.

"Do you want to come inside?" Maisy asked.

I looked down at her mouth, rosy and wet from our kiss. My body was screaming for me to accept. But I knew I shouldn't. I didn't think it would be fair to her when my head was still stuck on Ally.

I cleared my throat and shook my head. "I'd better go home."

Maisy stepped back, looking disappointed.

"I'll call you later, we'll try to have lunch," I said.

I kissed her gently on the cheek, lingering a bit longer than necessary.

"Good night, Maisy."

***

When I woke up the following morning, I had a few messages waiting for me on my phone, wishing me a happy birthday. I went running by the beach and, after a quick shower, rode my scooter to my parents' house for lunch. As usual, my mother had cooked a ten-people meal for the three of us, and I went back home late that afternoon with a few containers of food and a pack of blueberries for Colonel.

I decided a hot bath would do me some good, and I enjoyed the warmth of the water loosening my shoulders. I put on my sleeping pants, a T-shirt and my favorite hoodie. I didn't care that it was barely six. After all, it was Sunday, and my birthday, so I deserved a bit of self-indulgence. I went downstairs, grabbed a beer, the left-over birthday cake and the blueberries, and joined Colonel on the couch.

I watched the news, eating my birthday cake, and washing it down with beer. Every time Colonel gave me a nudge with his paw, I gave him a blueberry. When we had both finished eating, I switched off the TV and powered up my laptop. I opened the email account I had created for Ally. I hadn't logged on to it in a while—not since I had started chatting with Ally. But something tonight made me check the inbox. Maybe it was the way everything had soured with Ally, and the fact that I was having doubts about her. Or maybe I was feeling nostalgic because of my birthday. I didn't know why, but some part of my brain felt like this was something I needed to do.

I squinted at the screen, trying to make it less blurry. It had been a long day, and the bright light of the laptop was hurting my tired eyes. I grabbed my glasses on the coffee table and put them on. It really irked me that I needed them—but I supposed I'd better get used to it. Turning thirty-eight wouldn't make my eyesight better, would it?

With the glasses on, I could see I had a good fifty un-read emails. I scrolled down, skimming over the subjects, but didn't open any email. Until one caught my eye.

<Subject: Watch me.>

A flash of memory came to my mind, and I pictured a Post-it note stuck to a memory stick, bearing the exact same words. My heart started beating fast.

I opened the email. There was nothing in it but an at-tached video. My hands tingled in excitement. I opened the file, and Ally's beautiful face filled the screen of my laptop. My heart skipped a beat—or ten—at the sight.

"Hey, handsome."

A sound between a moan and a sob escaped my lips, and I pressed my fist to my mouth. I had almost for-gotten how bright her smile was, or how husky her warm voice sounded. It was good to hear it again.

"I heard your message in Danny's book." She rolled her eyes. "Obviously. I wouldn't be doing this if I hadn't, would I?" She shook her head and huffed a laugh. "Sorry, I'm a bit nervous. Anyway, I've thought about answering you for some time, and I decided that sending you a video was my best option. That way, you know for certain that it's me. With your looks and your voice, and the really sweet message you recorded, I'm pretty sure you received tons of emails." She chuckled. "I can't tell you how relieved I am that you don't seem to be mad at me. If the roles were reversed, I'd be livid. But you are a far better person than I am.

"I'm in Portland right now. I'm traveling south, so I should be near San Francisco in a few weeks. If you're still up for it then, maybe we can meet? I'd love to see you again. Here's my number." She held a piece of paper with a phone number written on it, and I quickly copied it down. "Text me whenever you want. Bye."

Warmth spread over my whole body. The room around me was spinning. I gasped in air, realizing I had been holding my breath this whole time.

I played the video again and focused on Ally's face. The lighting wasn't great. She seemed to be sitting in a park, and the sun was setting behind her, so her face was slightly hidden in darkness. But her piercing gray eyes and flashing smile were unmistakable.

I grabbed my phone and quickly typed a message without even thinking about it.

Me: <Hi, Ally. Just received your video. I'd love to see you when you are in SF. Steve.>

My phone pinged a minute later. I almost dropped it in surprise. I hadn't expected a reply so soon.

Maybe-Ally: <I haven't heard from you in a while. How are you?>

I froze. The text didn't come from the number I had just texted, but from the person I had been chatting with for three weeks. My hands grew cold. I had been right to be suspicious. Someone had indeed been playing me. I felt so stupid. I decided to play too.

Me: <I'm fine. Where are you now?>

Maybe-Ally: <In Texas.>

I frowned. Had I gotten everything wrong? There was a Portland in Texas, wasn't there? Maybe I was being paranoid? Ally could have two phone numbers. I did, I had a professional number and a personal one. But it was hard to believe that she would send the video if we were already in touch. She did say she was traveling south, not west, didn't she? I had to be sure.

Me: <Nice. In Portland? I hear it's a nice city.>

Maybe-Ally: <No, I'm in Dallas. I might go to Portland next.>

My stomach dropped to my feet. At least, now I knew. I had been duped.

Me: <Funny, I just got an email from you saying you were in Portland.>

Maybe-Ally: <Not from me. It must be someone pretending to be me.>

Me: <I'm sure it was Ally's face in the video they sent. Maybe you are the one pretending.>

I waited for a reply. And waited. As none came, I sent another text.

Me: <Who are you?>

Still no answer. I tried to call the number, but it went straight to voicemail. Well, that was that. I had indeed spent three weeks chatting with a stranger.

***

I spent the next few days on cloud nine. Ally—the real one—and I had been texting back and forth, and it felt right. Now, I recognized the positive woman I'd met in New York. On Thursday evening, I arrived early at Ocean Beach for our monthly beach volleyball game. Only Danny and Sam were there already, getting everything out of their car. I hugged them both and gave them a hand. When everything was settled on the picnic table, Danny opened a beer and handed me the bottle before sitting down and gesturing for me to join him.

"Okay, spill," he said.

"What?" I asked.

"Don't pretend," Sam said. "You're freaking us out, you're too happy. Who are you, and what have you done with Steve?"

I rolled my eyes.

"What happened?" Danny asked.

"Nothing," I said. I took a sip of my beer.

They were both scrutinizing me, and I looked away. Sam gasped.

"It's Ally!"

I choked, spurting beer on the table.

"You nailed it, love," Danny said.

He and Sam high-fived, and I scowled at them. Then I sighed.

"Fine."

I told them everything that had happened in the last few weeks—the texts from the fake Ally, the video from the real one, the radio silence from the fake one. I only skipped over what had happened with Maisy. Sam was so outraged that someone had toyed with my emotions, that she was gesturing wildly, her flaming hair flying all over the place. Danny, always the cool-headed writer, asked me if he could use my story in one of his novels.

Sam flicked him on the head. "He's your friend, not your muse, you jerk."

We heard someone call Danny's name, and we turned around to see three of our friends walking toward us. Danny lit the fire, kissed Sam, then dragged me to the volleyball net, and we started the first game of the night.

Later that evening, I was right in the middle of our third game when I heard Sam call my name near the fire. I turned to look at her. And the ball hit me hard on the head. I walked away among the peals of laughter of my so-called friends, rubbing my aching head, and joined Sam.

She handed me my phone looking a bit sheepish. "You've just missed a call from Ally."

I stumbled in shock. "What?"

"I'm sorry," she said. "I didn't mean to look at your screen, but your phone kept ringing, and I was trying to get it out of your jacket to give it to you, and I saw her name. I didn't mean to be nosy."

"No worries," I said. I took my phone from her hand and checked the screen. I had indeed missed a call from Ally.

I looked at Sam. "Should I call back?" I asked in a shaky voice.

Sam raised her eyebrows. "Yes, and right now! Hurry up, or I'll do it." She tried to take my phone from my hands, but I hid it behind my back. "Give me your phone!" she whined.

I grinned. "Chill out, woman. I'll call her."

"Can I listen?"

"Sure, and later tonight, I'll dance naked for you and Danny, would you like that?"

Sam scrunched up her nose. "No, thanks."

I walked away from the noises my friends were making and sat in the sand. I stared at the screen. My heart was beating frantically. I breathed deeply a few times, then pressed the call button. With shaking hands, I put the phone to my ear.

"Hey, handsome," Ally's soft voice answered.

My chest constricted at the sound of her voice. "Hey, Ally."

"Are you okay? You seem breathless."

"Yes, I'm fine." I cleared my throat. "I'm playing volley-ball with some friends."

"Do you want me to call you back later?"

"No, now is perfect. I needed a break anyway. How are you?"

Ally started telling me about her last few days. I hung my head low and rubbed my eyes with my thumb and forefinger. The relief that overcame me, sitting on the beach and listening to her telling me stories in a cheerful, enthusiastic tone, was almost too much. I had been hoping for this moment for five months after all.

We talked on the phone for a while. When we hung up, I sat there, trying to get over myself. In the distance, I saw a mane of thick red hair bouncing up and down as Sam was jumping on the spot, looking and waving at me. I chuckled, stood up, and walked toward her.

"So?" she asked when I was closer. Her eager eyes were wide open, as usual.

"So, nothing," I said casually.

"Mate, are you trying to kill my fiancée?" Danny asked. "Her head is going to burst if you don't tell us."

I shook my head. "There's nothing to say. She's in Salem at the moment, and she'll try to come here in a few weeks."

Sam looked at me expectantly. When I didn't say anything more, she asked, "And?"

"And that's it."

"Steeeeeeve!" Sam whined.

"There's nothing more to say."

"You're lying."

I narrowed my eyes. "I am not lying, *Samona.*"

Sam stilled, and her eyes opened wide. I sniggered. Danny frowned. He looked at Sam, then at me.

"Samona?" he asked. He looked at Sam. "Why is he calling you Samona? Did I miss something?"

Sam shook her head frantically, looking at me with pleading eyes.

I waved him off. "Nevermind. It's a stupid joke."

He looked puzzled. "I don't get it."

Sam laughed, a bit maniacally. "There's nothing to get. Steve's being stupid."

Jeffrey called after Danny, gesturing for him to join their game.

"You jerk!" Sam hissed when Danny was out of earshot.

I smirked and whispered, "You leave me alone, or I'll tell him."

"I hate you," she whisper-shouted. "Shit, I should never have told you the story."

I put an arm around her shoulders and kissed her head. "I love you too, Samona."

She shoved me and tried to punch me in the stomach, and I dodged, laughing.

Sam shook her head. "You're lucky I love seeing you happy, jackass."

Oh, she had no idea how happy I was. I was floating in a bubble of joy. Everything seemed so much better. The sky was bluer, the setting sun was brighter, and the sound of laughter was the most beautiful music. I was going to see Ally again.

9

EAGERNESS

Ally and I continued texting every day, but we didn't talk on the phone anymore. I wanted to call her, and I had to stop myself from doing so about five times a day. Instead, I focused all my energy on work. I had a couple of new recording contracts, and Danny had finally sent me his young-adult fantasy novel to proofread. Fantasy wasn't usually my jam, but to my surprise, I was hooked on his story. I knew it would make a great book. I was even considering asking Danny to let me handle the narration.

I had to wait for two weeks for another call from Ally. On Wednesday evening, I was sitting on the couch with Colonel curled up on my lap, when my phone rang. My heart leaped in my chest at the sight of Ally's name on the screen.

"I have some news for you," she said when I picked up.

She sounded cheerful, and I couldn't stop the smile that spread on my face.

"I hope it's good news," I said.

Ally chuckled. "That depends on you. Do you still want to see me?"

"Of course."

"Then it is good news."

Hope bloomed in my chest, and my whole body tensed. My hands crisped on Colonel's back. I didn't realize I was pulling on his fur until he meowed loudly in protest and sank his claws into my legs, piercing the fabric of my jeans.

"Is that Colonel Mustard?" Ally asked.

"Yes," I said, wincing and trying to pry his claws off my pants. "He's on my lap."

She chuckled. "What are you doing to him? Torturing him?"

I scoffed. "I'm the one suffering here. He's made minced meat of my thighs."

"Ouch," she said, sympathetically.

"To be fair, I pulled out a few hairs on his back."

"Oooh, poor baby," she cooed.

"What about me?" I asked indignantly.

"You got what you deserved."

I chuckled. "So, what's the good news? Are you coming to San Francisco?"

"Yes, I am." I could hear the smile in her voice. I lifted Colonel off my lap and sat him on the couch. "I should be there on Sunday afternoon."

I couldn't resist. I stood up, punching the air and making a silent victory dance à la Chandler Bing.

"Steve? Are you still there?"

"Yes." I cleared my throat. "That is good news. Where are you at the moment?"

"I'm staying at Lake Tahoe tonight. Tomorrow I'll go to Sacramento, and then I still want to see Oakland before I come to San Francisco."

"We can go to Oakland together if you want," I suggested. "It's only a bridge away from here." I was hoping she would come here a day earlier.

She hummed. "That's a good idea, actually. That way I'll have more time in Sacramento."

My shoulders slouched. Well, at least I'd tried.

"I'll call you on Sunday when I arrive in San Francisco," she said. "Maybe we can meet then, if you're free?"

"Sure."

We talked a bit longer, then hung up. I picked Colonel up and lifted him to my face.

"Well, buddy, what do you think? Should I thank Danny? It was his idea to record the message, after all." Colonel meowed, and I kissed him on the nose before setting him down.

Three days. I would see Ally again in three days.

It occurred to me then that, if I wanted to make the most of Ally's presence here, I needed to take time off work. I had no idea how long she would stay and I was afraid to ask—she never seemed to stick around in one place for long, and I didn't want to make her feel unwelcome. I wanted to enjoy her company for as long as she was here, and spending eight hours in my recording booth every day, only to see her in the evenings, wouldn't do it. I still had a few ongoing projects, and I needed to wrap them up before she arrived. So, I switched off the TV, quickly made myself a sandwich, and went back to work.

The next three days, I got up at five every morning, skipped my usual breaks, and worked until ten every evening to knock out as much work as possible. My lunch and dinner breaks were spent proofreading Danny's book, answering emails, and updating my social network accounts.

At long last, at five on Saturday, I was done. I quickly called Danny with some feedback on his book and fired a few last emails, then went grocery shopping. Back home, I tidied up and cleaned the house. At ten, I finally launched myself on the couch, feeling both exhausted and restless. I would see Ally tomorrow. I still couldn't believe it. And I wasn't sure what we would do together. I had suggested visiting Oakland with her. I might be able to stretch that into two days. But if I wanted to keep her around longer, I needed to find things to do. I sat up, grabbed my laptop on the coffee table, and started searching for ideas.

I woke up early the next day, after a restless night and went out for a much-needed run. I had spent so much time cooped up in my booth this week that my leg muscles were stiff, and I had a lot of energy to burn.

I was running along Fort Scott Field when my phone pinged. I didn't usually take it with me when I went running, but today wasn't a regular day. I stopped running to check the message, and my legs turned to jelly.

Ally: <Having breakfast on the beach.>

Attached to the message was a picture of a delicate hand holding what looked like a blueberry muffin. In the background, the Golden Gate Bridge was gleaming bright red in the morning light. I immediately knew where Ally was. That view could only be seen from Marshall's Beach, about half a mile from where I was.

My fingers hovered over my phone, pondering whether to reply or not. Ally and I had agreed to meet in the afternoon, but since she was already there, I couldn't wait anymore.

I put my phone back in my pocket without answering. I looked down at myself—new running shorts that fitted perfectly, and a tight T-shirt that highlighted my chest. I didn't look too bad. I sniffed my armpits. Good enough. I stopped by a coffee shop and bought two coffees, then made my way down to Marshall's Beach. There was only one way down to the small, secluded beach, and I knew the path well. I used to come here often after moving back to San Francisco. It was peaceful and never crowded, even in the touristy season. And the view of the bridge was my favorite, especially at dawn.

It didn't take me long to find Ally, sitting in the sand facing the bridge. Her back was to me, but I would recognize her anywhere. My steps faltered when I saw her and

I stopped walking. I watched her for a few long seconds, unable to move. My heart was pounding wildly in my chest. I almost couldn't breathe, I was so nervous. For five months now, I had fantasized about this moment. I had imagined a dozen different scenarios. What if it didn't go as I was hoping? What if she recoiled when seeing me? Should I hug her, kiss her, pat her back? Would she want the closeness we'd had in New York?

"Stop freaking out." I mentally slapped myself. "She wants to see you. You'll be fine."

I walked on the beach. Ally was still facing away from me and didn't see me. Her face was tilted up to the sky, and she seemed to be breathing in the morning mist. My footsteps couldn't be heard over the clapping of the waves on the rocks.

When I was close enough, I leaned down behind her and whispered in her ear, "Hey, you."

She started so much that she dropped the muffin she was holding. She snapped her head around and looked at me with wide eyes, one hand on her chest.

"Steve!"

She stood up and hugged me. It took my arms a few seconds to react and hug her back, a bit awkwardly since I was still holding the coffees. I breathed in her earthy scent before she leaned back. She punched my shoulder gently.

"You scared me." She looked up at me. "What are you doing here?"

"You said you were having breakfast, so I brought coffee." I handed her a cup. "A lot of milk, no sugar."

She took the cup and smiled. Oh, that beautiful smile.

"You remembered," she said.

I remembered just about everything about her. How her smile reminded me of the sun breaking through the fog. How her laughter sounded like music to my ears. How her body felt pressed against mine.

We sat in the sand, and she handed me the box of muffins. I chose one with blue icing, and Ally picked a chocolate chip one.

"How come you arrived so fast?" she asked, her mouth full. "Do you live nearby?"

"I live a few miles away. But I was running when you texted, so I was even closer."

"That explains the clothes," she said with a smile.

I grimaced. "And the smell," I said. "Sorry about that."

She chuckled. "You still smell like you, don't worry."

I smell like me? What is that supposed to mean? She remembers how I smell?

"You still smell like you, too," I said. "You look good."

And she did. She was wearing a baseball cap, but I could see that her hair had grown out a lot in the few months since New York. It was still wavy and a bit messy, but it was now in a bob cut and I could see a few bottle-green strands of hair underneath the cap. Her skin had a lovely golden tan.

But under all her natural beauty, I could see the exhaustion on her face. The dark shadows under her eyes brought out her cheekbones and her features were drawn. She was sitting cross-legged, her elbows resting on her knees, and her shoulders hunched slightly. Her outfit—denim shorts and oversized crop top—did nothing to hide the fact that she was quite thinner than she had been back in New York. She might not have lost more than a couple of pounds, but with her naturally slim complexion, it showed. She was still gorgeous, though.

"You look tired," I said softly.

Ally grimaced. "Yeah, I don't sleep much. There's too much to see around here, and I like hiking early in the morning, so my nights are short."

"So, you hike a lot?"

"Every day."

Maybe that was why she was thinner—a lot of physical exercise, not enough sleep. Also, being on her own for so long couldn't be good. I couldn't believe she wasn't feeling lonely.

I was surprised to hear that her French accent was thicker than it had been in New York. Was it a lack of practice, or the lack of sleep? I had no idea.

"I like your hair this way."

"Thanks," she smiled.

"I'm not sure about the cap, though." I pointed to her head and the Yankees cap she was wearing. "I'm afraid you'll have to take it off when you're with me."

Her smile turned into a grin. "Not a Yankees fan?"

I shook my head. "Definitely not. It's always been the Giants for me."

She turned the cap around, putting it back to front. "Is that better?"

I nodded. "Much, thanks."

I picked another muffin and pointed at her feet. "That's new, isn't it?"

Ally looked down at the words that were inked on the inner part of her left foot and nodded.

"This one, too," she said, lifting her right foot. There was a similar tattoo there.

I leaned closer and saw words I couldn't understand. I guessed they were in French.

"What do they say?" I asked her.

"Chaque seconde, chaque jour," she said lifting her left foot. "Jusqu'à la fin," she continued pointing toward her right foot.

It was the first time I heard her speak French, and her voice sounded very different. Deeper, in a way, and more sensual.

"It would translate in 'every second of every day, until the end'," she explained.

"What does it mean?" I asked.

She stayed silent for a few seconds, her fingers tracing the words on her feet. Then she said in a soft voice, "It means I want to live every second of my life fully."

I looked up at her. She kept her head down, but I could see the sorrow on her face. I was sure there was something else behind the ink, but I could feel her clamming up already, like she used to do in New York every time my questions became too personal.

In a way, it was frustrating, not being allowed to learn more about her. But I couldn't begrudge her for wanting to keep secrets, since I was keeping secrets too and didn't want to tell her about Nicole.

"How long are you staying in San Francisco?" I asked, changing the subject to distract her.

She lifted her head and seemed to shake herself up. "I don't know yet. A few days, I guess. Five days is the longest I've stayed in one place."

My chest constricted. "Only five days?"

Ally turned to me. "I might stay longer here," she said. Then she shrugged and looked at the ocean again. "I don't know. I told you, I'm not planning anything."

"I know," I replied softly. "Where were you, those five days?"

"Yellowstone. I loved it."

I took a bite of the muffin. "Where are you staying while you're here?"

She turned to me, looking puzzled. "What do you mean?"

"I mean, which hotel are you staying in?"

"None." She stared at me as if I was supposed to know that. "I sleep in my car."

I paused and looked at her, baffled. "What?"

"I sleep in my car," she repeated, smiling.

"You sleep in your car." I parroted. I said this as a statement, not a question.

"Yes."

"Every night." Again, not a question.

She started laughing at the look on my face. "Mostly, yes. I sometimes get an Airbnb or a room in a motel, so I can take a shower and have a good night's sleep, but that's all. Sleeping in the car gives a lot of freedom. I can stop whenever and wherever I want."

I looked back at the ocean. "Well, you won't be sleeping in your car while you're here."

Her smile turned sly. "I won't?"

I shook my head. "You're staying with me."

After a brief silence, she asked, "What if I don't want to?"

I snorted. "You're telling me you don't want to spend a few nights in a real bed and take a shower every day, have a few hot meals, maybe wash a few clothes?"

She bit her lower lip, looking away at the ocean.

I suddenly worried that she might have misunderstood me and hurried to add, "I have a guest room."

The corners of her lips lifted. "I'm not worried about that. But I don't want to intrude, with your work and stuff."

"I invited you, didn't I?"

"What if I decide to stay for a few weeks instead of a few days?"

Please, do stay for a few weeks.

"I won't mind," I said casually.

"And a few months?"

"I'm pretty sure you won't stay that long." My chest ached as I said that, a bit too aware that this was the truth.

"You're probably right. But what if I do?"

I shrugged. "I'll call immigration."

She burst out laughing. "You know I have a visa."

"Speaking of, isn't it expiring soon?"

"I applied for a second one, so I've got six more months before I have to go back to France."

"So, you'll be staying at my place, right?"

She shook her head. "I don't have a choice, apparently." She turned to me, a soft smile on her lips. "Thank you, Steve."

"No problem. Colonel will be happy. He was looking forward to meeting you."

"You told him about me?" she asked.

I nodded.

"I'm looking forward to spending time with him, too," Ally said softly.

I finished my muffin. "What are your plans for the next few days?" I asked.

She shrugged. "I don't have any."

"Oh right. No planning."

"Exactly." She grinned. "Anyway, I thought I'd let you do the work and show me around." She paused, frowning. "That is, if you want to, and have time after work."

"I don't have to work next week. I'm between projects and I need a break, so I'm taking some time off."

A slow smile spread on Ally's face. "What a coincidence. It's lucky I chose this week to come, isn't it?

My face started to burn, and I looked down to hide my blush.

"You can show me your favorite places, then."

"Just like in New York?"

"Just like in New York."

10

RESENTMENT

I wanted to start our first day together immediately, but I desperately needed a shower first. Ally offered to drive me home, so we left the beach and walked the path up to the street. When we arrived at her car, Ally got in and quickly removed a few things from the passenger seat before I could climb in.

"Sorry for the mess. I wasn't expecting company in the car."

When she turned on the ignition, the radio turned on automatically, and a very familiar voice blasted through the speakers. Ally fumbled with her phone, and the radio fell silent, but not before I could recognize the voice.

I turned to Ally. "Was that... me?" I asked, my lips stretching into a slow smile.

Ally bit her lower lip. Her cheeks had gone rosy, a lovely color I hadn't seen on her before. "Yeah, I wanted to hear your voice on the way here." She smiled sheepishly. "I forgot that Bluetooth connects automatically."

I pursed my lips to try and contain my smile, but she saw right through me.

"Feeling a little smug?" she teased.

"Maybe."

I gave Ally directions to my house, and we set off. I had a quick look around. In the back of the car, Ally had folded the seats down. There were a cushion and a small blanket, next to her suitcases and bags. Everything was tidy, but it was definitely cramped. Scratch that, it was tiny. As in shoebox-sized. I couldn't believe she was sleeping in here. There was no way she was able to stretch out completely—I wouldn't be able to, and Ally was not much shorter than me.

"It's good enough," she said when I asked about it. "I don't sleep much anyway."

"You said that before. What does it mean? How much is not much?"

"A few hours a night."

I frowned. "Do you have insomnia?"

She shook her head. "I just find it hard to relax at night, that's all."

I raised a sarcastic eyebrow. "I can't imagine why. Sleeping alone in a car in a foreign country, that's like a yoga retreat."

She barked out a laugh. "It's not because I'm scared."

I was scared enough for both of us, I guessed.

"Should I turn left or right?" Ally asked.

"Right. So, if you're not scared, how come you don't sleep?"

She shook her head again, chuckling softly. "It's nothing, really. It's just that darkness brings weird thoughts, and sometimes I have night terrors."

I frowned.

"I prefer having naps during the day when I feel too tired," she continued. "And I love walking around cities at night, it's so peaceful."

"You have night terrors?" I asked softly.

Ally winced, and I had the feeling she hadn't meant to say that.

"Never mind," she said, waving a hand. "Where should I go?"

I watched her for a long second, then looked around. "Turn left here," I said. "My house is at the end of the street."

A minute later, Ally parked in front of my place, and we got out of the car.

"It looks nice," she said appreciatively, looking at my house.

It was a two-story house with two bedrooms and one bathroom. It wasn't big, but it was comfortable, and it was home. I had it redecorated two years ago after I had moved back to San Francisco, and it was now modern and fully equipped. It didn't have a garden, apart from the small patch of grass at the front, but there was a nice wooden deck at the back, and the view of the Pacific Ocean from there was breathtaking.

"I don't even want to know how much the rent is on a place like this," Ally said. "I heard real estate in San Francisco is ridiculously expensive."

I chuckled. "It is. But I'm not renting, I own it."

Ally whipped her head around and stared at me with wide eyes. "You do?"

I nodded. "My aunt died ten years ago, and she left me the house. I didn't even have to get a mortgage. The house's all mine."

"Wow. She must have love you a lot."

We walked to the front door.

"She used to take care of me when my parents were at work, and she didn't have children of her own. In a way, she was like a second mother to me."

I unlocked the door and stepped in, keeping the door open for Ally. I kicked off my shoes, and she did the same. I put them safely in the cupboard away from Colonel's reach.

Ally turned and looked around, and I did the same, trying to see my house through her eyes. The entry hall was tiny, barely large enough for the cupboard I used to store coats and shoes. But it opened into a large living area painted in soft colors—light terracotta with a few touches of aquamarine. The room wasn't over-decorated. There was a huge cactus in a corner—a cactus that had belonged to my aunt—and a few other houseplants on the window sill. A picture hung on the wall behind the couch. A tinted glass wall separated the room from the modern kitchen, which was painted in clear taupe and again, touches of aquamarine. The stairs in the living room, leading to the upper floor, were made of dark brown wood. On the other side of the living room was the door to the laundry room. I always left that door open for Colonel, and we could hear the soft hum of the washing machine.

Ally turned to me. "It's a beautiful home," she said. Then, she looked around again, as if searching for something. "Where's Colonel Mustard?"

I looked around for him. "Probably hiding somewhere."

At that moment, a soft meowing had our heads spin to the left, as Colonel's yellow face peeked around the laundry room door.

Ally squatted down and cooed, "Hi, handsome. How are you?" She held out her hand to him, coaxing him to come closer. Colonel didn't move and kept watching Ally.

"He's very shy, so he might not—" I broke off when Colonel started purring. "Huh."

Colonel came out of the laundry room and trotted toward Ally, tail held up high.

"Oh my, he's huge!" She turned to me. "Are you sure he's a cat?"

I barked out a laugh. "What else could he be?"

She looked back at Colonel. "I don't know, a baby tiger? He has the right color. Or a dwarf lion. Have you seen his mane?"

I looked at my cat. I had to agree, he did look like a small-sized lion. Even his wide muzzle wasn't really cat-like.

Colonel reached Ally and started rubbing his head on her hand.

She chuckled. "He's shy, you said?"

"Yeah, he's usually not that affectionate."

"He's a Maine Coon, right? He's gorgeous."

She picked Colonel up and hugged him tightly, putting her face in his soft fur. Colonel purred loudly. Okay, so it was ridiculous to be jealous of a cat, right? Good thing I wasn't. Not at all.

"I'll leave you two to get acquainted. I just need to take a quick shower, then we can go to the city."

"Sure." Ally let Colonel go, but he stayed near her, rubbing against her legs.

"Make yourself at home. You can bring your bags in if you want."

"Should I watch Colonel, so he doesn't go out?" she asked.

I shook my head. "Keep an eye on him, but don't worry too much, he rarely goes out."

I went upstairs and showered as quickly as possible, then crossed to the bedroom and put on a fresh pair of shorts and a T-shirt. When I went back downstairs, I found Ally on the deck, leaning against the wooden rail, looking at the ocean. I joined her.

"This is my favorite room," she said when I was side by side with her.

"You haven't seen the whole house yet."

She shook her head. "I don't need to. This is perfect. I love the sound of the ocean."

"If you're ready to go, we can go to the waterfront, and listen to the ocean all day."

"That would be nice," she said.

An hour later, we were sitting on the pier near Fisherman's Wharf, our feet dangling over the water, eating fish and chips. Ally was telling me about all the places she had seen in the last six months.

"And in six months, you've never been scared?" I asked her.

She shook her head. "There were a couple of places where I didn't feel safe or comfortable, so I kept driving. I've been anxious or worried a couple of times, but never really scared."

"Like when?"

"Like when I had a flat tire in South Dakota. I was on a small dirt road in the middle of nowhere, and there were no other cars around, and no houses where I could ask for help. And of course, no phone signal either."

I winced. "What did you do?"

She answered matter-of-factly, "I changed the wheel."

"You did?" I had never changed a wheel in my life. I wasn't sure I would even know where to begin.

"What else could I do? I was stuck there for an hour, and I didn't see anyone. I had to do it."

"That's kind of amazing." I felt a weird sense of pride toward her.

She shrugged it off. "Not really. When you're lost in the middle of nowhere, you don't have a choice, do you? But I have to admit I was worried I would mess it up."

"So, you never feel in danger?"

She shook her head. "The only thing I don't like is when I have no phone signal. When that happens, I just keep driving. I sometimes drive all night long and only stop when I get a signal again."

"How can you manage without sleep?" I wondered.

"I'm used to it. And I nap a lot."

As I was listening to her telling me about her journey, I started feeling a bit dizzy. I usually considered my life to be interesting, or at least interesting enough. But now, it felt dull. Ally truly was fearless. She didn't hesitate to go on twenty-mile-long hikes on her own, or to raft down rivers.

"You've had quite a lot of adventures," I pondered.

Ally shrugged one shoulder but didn't say anything. I stole a few fries from her packet, and she swatted at my hand.

"Hey," she said indignantly. "Don't steal food from a lady, you monster."

I laughed and put the fries into my mouth.

"That's the fastest way to lose a woman's affection, you know," she said scowling.

"I'll buy you an ice cream."

"You will?"

I nodded.

She hummed. "Fine, you're forgiven." She handed me her fries. "Here, you can finish them. I'm done anyway."

"So, you just blackmailed an ice cream out of me for no reason?"

She grinned broadly. "Ice cream's a good enough reason."

I sipped my soda. "Don't you sometimes feel... I don't know... lonely? Or depressed? I mean, you're on your own all the time."

"I don't mind being on my own. Sometimes I have a rough day and think of going back to France, but then I meet wonderful people and they manage to cheer me up and keep me going." She threw me a sideways glance, smiling softly. "And sometimes I listen to you, and I feel better."

My face started to heat up, so I looked down and took a few fries.

As I had promised her, I bought some ice cream, and we walked along the ocean all afternoon, before riding my scooter back to my house in the early evening. I showed Ally the guest bedroom and the bathroom so she could shower, and went back to the living room. Ten minutes later, I still couldn't hear the water running upstairs. In fact, I couldn't hear anything. I climbed the stairs, calling for Ally in a soft voice. The door to the guest room was ajar, and I peered inside. Ally was sprawled on the bed, still in her clothes, and fast asleep. I listened to her soft snores before closing the door quietly. I went back downstairs to tidy up the house and feed Colonel, before turning in myself.

***

The following morning, I woke up feeling content. I had a whole day to spend with Ally. I knew she wouldn't stay for long, and I was determined to enjoy every second of her presence here.

I put on sleeping pants and a T-shirt, and got out of the room. The door to the guest bedroom was wide open. I called Ally's name and peered inside. The bed was made. There were no clothes on the floor, no bag near the door. No trace of Ally. It was as if the room hadn't been slept in at all.

A feeling of foreboding crept into my chest. I went down the stairs so fast I tripped on the last step and almost fell face down on the living room floor. Colonel lifted his head from his cushion on the couch when he heard me swear.

I called for Ally again but received no answer. A cold chill ran down my spine. Ally wasn't in the kitchen or the living room. I looked around for her shoes, some clothes, or even a goodbye note, but didn't find anything. The truth hit me hard in the chest. Ally was gone. Once again, she had left without saying goodbye. I grabbed fistfuls of my hair and pulled. How had I not seen this coming?

I stood there, in the living room, hands in my hair, my heart breaking into pieces. A noise behind me snapped me out of my daze, and I whirled around. The front door opened, and Ally came in. She was dressed in leggings, a sports tank and an unzipped hoodie, sneakers on her feet, carrying a small duffel bag and a water bottle.

I dropped my hands to my mouth and choked back a sob.

"Hey, handsome," Ally said.

I let my hands fall to my side and clenched them into fists. "Where the hell have you been?" I almost shouted, half enraged, half relieved.

Ally's steps faltered. "What?"

"I woke up and you were gone, your room was empty, I couldn't find your bag or a note, or anything. I thought you left."

"Steve, I—"

I cut her off. "Have you even thought of what I would feel, knowing you were gone when I woke up? Or don't you care at all? You're being selfish, Ally."

Her face closed up. She stared at me with a glacial look in her eyes. "I was up at four this morning," she said through clenched jaws. "I wanted to go running, and I didn't want to wake you up. I'm selfish that way, I guess."

I slowly unclenched my fists. "You could have left a note to tell me where you were going," I said, trying to control my voice.

Ally dropped her bag and walked up to me. "Let's get one thing clear," she said icily, poking me in the chest. "I never let anyone dictate what I can or can't do. Where I go or what I do is my business, not yours," she said in a steely voice.

"It's mine when you're staying in my house," I snapped back.

Ally folded her arms across her chest. "Then I don't think I'll be staying here very long."

My anger evaporated at her words. "Ally, I'm—"

She cut me off. "I went to the park to work out because I couldn't sleep. If only you had looked outside, you would have seen my car. It's parked right in front of your house. And my bag is in the wardrobe in the guest room."

My eyes snapped to the window. I could indeed see her car. I could have slapped myself for not checking. My shoulders slumped. "I didn't think—"

"Clearly, you didn't." She picked up her bag. "If this is how it's going to be, Steve, I don't think I want to stay here."

She turned to walk through the door. I stepped forward and caught her by the arm to stop her. She turned to me.

"Ally, I'm sorry." I let out a harsh breath. "I thought you left again. I was so happy when I woke up, knowing we'd spend the day together, and I freaked out when I couldn't find you. I'm so sorry. Please, stay."

Ally's face was still stern, but her eyes softened at my words. She flicked me on the forehead. "Next time, use that fantastic brain of yours instead of freaking out, you big dummy," she said in a low voice. "Did you really need to talk to me that way? Couldn't you just have asked, like a normal human being?"

I winced and dropped my head. "I'm sorry. I don't know what got into me, I'm not usually a jerk. Ask Danny, he'll tell you I'm a real doormat most of the time."

Ally huffed out a soft laugh. She put a finger under my chin and lifted my head to look into my eyes. "I really hurt you in New York, didn't I?" she whispered.

I swallowed thickly.

"I'm sorry about that." She dropped her hand and took my hand in hers. "You know I'm going to leave at some point, don't you? I can't stay here forever."

I nodded.

"And whenever I decide to go, I need you not to hold me back."

I stared at her in silence.

"Can you promise you'll let me go?" she asked.

"Yes," I whispered, knowing that, when the time came, I might not be able to hold my promise. I would try, though. I owed her that much. "Will you promise me something in return?"

She looked unsure, but nodded.

"When you do decide to leave, can you tell me the day before? So I can get my head around it and say goodbye."

After a short silence, Ally agreed softly. "Can I hug you?" she asked.

I didn't answer, but took her in my arms and kissed her forehead.

Ally spoke, her voice muffled by my T-shirt. "Can we pretend this didn't happen?"

I squeezed her tighter. "Did something happen? I didn't notice."

She chuckled into my chest and I felt the vibrations in my whole body. A soft meow came at our feet. Ally stepped back and picked up Colonel. Oh, that damned cat.

11

BLISS

Over the next three days, I took Ally around San Francisco and the surrounding areas. Ally was always so enthusiastic that I couldn't help but see my city, one that I had known all my life, in a new light. It was intoxicating. Being with her was like having a dose of heroin coursing through my veins every second. She was my own private sun—warm, bright, comforting.

At the same time, it was becoming unbearable to spend so much time with her without touching her, holding her hand, kissing her. Apart from hugging me twice, she hadn't initiated any physical contact—and I was too chicken to make a move myself, not knowing where we stood.

So much for being bold, Steve.

I'd had a very difficult time keeping my hands to myself on Ally's second night at my place. The first night had been easy since she had dropped dead on her bed as soon as she had lain down.

But on the second night, Ally came out of the bathroom in the evening, wearing short pajama shorts and a Harry Potter top, and I found myself unable to stop staring at her. Ally saw me gawking, and she smirked. Trying to cover it up, I pointed at the Harry Potter design on her top.

"Ravenclaw, huh?" I said. "I would have thought you were a Gryffindor."

Her face lightened up. "Oh, another Harry Potter fan."

I chuckled. "Guilty."

"I'm definitely not a Gryffindor, though. I have a bit of Slytherin in me, but for the most part, I'm all Ravenclaw."

"Yeah, me too, I suppose."

She hummed. "When you wear your glasses, you do look like a Ravenclaw. But you're also a Hufflepuff, I think. Loyal and kind. I like that about you."

My cheeks grew hot, which was becoming a very annoying habit when I was around Ally.

That night, we had watched a film together, and I hadn't understood a word of it. I had been too focused on keeping my brain and body under control.

On Ally's fourth day in San Francisco, something snapped in me. I couldn't take being in this in-between state with Ally anymore. I had to know where we stood.

At breakfast on Wednesday morning, I told her, "I'd like to take you out today."

She looked up, her mouth full of cereals, then swallowed. "That's what we've been doing for three days, isn't it? Going out?"

I shook my head. "I mean, I'd like to take you to dinner. Tonight." My cheeks grew hot—again—and I ducked my head.

After a few seconds of silence, Ally said in a soft voice, "Like, on a date?"

I squirmed on my chair, keeping my eyes on my coffee. "If you want."

I knew her eyes were fixated on me, I could feel her stare burn a hole in my head. But she didn't say anything.

"I mean, if you don't, that's fine," I rambled on. "I don't want you to feel obligated. And I won't be mad or awkward about it. I just thought, maybe—" I lifted my head when she started chuckling. "What's funny?"

"Nothing." She shook her head and tried to keep a straight face. She put a hand on mine. "I'd like to go on a date with you."

I turned my hand over and interlocked our fingers.

"I was wondering about it," she said. "Whether you'd want us to be together that way again. I was afraid to ask."

"You, afraid?"

She snorted. "Yes, Steve, it happens to me, too." She shrugged a shoulder. "I like you. It would hurt me if you rejected me."

"I like you too. A lot."

My face burned hotter. Ally lifted her other hand and gently touched my cheek with the tip of her fingers.

"I like that color on you," she said softly.

I huffed out an embarrassed laugh. "Shut up, I can't help it."

After breakfast, we packed backpacks with sandwiches and snacks, and rode my scooter to McLaren Park. We walked around the park all morning, watched people on the ropes courses, and went to see the blue Water Tower and the amphitheater.

At one o'clock, we found a secluded corner near the lake, sat down on the blanket I had brought, and had lunch. We spent the afternoon simply sitting there, chatting and enjoying each other's company. The park was quiet. We could hear the chatters of families at the playground nearby, but they were out of sight, and the only company we had were a few ducks waddling around the lake.

After a while, Ally took out a book, crossed her legs, and started reading. I lay down on the blanket with my hands beneath my head, pretending to rest. I kept glancing at her out of the corner of my eye. She seemed unable to concentrate on her novel. Instead, she often threw me a glance, as though checking if I was still there. When our eyes met, we smiled at each other. She gave up trying to read after ten minutes, and lay down, putting her head in the crook of my shoulder.

My hands went to Ally's head on their own accord, and started stroking her hair. She sighed. I tentatively ran my fingers on her cheek and along her jaw. I could feel her relax even more, so I continued tracing the lines of her sculpted face, her turned-up nose, and her slightly chapped lips, studying her features with my fingers. Her hand ran over my chest and stomach, then slid under my shirt. A shiver ran through me when her hand touched my bare skin and played with the hair on my chest.

I had to suppress a moan when she climbed on my body, straddled me, and pressed her chest to mine. She kissed my neck, slowly moving up to my ear, and gently bit my earlobe. This time, I couldn't stop the sound—half whimper, half groan—that came out of my throat. I pulled her closer, and she started rocking on my lap. She kept her head buried in my neck, kissing and biting my skin. My lips were burning with the need to feel hers, but she never kissed me.

After a few minutes of grinding, I could feel my control slipping away. We needed to calm down before we got arrested for public indecency. I rolled us over, laying Ally on her back, and lay on my stomach next to her.

"We need to stop," I told her, slightly out of breath.

"You're probably right," she panted.

We turned our heads and locked eyes. Her cheeks were pink and her eyes bright. I imagined I didn't look any different. We started laughing.

When we had come down from our high, I sat up and said, "We should probably go home. I have a date tonight, I don't want to be late." I winked, and Ally laughed.

We packed our stuff, making sure we left nothing behind, and rode back home.

I had decided to take Ally to one of my favorite places in the city. It was not the most romantic or classy restaurant, but the food was excellent, and the terrace overlooked the San Francisco Bay and the Bay Bridge.

When Ally was out of the bathroom, I quickly showered and put on a fresh pair of black jeans and a buttoned-down shirt. Ally joined me in the living room five minutes later, wearing a green and gold summer dress and flats. The green in her dress perfectly matched the strands in her wavy hair, which was hanging loose. She had put a bit of makeup on her eyes, making the gray look even lighter than usual. I looked at her, taking in her appearance, unable to speak.

"You look nice," she said, looking me up and down. When I didn't answer, she looked down at herself, fidgeting with the hem of her skirt. "I'm sorry, I don't have anything fancier to wear. I hope this is good enough for where you're taking me."

I walked toward her and gently lifted her face. "You look gorgeous, Ally," I said, my voice hoarse.

Her cheeks grew pink, and my heart melted. In all the time we had spent together, both here and in New York, she had never blushed. I didn't seem to be able to get rid of that nasty habit, but Ally always was confident and sure of herself. Now, seeing the color on her cheeks, I wondered whether that confidence was real, or just a mask she put on for the world to see. A rush of protectiveness and hunger came over me.

I touched her cheek. "I like that color on you."

She swatted my hand away playfully. "Shut up."

At the restaurant, we chose a small table on the balcony, so we had a perfect view of the ocean. The sun was starting to set, casting a glowing, orange light over the Bay Bridge. There was no light on the balcony, except for the candles on the tables. On second thought, this was extremely romantic.

While we were waiting for our dinner to arrive, I asked Ally something I hadn't even thought of asking before.

"By the way, what did you think of Danny's book?"

Ally took a sip of her wine, then said, "It was different from his previous books. He's usually more mellow."

I chuckled. "I told you it was a thriller, didn't I?"

"You did, but I still didn't expect this. I've read psychological thrillers, even horror stories, that were less nerve-racking."

"So you didn't like it?"

She smiled slyly. "I loved it."

Our food arrived then, and we stopped talking for a while. The sun had completely set now, and we were in almost darkness but for the light of the full moon. The dancing flames of the candles illuminated Ally's face in a soft glow, shading the dark circles she still had under her eyes.

Ally had only eaten half her plate when she put her cutlery and napkin down on the table.

"Are you finished?" I asked.

She nodded. "I'm full."

"You haven't eaten much."

She really hadn't. Her share of risotto was small—I'd worried that she wouldn't have enough—and she had only eaten half of it. "We can order something else if you don't like it."

"No, it's really good, but I can't eat anymore. I shouldn't have eaten so much this afternoon."

I frowned, thinking back at our day in the park. She hadn't eaten that much. A sandwich and a soda for lunch, and an apple in the afternoon. I wasn't even sure she had finished the sandwich.

I watched her carefully. "Are you feeling sick?"

She shook her head. "I'm fine. I'm just not that hungry."

I stared at her, my lips pursed. Now that I was thinking about it, in the three days since she had arrived, she had never eaten much.

Ally rolled her eyes. "Stop worrying, Steve. I've never been a big eater, so really, don't make a big deal out of it."

Except she had been eating when we were in New York.

"I can't help it if I'm worried about you," I said softly.

"Well, try to help it." Her tone was getting sharper. "I don't want you to worry, there's no need for that. I'm not here to be taken care of, or bossed around, or whatever. I just want to have a good time with you."

Ally leaned back in her chair and put her hands on her lap. I could feel she was pulling away from me again.

"Okay, I'll leave it alone," I soothed. I inched forward and put my hand on the table, palm up. "Do you want some dessert?" I asked her.

Ally breathed in slowly, then put her hand in mine. "No, thanks," she answered. "But you can get some if you want. I'd like some more wine, though."

I ordered another glass of wine for Ally, and mint tea and a chocolate cake for me. I didn't let go of her hand, and she didn't withdraw it either. I let my thumb run over her knuckles, then her wrist, and noticed the goosebumps on her arm.

"Are you cold?" I asked.

"No," she whispered. Her eyes were fixed on me, dark and shining.

I was about to move my hand up her arm when the waiter arrived with our order, interrupting our moment, and I let her hand go instead. When Ally saw the dark chocolate lava cake on my plate, she hummed and licked her lips. I chuckled and shook my head. Scooping a forkful of cake, I moved it toward her mouth. When she tasted the bitterness of the chocolate, she moaned, making me squirm in my chair.

I shared the rest of the cake with her, then we finished our drinks and left. When we were out of the restaurant, I took hold of her hand, and we walked along the waterfront, then on Pier 7. At the end of the Pier, we stopped and leaned against the railing, facing the bay.

"It's beautiful here," Ally said in a soft voice.

I looked around. The full moon was reflecting on the surface of the calm water of the bay, and the lights from Oakland seemed to flicker in the dusk. It was beautiful. But it was nothing compared to the woman standing next to me.

"You are even more breathtaking," I said softly.

Ally turned to me and smiled. I straightened up, put my hands on her hips, and turned her, so her back was against the railing. I pressed my body against hers. I kept one hand planted on her hip, and cradled her face with the other, gently tilting her head. I softly brushed my lips with hers. When I leaned back and looked at her, her eyes were closed.

"Steve," she said on an exhale.

I crushed my mouth against hers then, and sensations overwhelmed me. We kissed, swiping our tongues against each other's, swallowing each other's moans. Ally's hands were fisted at my waist, pulling me closer.

I pulled back, panting, and put my forehead against hers. "We have a habit of losing control, don't we?" I said breathlessly.

Ally laughed shakily.

I looked into her eyes. "Let's go home."

We almost ran back to my scooter, and I rode as fast as the bike would go, being all too aware of her hands under my shirt, lying flat on my stomach. When we arrived home, I helped Ally down the bike, took her hand, and we marched toward the front door. As soon as it was open, we were kissing again.

We ignored Colonel's meow of greeting. Clothes were flying all over the living room and the stairs, and we were already in our underwear when we got to my bedroom. I lay her on the bed and took my time learning the earthy smell and taste of her body all over again.

I hadn't thought it possible, but the night was even more intense than the one we'd had in New York. Intensely, that was how Ally seemed to be going through life. She gave herself completely to everything she did. That night, I tried to give her all of me.

When we were ready to sleep, we lay in bed again together, and I curled my body around hers. We fell asleep spooning.

12

DISARRAY

I woke up with a start at the sound of muffled crying. I looked at my alarm clock. Two a.m. I sat up. Ally was lying on her side, her face buried in the pillow. I had forgotten to close the blinds when we went to bed and in the soft light of the moon, I could see her entire body shaking.

I gently put a hand on her shoulder. "Ally?"

She jumped upright with a cry and sat up. She had a wild look on her face, and her gray eyes were wide open and shining with tears. She looked at me confused.

"Hey, it's okay, it's just me." I gently rubbed her back.

"Steve," she whispered. Then she started crying in earnest.

I hugged her, and she locked her arms behind my back, burying her face in my chest. We stayed silent, Ally crying softly, me gently rocking her.

"What's wrong?" I asked after a while.

"Nothing." She sniffled and pulled away, wiping tears from her cheeks. "Sorry."

"Don't apologize."

I took the box of tissues from my nightstand and handed it to her. She took one and blew her nose.

"Did you have a nightmare?" I asked.

She winced. "Kind of." She got off the bed, picked up my T-shirt on the floor, and put it on. "I need to get some air. Go back to sleep. I'm sorry I woke you up."

"Don't apologize, Ally, it's fine."

She left the bedroom in silence and closed the door behind her. I wanted to go after her, but I understood she needed some space. I would talk to her when she came back to bed.

Except that an hour later, she still hadn't come back. I stood up, put on my sleeping pants, and went downstairs looking for her. I found her on the deck. She was sitting on the bench, hugging one of the cushions and looking at the ocean. Her phone was next to her, and she had her earphones on. She turned to me when I called her and took them off. Her eyes were still red-rimmed, but she had composed herself and was smiling her usual, bright smile.

"Hey. Are you okay?" I asked.

She nodded.

I sat next to her and pointed at her phone. "What are you listening to?"

"A Stephen King novel. It's perfect to take my mind off things. Why aren't you sleeping?"

I tucked a lock of hair behind her ear. "I was worried about you."

"I'm fine. It's nothing unusual." She looked down. "I'm sorry I woke you."

"Stop apologizing."

Ally turned to me, her piercing eyes examining my face. She leaned closer and kissed me. The kiss started soft and sweet. But when she climbed onto my lap, straddled me, and deepened the kiss, my body reacted immediately.

Ally's lips moved to my jaw, then my ears. She nibbled my earlobe and murmured, "Are you clean?"

It took my foggy brain a second to understand her question. "Umh... yes. Why?"

"I want to taste you." She kissed her way down my bare chest, my stomach, then knelt between my legs and pulled down my pants. I wanted to stop her, but when her soft lips touched me, my mind blanked out, and my head fell back against the wall.

I came down from my high when the cushion dipped next to me. I opened my eyes again. Ally was watching me, her lips curved in a soft smile.

"You're beautiful when you come," she said.

I blushed furiously and her grin broadened. I pulled my sleeping pants up again, covering myself.

"What was that for?" I asked. "Not that I'm complaining, but—"

Ally kissed my lips. "I hadn't had the privilege to do that yet, and I wanted to."

"You know you didn't have to."

"Yes, I know. But you have such a beautiful dick, it would be a shame not to do that."

I groaned and covered my face, making her laugh.

I scowled. "You're making me blush on purpose, aren't you?"

She bit her lower lip, still smiling, and nodded. "You're so cute when you blush." She touched my cheek gently. "Go back to bed. I still need some time out here."

She pecked my lips. I cradled her face and stared into her eyes. "Are you sure you're all right?"

"Yes." She kissed me again.

"Okay." I stood up. "Call me if you need anything."

When I woke up at seven, I was still alone in bed. I got up and went downstairs. Ally was still on the deck, lying on the bench, soundly asleep. She was half-naked, wearing only my T-shirt and her underwear, so I went back inside and picked a blanket from the living room. I tried not to wake her up when I covered her with it. She clearly needed some extra sleep. I went into the kitchen to make breakfast.

An hour later, the pancake batter was ready and the coffee machine was brewing, so I went back on the deck to watch over Ally. She opened a blurry eye and spotted me in the doorway.

"Hey," she said in a voice hoarse with sleepiness.

"Good morning. How are you?"

She lifted from the bench and sat up. "Fine. Did I fall asleep here?"

I chuckled. "Yes. It's almost eight."

She stretched and yawned.

"Coffee's almost ready," I added.

"Thanks. I'll be right there."

I went back into the kitchen and prepared a cup of coffee the way she liked it, then I started making the pancakes. Ally joined me a few minutes later and took the coffee, looking grateful.

"Sorry again, for last night," she said.

"I've told you already, you don't need to apologize." I poured some batter into the pan. "I hope you like pancakes?"

Ally shrugged. "Who doesn't?"

"Do you want bacon and eggs with them?"

She scrunched up her face, her nose crinkling. "Ugh, no."

I snorted. "What's wrong with bacon and eggs?"

"They don't go with pancakes."

"Have you ever even tried it?"

She shook her head adamantly. "No, and I don't want to." She sipped her coffee. "Pancakes need sugar, not grease."

I held up my hands in surrender. "Okay, something sweet, then."

"Do you have maple syrup?"

I nodded.

"And maybe some whipped cream?"

"I think so. There are blueberries in the fridge, too, if you want some."

"That would be perfect."

I poured another ladle of batter into the pan and turned to watch her. She was leaning against the counter. She looked more edible than the pancakes I was making.

I went to her, grabbed her legs to lift her, and sat her on the counter. She made a soft yelp when her thighs touched the cold granite countertop. Standing between her legs, I let my hands slide up her thighs until they rested on her hips. She put her cup down on the counter. I leaned in to kiss her, but she turned her head away from me.

"Morning breath," she whispered.

"I don't care." I took her face in my hands and kissed her. "Mmh, you're right." I pursed my lips. "Morning breath, mixed with coffee. Lovely."

She smirked. "Told you."

I shrugged. "I like it."

"Weirdo."

"No, really." I leaned closer to her and pressed my body against hers, so she could feel exactly how much I liked it.

"Nice morning wood," she joked.

I shook my head. "That's not morning wood, that's Ally wood." I scrunched up my face. "Okay, that sounded creepy. Forget it."

She burst out laughing. "Your pancake's burning," she said, pointing to the pan.

I stepped back reluctantly. She started moving to get down the counter, but I glared at her and said, with as much authority as I could muster, "Stay."

She smirked. "Yes, sir."

I moved to the stove to flip the pancake. "You like it when I'm being bossy, don't you?"

"You've noticed."

"You should call me *Sir* more often."

"Yeah, right," she scoffed. "I don't actually like being bossed around. I need my man to be in charge in the bedroom, but I will never submit to anyone."

"I could make you," I said.

"You could try," she answered.

I chuckled. "I thought I had to be in charge?"

She rolled her eyes in response.

"And anyway," I continued. "This morning on the deck, you were the one in charge."

She shrugged one shoulder. "Yes, well, sometimes that's fun too."

"I won't say otherwise." I waggled my eyebrows, and she chuckled. "I kind of feel guilty, though."

"About what?"

"About this morning. You didn't get anything."

She lifted an eyebrow. "And?"

"Well, it's not very gentlemanly. And it's not in my habits."

"I don't need a gentleman," she said. "And sometimes, it's okay to take without giving anything in return. There's nothing wrong with being selfish from time to time." I must have looked unconvinced, because she added, "Anyway, you're already giving it back, you're making pancakes."

I barked out a laugh. "You can't compare pancakes and a blow job."

"Why not? Pleasure doesn't have to be sexual. I haven't had pancakes with syrup in ages, so it's perfect."

I pretended to be focused on the pancake I was flipping, and asked, "Do you want to talk about what happened last night? You had a nightmare?"

"Not a nightmare," she said in a strained voice. "I have night terrors. And no, I don't want to talk about it."

I turned to her. "If you change your mind, you know you can talk to me, right?"

She nodded.

"But you won't," I stated.

She shrugged. "Probably not." She slid down the counter and started laying the table, effectively putting an end to that conversation.

I had already gathered that something bad had happened to her, but I couldn't figure out what. I wished she would confide in me. Maybe with time—if we had time.

As we were eating breakfast, Colonel Mustard came out of his hiding place and jumped onto Ally's lap. She humph-ed from the weight, and I laughed.

"He's still smitten over you, I see."

But Colonel didn't let her pat him. Instead, he put his front paws on the table and launched himself towards her plate, eating some of her blueberries.

Ally gasped. "You little thief," she said, outraged.

I burst out laughing. "I should have warned you, he loves blueberries." I pointed my fork at Colonel. "Don't steal food from a lady, buddy, it's the best way to lose her affection."

"Damn right, it is," Ally mumbled. She lifted Colonel and looked at him sternly. "That's mine, no touching." Then, she kissed him on the nose and put him down on the floor. "Go play, you monster, and let the adults eat."

I couldn't help the warm feeling that bloomed in my chest from the way Ally cared for Colonel. I could see she was really fond of him. And I loved it. No matter how often I complained about my cat, he was one of the most precious things in my life. And he had suffered enough already, he deserved all the affection in the world.

We spent the morning at home, since I had some things to catch up on. I called my parents, and texted Danny and Maisy, then did some housework. Despite my telling her to rest, Ally helped. Well, sort of. Colonel kept following her around, and she would always drop what she was doing to scratch his head or play with him.

At eleven, I opened the front door to let in some fresh air, and found myself face-to-face with familiar blue eyes. My smile vanished and all my blood drained from my face.

"Nicole."

Why was she here? I didn't remember agreeing to see her again. And with Ally in the house, no less. Ally didn't know about Nicole. I had mentioned the divorce when we were in New York, but hadn't gone into details, and Ally had never asked. I wasn't sure she even remembered.

"What are you doing here?" I said in a hushed voice. "Now is not a good time."

Nicole didn't listen and pushed around me, walking into the living room. I was too stunned to stop her on time.

"Oh," I heard behind me.

"Shit." I winced. I turned around and joined Ally in the living room.

Nicole turned to me. "I didn't think you would have company." Then, turning to Ally, she said, "I'm Nicole, Steve's wife."

A spark of anger flared in me. "Ex-wife," I said harshly.

"I should have known you were lying when you said we would try again."

I gaped at her, brows rising and jaw dropping. "I never said such a thing," I spat.

Ally spoke then in a soft voice. "I'll leave you two alone."

I grabbed her hand before she could walk away. "Please, stay."

She withdrew her hand gently and shook her head. "You two need to talk. I'll be back later, I promise. I'll just go and buy something for lunch." She quickly put on her shoes, grabbed her car keys, and walked out.

I turned to Nicole, fuming. "Why did you say that?" I said through clenched jaws.

She walked close to me and cradled my face with both hands. "I wanted to see you."

I pushed her hands away and took a step back. "Why are you here?" I asked again.

"Is she your girlfriend?" she asked.

I scoffed. "That's none of your business. Answer my question."

"It is my business, Steve. I still care a lot about you."

I crossed my arms. "Answer me or leave. What the fuck are you doing here?"

"I'm visiting my parents," she said. "I thought I would come by and see if you've considered what we discussed."

"You mean, you asking me for money?"

She flinched. "No, I mean, me asking you to help your wife get out of a difficult situation."

"Ex-wife," I corrected again. "And you put yourself in that difficult situation. You can deal with it yourself."

"Please, Steve. You owe me, after everything I did for you during our marriage."

"Are you kidding me?" I sputtered. My hands started shaking, I was so angry. "And what exactly did you do for me? Except make me abandon my cat and my house, leave my home city, or refuse contracts because you didn't like the genre of the novels? Oh, and let's not forget the minute detail of your cheating on me." I shook my head. "I don't owe you anything, Nicole. You and I are over, and that's that." I walked to the door and opened it. "Leave."

Nicole's face closed up and she curled her lips. "Think carefully before blowing me off, Steve. I can do a lot worse to you than just asking for money."

Finally, she was showing her true colors. I sneered and shook my head in disgust. "I don't care for your threats. There's nothing you can do to me that would change my mind. I'm not going to tell you again. Get out of my house."

Nicole glared at me for a few seconds, then walked out the door and left.

I slammed the door behind her. I walked back to the living room to get my phone and call Ally. I heard a sound coming from the kitchen and walked in to find Ally's phone on the table. I hung up and stopped myself from throwing my phone against the wall. That wouldn't help at all, now, would it?

I spent the next ten minutes pacing the house, praying for Ally to come back. At last, her car stopped in front of the house. I ran out, barefoot in the gravel, and joined her.

"Ally, please, I can explain," I said. I didn't care that I was begging. If she left because of Nicole, I didn't know what I would do.

She looked up at me. "I'm not going anywhere, Steve." She smiled softly. "I bought Chinese food."

She lifted the bag she was holding, and I sighed in relief.

As we ate, I told her about the divorce, the situation Nicole had got herself into, and her demands for money.

Ally never spoke, but gasped her indignation in all the right places. When I stopped talking, she sat back on the couch and looked at me in a contemplative way.

"I kind of feel for her," she said. "I mean, what she did to you was horrible. But she doesn't deserve to be black-mailed, does she?"

I sighed. "I know. But does it mean I should clean up her mess?"

"It depends, I suppose."

I frowned. "It depends on what?"

"Whether you still have feelings for her or not."

I gaped. "Of course I don't have feelings for her."

"Are you sure you're not mourning your relationship anymore?" At my shocked expression, Ally added, "It's alright if you are. We are all mourning something in life, aren't we? I know I am." She chuckled softly, but her eyes were filled with sadness.

I shook my head. "I'm not. Sure, I'm still furious for everything she did to me, and still does. But that's all."

I stood up and started clearing the table.

"I'm sorry she's making things difficult for you," Ally said. "You don't deserve that."

I shrugged.

Ally stood up and joined me. "No, really, you don't." She put her arms around my neck. "You are caring, generous, protective. You need to be with someone who sees that and gives it back to you."

At Ally's words, something uncurled in my chest, as if my failed marriage had left a rope wound tight around my lungs, and finally, after more than two years, it uncoiled and I could breathe deeply again.

I stared at Ally. Her gray eyes pierced my heart. And I knew then that she saw me. I leaned down and kissed her gently.

"Thank you," I murmured against her mouth.

Her lips stretched into a smile.

13

PEACE

Time went by too fast. Before I realized it, Ally had been here for a week. I secretly rejoiced that I had beaten Yellowstone. I didn't dare remark it out loud, in case Ally took it as an invitation to leave.

On Sunday evening, we were sitting on the deck, watching the sun set over the ocean. Ally's feet were on my lap, and I was gently rubbing the soles.

When I started tracing the lines of her tattoos with the tip of my finger, she moved her feet to the ground and sat up, looking ahead in the distance, her face drawn. Then she cleared her throat.

"You're getting back to work tomorrow, right?" she asked.

I nodded.

"Do you work from home?"

"Most of the time, yes."

"What's your schedule like?" she asked me, turning to face me.

"I usually get to work around eight and stop at five or six in the evening. Lunch break at twelve, coffee breaks around ten and three."

"And you spend all that time in your recording booth?"

I shook my head. "Only if I'm recording or editing. If I'm preparing a new book or negotiating contracts, then I can work wherever."

"Do you want me to leave, so you can work properly?" she asked.

I whipped my head around and stared at her. "No," I said a bit abruptly.

Ally frowned. "I don't want to interfere with your job, Steve."

"Then stay. If you leave, I won't be able to concentrate," I said honestly.

Ally chuckled softly.

I took her hand. "I'm not asking you to stay in the house the whole day. But there are a lot of things to do and see in the area. So maybe you can do your own stuff during the day and come back and spend the nights here?"

Ally turned to look at the ocean again. She finally nodded. "That sounds like a good idea."

I fought the urge to punch my fist in the air. I had thought it would take some effort to convince her. I had a whole argumentation prepared in my mind, which included the hot meals I would cook for her, the hot showers she could take, and the real bed to sleep in—and Colonel's company, of course. But in the end, it had been easy.

I was still feeling giddy when we went to bed a few hours later.

***

When I walked into my recording booth on Monday morning, after Ally had left for an excursion at Big Sur State Park, I couldn't help but blush at the memory that came to my mind. The night before, Ally had had another night terror and had gotten up in the middle of the night. When I walked around the house looking for her, I found her sitting on my desk chair in the recording booth, fiddling with the material. I watched her in silence until she spun the chair around and spotted me.

"Having fun?" I said with a smirk.

She smiled playfully. "Nice chair you've got here, very comfy."

I walked into the room. "I spend a lot of time on it, so it'd better be."

She spun the chair around again. When the chair stopped spinning, her smile had turned mischievous. "Have you ever tried it for other things?"

"Like what?"

She spun again. When she was facing me again, I put my hands on the armrests to stop her.

She looked up at me and wiggled her eyebrows. "Like trying out a few scenes from the books Saul narrates?"

My body reacted immediately and I growled. "Not until now," I answered in a low voice.

I bent down and kissed her. Very quickly, our kiss had turned frantic, and we had lost control. And we had indeed tried the chair for other things. Several times.

So now, I was faced with the need to concentrate on my work when all I could think of was what we had done here the day before.

It took me a while, but I finally managed to get some work done. When Ally came back in the evening, we went out for dinner and she told me about her hike in Big Sur.

We repeated the same routine over the next few days, and quickly found a rhythm that suited us both. Every morning—sometimes very early in the morning—Ally would take her car and go on hikes, visit National Parks or cities, and I would get to work. Every evening, she would come back, and we would go for a run or out for dinner, then take a shower together, and go to bed. Sometimes, Ally left for two or three days, and I found myself in an empty house again. But we texted a lot, and she always came back with a ton of photos and stories to share.

I had already gotten used to having her in my home and sharing my life with her. I was bewildered at how easy and natural it was to live with her. And I was already dreading the day it would end. She didn't seem to consider leaving at the moment, but I knew the time would come when she would.

One evening, we were walking on the beach when I received a text from Danny.

Danny: <Are you free tomorrow evening?>

Me: <I'll be with Ally, but we don't have plans. What's up?>

Danny: <We'd love to have you both for dinner. What do you think?>

I showed Ally the text. Her face brightened.

"Dinner with Danny Mitchell?" Her voice rose on the name. "Oh my God," she almost squealed. "Can we go? Please?"

I laughed. "You're such a nerd!"

She swatted my shoulder. "Shut up! I'm a big fan, and you know it. It's like having dinner with Chris Hemsworth."

That made me laugh even more. "You've seen Danny, right? He looks nothing like Chris Hemsworth. They're as different as night and day. Literally."

She waved her hand. "Oh, you know what I mean."

I shook my head. "Fine, we'll go."

So, the following evening, we went to Danny's house together. Ally had put on the dress she had been wearing on our first date together. She seemed uncomfortable when she came out of the bathroom.

"I'm sorry, that's the only dress I have with me," she apologized.

I went to her, cradled her face in my hands and kissed her softly.

"You don't need to dress up, it's only Danny."

"Are you kidding me? It's Danny Mitchell! Of course, I need to dress up. I want to make a good impression."

I snorted. "Then you look perfect." I shrugged. "You could be wearing rags and you would still look gorgeous."

She blushed—something that seemed to happen more and more often as time went by. I touched her cheek, smiling softly. Seeing her pink cheeks now did something to my heart, something I didn't want to analyze just yet.

We took an Uber to Bayview. On the drive, Ally kept fidgeting with the hem of her dress, looking out of the window. Halfway to Danny's house, I took her hand.

"Are you okay?"

She puffed out her cheeks and let out a sharp breath. "I'm nervous."

I frowned. That wasn't like her to be nervous.

"Why?" I asked.

She turned to me. "I suppose you told Danny about me?"

I nodded.

"So—" She trailed off. Looking down, she asked, "You also told him how I left you in New York?"

"I did."

She bit her lower lip, keeping her eyes down. "What did he say?"

Comprehension dawned on me then—she feared what Danny would think of her.

I squeezed her hand. "He's not going to think badly of you."

"How do you know?" Her voice quivered.

I shrugged. "Because I know him. Danny knows everyone has baggage, and he's not one to judge." With the tip of my fingers, I lifted Ally's chin so she would look at me. "You know, the message I recorded at the end of his book was his idea."

"Really?" She sounded surprised.

I nodded. "He had to push hard to convince me to do it. I was sure it was a terrible idea, but he said it would work. It turns out he was right." I grimaced. "I hate it when he's right. He never lets me live it down."

Ally laughed softly and seemed to relax a little. "So I have to thank him for seeing you again, then."

I shuddered. "Please don't. He's smug enough without that." I leaned down and kissed her. "You don't need to worry, I'm sure they'll love you as much as I do."

Ally's nose crinkled and I froze, playing the words in my head again. My eyes opened in shock, realizing what she must have heard. Did I just tell her I lo—? No, I couldn't. I didn't. Did I?

Before I could figure out how to save the situation, Ally leaned closer and whispered, "I'm sure they're both charming, but I don't think I'm ready for a foursome."

Relief swept over me, and I laughed. "Your mind goes to weird places sometimes, you know?"

She grinned. "Yeah." She leaned back in her seat and sighed. "So, is there anything I should know about them?"

I shrugged. "Not really." Then I took a second to think. "Maybe I should warn you about Sam. She's sweet and all, but she's also spontaneous and very, *very* enthusiastic. Sometimes when you spend time with her, you come out of it feeling as if you've been swept away by a hurricane."

Ally smirked. "I think I'll survive."

I shrugged. "Don't say I didn't warn you."

She chuckled. "What about Danny?"

"He likes yanking everyone's chain—except Sam's, I think he's secretly scared of her. But he's a great person. I'm sure you'll get along."

When the Uber parked in front of the house, Ally was back to her true self, relaxed and with her usual bright smile on her face.

Sam opened the door as we were walking up the alley, and her face split into a huge smile. She almost ran out to meet us and surprised both of us by hugging Ally tightly.

"It's so good to see you again, Ally," she said in her usual chirpy voice, the sound of her Cajun accent spicing her words sweetly. She let Ally go and bounced on her toes. "We've heard so much about you, as you can imagine, and I'm dying to get to know you better." She gestured for us to follow. "Come in."

Ally chuckled. I walked up behind her and put my hand on the small of her back. Sam turned around and went inside. Ally turned to me and whispered, "I see what you meant. Hurricane Samantha, right? I'm tired already."

I grinned, and we walked in.

Sam and Ally immediately clicked. Five minutes in, and they were already laughing—mainly at Danny's and my expense, but I didn't mind. Seeing her get on so well with my best friends had my heart leaping in my chest. We went on a tour of the house, then settled in the garden. I joined Danny at the grill while Sam and Ally kept talking at the table.

After dinner, Sam and I cleared the table. I softly kissed Ally's lips before following Sam to the kitchen to load the dishwasher.

"So, she's still here," Sam said. "It's been three weeks, right?"

I nodded.

"I thought you said she didn't stay put very long."

"She usually doesn't."

Sam leaned against the kitchen cabinet and watched me. "How come she hasn't left yet?"

I shrugged. "I don't know. Maybe she likes it here."

"Or maybe she likes you," Sam said.

That thought made my heart leap in my chest, but I gave a dismissive wave of the hand. "I have nothing to do with that. Ally does what she wants."

Sam nodded. "Exactly. So she wants to stay with you."

I finished loading the dishwasher, not answering. Sam turned it on, then turned to me.

"So, now that you got to know her better, how is she?"

"She's great." I tried to keep my face blank and to sound casual. "We get on really well, and it's easy to have her in the house."

Sam threw me a knowing look. "You love her," she said in a playful tone, wiggling her eyebrows. "Ally and Steve, sitting in a tree—"

I put my hand on her mouth to cut her off, and shushed her, looking behind me to make sure Ally wasn't near us.

Sam swatted my hand away. "Oh my God, you do love her!" she exclaimed cheerfully—and very loudly. She jumped on the spot and clapped her hands enthusiastically.

"Shut up," I whisper-shouted. "She can't know that."

Sam stopped jumping and cocked her head, looking confused. "Why not?"

I cringed. "I think it would scare her away."

She started laughing but stopped when she saw the serious look on my face. "What do you mean, it would scare her away?"

"I don't know." I ran my hand over my face. "There's still so much I don't know about her. She won't talk about her life in France, her past, or even her family. Every time I mention it, she shuts up completely."

Sam looked at me, her brows drawn together. "Why?"

"I don't know." I scratched the back of my neck. "I'd love to have the full picture of her life. I wish she would trust me, you know? Or maybe just like me enough to talk to me."

"Oh, I think she likes you quite a lot."

I shook my head. "No, she doesn't. I mean, she likes me just fine, or she wouldn't be here anymore, but not like *that*. She even told me she would have to leave and made me promise not to hold her back."

"That doesn't mean she doesn't like you, dumbass."

I stared.

Sam gave me her best *duh* look. "Really, Steve? After all those romance novels you read, you're still that clueless?" She chuckled. "When we go back out, watch her and you'll see. She always seeks you out. She turns halfway toward you all the time, like she's gravitating around you." She poked me in the arm. "You do the same. It's obvious you both have it bad for each other."

We stood there in silence for a few seconds, then she shook herself up and sighed dramatically. "Okay, I promise I won't tell her you love her." She went back outside, leaving me to ponder her words.

Did I love Ally? Getting to kiss her goodnight and waking up every morning next to her certainly was the best feeling in the world. And the thought of her leaving did stab me in the heart every time it crossed my mind. I had been obsessed with her for a long time now. But did I love her? I wasn't so sure. I had never believed in love at first sight, and since my divorce, I wasn't sure I believed in love at all. So I didn't think I could fall for someone in only a few weeks, even someone as memorable as Ally.

But maybe I was wrong. I had been wrong before—very often. I had never been good at reading my own feelings, let alone other people's. Sam was right about one thing—I really was clueless.

I shook my head, trying to get back to reality, and went back outside. Ally, Danny and Sam were roaring with laughter. I gave Sam a look of concern, worried that she had spilled the beans.

But Danny said, "I was telling Ally about the time you kissed a drag queen."

That had happened shortly after Nicole and I had split up, and I had moved back to San Francisco. Danny had taken me to a bar, not knowing it was a special, drag night. I had gotten drunk, had danced, and had ended up kissing someone, not realizing they were a man in drag. Danny had to pull me away and out of the bar to get me home. He hadn't told me about it until the next day when I had sobered up a bit.

I cringed at the memory. "Yeah, that wasn't my best moment," I mumbled.

Ally laughed. "How was the kiss?" she asked.

I sat down on the chair next to her and put my hand on her thigh under the table. I squeezed her leg gently. "Really good. I remember wanting to take them home with me. But I was wasted so I might have embellished the memory."

They all laughed at my expense.

I cleared my throat. "Can we change the subject now?"

"Yes," Danny said. His face grew stern, and he scowled at me. "I have a bone to pick with you, mate."

I froze. "What did I do?"

"You still haven't said you'll come to my birthday party."

Oh, right. He had texted me repeatedly about it, but I still hadn't RSVP'd.

I let out a breath. "That's what you're mad about? A bit over-reacting, aren't you?" I chuckled at Danny's look of indignation. "I'm sorry, man, I still don't know if I'll be able to make it."

Ally sat up straight in her chair. "When is it?"

"Next Friday."

Ally turned to me. "Why aren't you going?"

I shrugged. I couldn't tell her I was reluctant to make plans, not knowing when she would leave. If she left before the birthday, I wouldn't be in the right mood to go out, and I wouldn't want to spoil Danny's party. In a way, I hated how my life was now revolving around her because when she decided to go, she would leave a huge, empty space behind her.

Ally looked shocked. "You're seriously going to pass on your best friend's birthday?" Turning to Danny, she asked, "What do you have planned?"

"Nothing fancy," he said. "It's pretty much like our usual volleyball game at the beach. There'll be beer, meat, and a lot of people."

Ally turned to me again. "You have to go, Steve."

"Yes, you have to go, Steve," Danny repeated.

I scowled at him. He completely ignored me and turned to Ally.

"You're invited too, Ally."

Her head snapped back to Danny. "I am?"

"Of course," Sam said.

Ally smiled broadly. "I'd love to come, thanks." She turned to me. "I'm going to Danny's birthday party." She turned to Danny again. "Can I bring a date?"

Danny winked. "Of course."

"Hey, Steve," Ally said, tapping me on the shoulder. "Do you want to go to Danny's birthday party with me?"

I snorted. "Fine, count me in."

"Jeez, could you be more excited?" Ally huffed.

I chuckled and leaned in to kiss her cheek. "I'd love to go."

Danny clapped his hands together. "Great. Let's move inside for dessert, it's getting chilly."

When Danny hugged me goodbye an hour later, he whispered, "I'm glad to see you happy."

Yes, I was happy. My chest hurt, my heart was so full of joy. And Ally going to Danny's party meant she was planning to stay an extra week. That thought almost brought me to my knees.

14

GRATITUDE

"Are you ready?" I called out to Ally.

The week had gone by in a flash. It was Friday evening already, and high time for us to leave for Ocean Beach. I was sitting on the armchair, putting on my shoes. Colonel was lying on the coffee table, glaring at me, his tail slowly thumping the wood. He knew we were going out and was giving me the stink eye. He had gotten too used to spending the evenings on Ally's lap and knew that wasn't going to happen tonight.

When Ally climbed down the stairs, wearing high-waisted denim shorts and a gray crop top that hid nothing of her perfect stomach, my eyes stuck on her and my brain misfired. I stayed motionless, bent at the waist with a half-tied shoelace in hand, mouth wide open, gawking at Ally in silence.

She was busy putting on her bracelet, so she didn't notice me staring.

"Where is the party again?" she asked.

I snapped my mouth shut and shook my head, trying to come back to reality. "Ocean Beach," I croaked.

She raised her head at the husky sound of my voice and caught me staring. She smirked.

I cleared my throat and looked down to finish tying my shoe. "Are you really going to wear that?"

"You don't like it?"

I looked up at her with raised eyebrows. She knew damn well I loved it. I could see it in the cheeky gleam in her eyes.

"Something's missing," I said.

I stood up and went to the chair where her new Giants jersey was draped. We had gone to see a game earlier that week, and I had bought one for her, to make up for the Yankees cap she had decided to wear. I took the jersey and put it on Ally's shoulders.

"Now, it's perfect."

She snorted. "What is it with you and the Giants?"

I smiled. "They were the first team I ever watched live."

Her smile softened. "How old were you?"

"Five or six? My aunt took me to my first game, and the Giants won."

"The same aunt who left you this house?"

I nodded.

"So... you like my outfit?"

A slow smile spread across my face. I bent down and kissed her, then lifted her and took her to the couch. When I started unbuttoning her shorts, Colonel meowed and Ally tried to stop me.

"We've got an audience," she panted.

"I don't care." I kissed down her stomach.

"He's going to be traumatized." Her hands were in my hair, pulling lightly.

"He's seen worse." I slid her shorts down.

"We'll be late," she moaned.

"Let's be quick, then."

Needless to say, we weren't quick. By the time we arrived at Ocean Beach, everyone was there, the fire was burning strong, and a volleyball game had started. Danny was talking with Jeffrey. He waved when he saw us arrive. We joined them, and I hugged Danny.

"Sorry we're late," I said.

"We're not sorry," Ally said.

Danny winked at her. "I'm sure you're not. You're both glowing."

My cheeks heated.

"Especially Steve," Ally said, completely unfazed.

Danny laughed and kissed her on the cheek.

I looked around at the people present. Sam was chatting with her cousin Jill, and Maisy. Sam spotted us and waved frantically, making Maisy turn around. When she saw us, Maisy froze and her smile faltered. I couldn't blame her. We had texted a bit in the last few weeks, and she knew that Ally—the real one—had finally contacted me, but we hadn't seen each other since my birthday. She recovered quickly though, and she smiled and waved at us.

I took Ally's hand, and we went to the group of women. Sam hugged us both. I kissed Maisy and Jill on the cheek, and introduced Ally to everyone.

"It's nice to meet you," Maisy said. "I've heard so much about you."

Ally's eyes darted to mine, then she turned to Maisy and smiled back. "It's nice to meet you too."

"This is Jill, Sam's cousin," I said, gesturing toward the red-haired woman.

"What do you want to drink?" Sam asked us. "We've got beer, wine, soft drinks, and there's a pitcher of margarita."

"I'd love some margarita," Ally said.

"I'll go get the drinks." I leaned down and kissed her temple. "Will you be okay here?" I asked in a whisper.

Ally nodded.

When I came back with the glasses, all four women were chatting animatedly. I handed Ally her drink and leaned toward her, putting my hand on the small of her back.

"You okay?" I whispered in her ear.

She turned and winked. We chatted for a while, waiting for the game to end. When the players scattered around, laughing, one of them—a tall guy with dark hair who seemed vaguely familiar—walked toward us and put his arm around Jill's shoulders.

"Guys, this is my boyfriend, Simon," Jill said.

Under my hand, Ally tensed. I threw her a quick glance. Her face had paled, her lips pinched, and the corners of her eyes tightened. She almost took a step back.

"Simon, this is Steve, Danny's best friend, and Ally," Jill continued, unaware of Ally's reaction.

I shook Simon's hand. After a few seconds of awkward silence, Ally did the same. She smiled a weird, strained smile and said nothing. I couldn't understand her reaction. I'd never seen her be anything but open and jovial when meeting new people. What was going on? Had she met Simon before? Or did she know someone who looked like him?

Sam was also looking at Ally, her brows furrowed. She looked at me quickly and opened her mouth to say something, but I shook my head slightly, silently asking her not to say anything.

I tightened my grip on Ally's waist. "Let's go get another drink," I said.

Ally followed me in silence. She seemed lost in thoughts.

"Are you alright?" I asked her when we were out of reach of prying ears.

She started slightly. "Of course," she said, not looking at me.

We reached the table with the drinks. I filled her glass with margarita and grabbed a beer from the cooler.

"Have you met Simon before?" I asked.

"What?" She turned to me. "Of course, not. Why would you think that?"

I tucked a strand of hair behind her ear and shrugged. "I don't know. You had a weird reaction when you saw him."

Ally shook her head. "It's nothing, he just reminded me of someone."

I frowned. "Who?"

She shook her head again but didn't answer. She closed her eyes and took a deep breath. When she opened her eyes again, they were clearer, and her face relaxed. "I'm sorry, it was just a blast from the past." She smiled a smile that looked more like her usual sunny one, though not completely yet. She stepped on tiptoes and kissed me softly. "Don't worry, I'm fine."

"Okay," I said.

Of course, she was fine.

But what happens when fine isn't good enough, Ally?

We joined Danny near the fire, where he had started grilling the meat, and sat down in the sand. Sam joined us after a while and gave me a pointed look. I smiled and winked.

Sam turned to Ally. "Boys against girls, are you in?"

"I wouldn't miss that," Ally said, jumping to her feet. She took off her Giants jersey and handed it to me. "Can you keep this for me?"

I watched Ally and Sam join Maisy near the net. She played with a lot of enthusiasm, diving for the ball, smashing it to the other side, and laughing. When she came back to sit with me at the end of the game—that the women won hands down—her cheeks were pink and her eyes were shining brightly. She was still laughing. I kissed her before draping her jersey over her shoulders and handing her another glass of margarita.

Everyone gathered around the fire to eat. Ally took a few pictures of Danny and Sam, then tried to take some of me, but I took her phone from her. We took a few selfies instead, making the most stupid grimaces possible to the camera, sticking out our tongues, and bulging our eyes.

When it was getting dark, I took Ally's hand and pulled her to her feet.

"Let's walk," I said.

We walked away from the sand, toward the cliff at the end of the beach. When we were far away from the group, I put my hands on her waist and backed her against the cliff. I leaned against her and kissed her. As it was our habit, the kiss started softly but quickly turned passionate. When she felt my hard body pressing against her, she rolled her hips, making me moan. I broke the kiss.

"Stop that," I panted. "I've been on edge all evening." I looked at her bright eyes. "You look happy."

Her chest was rising and falling against mine. She ran a finger along my jawline and smiled, but didn't say anything. So I kissed her again. We made out in the darkness for a while until I heard someone call after me. We broke our kiss, both breathing hard.

"Fuck," I whispered, leaning my forehead against hers.

"We'd better go back before they come looking for us." She patted my chest.

"Yeah," I mumbled, taking a step back. I winced. "I just need a minute to—you know." I gestured vaguely.

Ally chuckled softly.

We walked back to the fire, hand in hand, laughing like goofy teenagers.

Danny was watching us, a knowing smirk on his face. "Sorry I interrupted whatever you were doing," he said when we joined them.

My cheeks got warm. "Shut up."

"Are you up for a one-on-one game?" Danny asked me.

"It's too dark to play," I said.

"Are you scared of losing?" he smirked back.

I scoffed. "I'll bet you fifty I win."

"You're on," he said with a devilish grin.

I turned to Ally. "Do you mind?"

She gave a dismissive wave of the hand. "Not at all."

"I'll keep her company," Maisy said. "We haven't had time to talk much yet."

I looked at Maisy, feeling inexplicably worried, but she wore a friendly expression and winked at me.

During the game, I took a few balls on the head because I kept turning to the fire to watch Ally and Maisy. They were sitting in the sand, a bit further from the fire. They seemed to be having a friendly chat, gesturing and laughing, occasionally pointing at us. I'd been afraid Maisy would be cold, or downright unpleasant toward

Ally, but I shouldn't have worried. As always, Maisy was friendly and welcoming.

"That's fine, keep looking at Ally," Danny smirked. "I need those fifty bucks."

I gave him the finger and tried to concentrate on the game. And I ended up winning. Danny tackled me in the sand in revenge. We struggled for a while until I got him in a headlock and he surrendered. I helped him stand up, laughing at his sour look.

"Come on, let's have a beer," I said, slapping his shoulder.

"Yeah, I need Sam to lick my wounds."

We walked back to the fire. Maisy and Ally were still sitting together. I grabbed a beer and sat down on Ally's side. My head was spinning. Not from the alcohol—I'd only had a few beers—but the adrenalin of the game and the joy of being with Ally, of seeing her so happy; all of it was intoxicating.

Maybe that explained why I didn't notice something was wrong.

It was past midnight when I realized Ally wasn't sitting next to me anymore. I looked around. Most of Danny's friends had gone home, so I easily spotted her standing in the shallow waters of the ocean. I joined her.

"Hey," I said softly. "I'm sorry, I didn't notice it was this late."

She shrugged. "No worries."

I looked at her stern face. "Are you alright?"

She nodded. "It's been a long day, that's all."

There was something else, I could see it. Her eyes had lost their bright spark. Or maybe I was being my usual Downer Dan.

I kissed her gently. "Let's go home, then."

We called an Uber. Ally stayed silent in the car. She was sitting on the far end of the backseat, looking out of the window.

I leaned toward her and asked, "A penny for your thoughts?"

She jolted and turned to me. "What?"

"You seem lost in thoughts."

She shook her head. "I'm fine." She put her hand on mine and smiled, but it didn't reach her eyes. "I'm just tired." She squeezed my hand and let it go. She put one foot on the seat and crossed her arms around her knee, physically closing up. We didn't speak another word for the rest of the journey.

Back home, Ally took off her sneakers and turned to me. Her eyes were fixed somewhere over my shoulder. "I'll sleep in the guest room tonight if you don't mind."

My stomach dropped to my feet. I didn't like the sound of that.

"Why?" I asked her.

"I think it will be a bad night. I don't want to wake you up if I have night terrors."

I shrugged. "I don't care if you wake me up, Ally. In fact, I'd rather you do."

"You need to catch up on sleep."

Ally still wasn't looking at me. My hands started shaking. Ally turned around and started toward the stairs, but I grabbed her hand and stopped her.

"Did I do something wrong?" My voice shook slightly.

She finally looked at me. Her eyes were shining with the beginning of tears. She shook her head. "Of course, you didn't."

"Tell me what's wrong, then," I pleaded.

Ally looked away.

All the blood left me, and my body almost went limp as, at last, my brain caught up. The room seemed to shrink down on me.

"You're going to leave," I whispered.

Ally shut her eyes tight and lowered her head. I put my fingers under her chin and gently lifted her head.

"Why now?" I whispered. There was a huge lump in my throat. I didn't dare speak loudly for fear of my voice breaking on the words. "Did something happen tonight? Did I say or do something to upset you?"

She shook her head, keeping her eyes closed. "No. It's just that I've stayed here long enough."

"You've only just arrived." My voice quivered.

She shook her head again. "I never planned to stay here this long. I got caught up in us and lost track of time. I need to move on." She opened her eyes. They were brimming with tears. "And I think you do, too."

My heart squeezed painfully. "Will you at least stay until tomorrow?" I asked in a shaky voice.

She nodded.

"Sleep with me tonight. Please."

She hesitated, then nodded again. I leaned down and kissed her softly. We went straight to bed.

That night, we didn't have sex—we made love. It was soft, tender. I tried to convey my feelings for her with my body. I couldn't lie to myself anymore. I had fallen in love with Ally, and I needed her to know. Every kiss was an *I love you*; every caress, an *I'll miss you*; every sigh, a *Don't leave me yet.* And I was probably deluding myself, but I thought that her eyes were saying *I love you, too.*

She fell asleep in my arms. I didn't dare follow her in slumber. I was scared that she would leave and I wouldn't wake up to see her go. There was a pit of despair in my stomach and I feared I would fall into it and break into pieces. So I stayed awake, fighting back tears, and tried to commit to memory the feel of Ally in my arms; how her lean body fitted against mine; how her chest rose under my arm with every breath she took; how her earthy smell reminded me of rain in the spring.

And I slowly made my peace with watching her walk away. I decided to be grateful for having met her and having spent so much time with her. I had never expected her to stay this long. I knew that her departure would wreck me. But she had awakened something in me, a spark of life that Nicole had smothered. That was what I would keep from my time with Ally.

When Ally woke up a couple of hours later, the sun was already up, and I was still awake and holding her tight. She turned to me and kissed me.

"Hey, handsome."

"Good morning, beautiful."

There was a tinge of sadness in the smile we exchanged. We got up and showered together. Then I let Ally pack and went into the kitchen. When she came downstairs ten minutes later, holding her suitcase and backpack, breakfast was ready on the table.

We ate in a silence heavy with sorrow and—for my part—dread. When Colonel joined us, Ally picked him up and hugged him, telling him things I couldn't hear. He meowed softly in answer, pawing her hair.

She let him go and stood up, not looking at me. She picked up her bags and went out to load her car. I followed her and watched her, feeling numb. My arms were heavy, my head spinning. How was I supposed to let her go? I had promised not to hold her back. But it was too damn hard.

She came back inside and walked toward me.

"Ally—" My voice broke. I swallowed thickly. "I don't know how to let you go." My throat was so tight that the words came out strained.

Ally looked up at me. "You promised, Steve."

I closed my eyes. She stroked my cheek and I leaned into her hand. I had to tell her. I hadn't said the words to anyone in ages. But she deserved to hear them.

I opened my mouth to speak, but her lips swallowed my words. We shared a desperate kiss.

When we parted, I blinked a few times, trying to keep my eyes dry. Ally's cheeks were wet. She smiled softly.

"I know," she whispered.

Then she dropped her hand, turned around and went out. I watched her climb into her car and start the engine. She smiled at me one last time. Then, she was gone.

I went back in, slowly closed the door, and looked around me. Colonel was watching me, meowing softly, his head tilted to the side as if asking where Ally had gone.

I picked him up and we went upstairs. The guest room door was open and I walked in. The bed was made. On top of the covers, was a neatly folded Giants jersey and a small piece of paper. I unfolded the note with one hand. There were only two words on it, written in Ally's loopy handwriting. "Thank you."

I picked up the jersey and brought it to my face. It smelled like Ally. I put it back carefully on the bed and left the room, closing the door. I went to my room and found my phone on the bedside table. I sat down on the bed, put Colonel down, and dialed Danny's number.

"Hey, mate," he answered in a sleepy voice. "What's up?"

"Ally's gone," I said.

I squeezed my eyes. And the tears finally rolled down my cheeks.

15

EMPTINESS

October

Three weeks had passed since Ally had left—three weeks that had gone by in a fog of which I kept very few memories.

After I had called him, Danny had come to my place, and he had stayed with me until I had fallen asleep on the couch in the evening. In the days that followed, he came by every evening, made sure I ate, and dragged me out of the house for a walk. I had some recollection of that time, but most of it was a blur.

It had taken Colonel Mustard a whole week to stop pouting and being mad at me. My arms were finally recovering from the scratches and bite marks he had given me, and he was back to his sweet, shy self.

For my part, I was still trying to find balance. It was hard to concentrate on work. I had lost a couple of work projects because I had missed deadlines or had forgotten to reply to emails. I couldn't help thinking about the way Ally had left. I was convinced that something must have happened at Danny's birthday party. She had been perfectly fine during most of the party, but had clammed up somewhere near the end, and I couldn't figure out why. I had asked Danny and Maisy, but they had no idea what had happened either. More than anything—more than the fact that she was gone—not knowing the reason was driving me crazy.

I had texted her a few days after she had left, but the message had remained unread. So I'd tried calling her. When I'd heard the voice telling me the number wasn't assigned, I'd fallen to pieces again. For the second time, she hadn't left me any means of contacting her.

One morning in mid-October, I was woken up by the ping of an incoming text. I scrambled out of bed to grab my phone, trying to quench the spark of hope blooming in my chest.

Maisy: <I heard about Ally. I'm sorry.>

My heart squeezed painfully and sighed. I closed my eyes for a second and took a deep breath before typing an answer.

Me: <It's fine. I knew it would end someday.>

Maisy: <I'm here if you need to talk.>

Me: <Don't worry, I'm fine.>

I stopped myself before I hit send. I couldn't lie anymore. I wasn't fine. Maybe going out would do me some good. I backspaced and typed another message.

Me: <I'd like that. Can we meet tonight?>

We agreed to meet at a pub later that day. But even though it had been my idea, when it was time to leave, I hesitated and almost canceled. Telling myself that I had let Maisy down before and couldn't do it again, I dragged my feet out of my house and rode my scooter to the pub.

In the end, I was glad I had gone. I ended up having a great time. Maisy was a really good listener. I must have talked her ears off, talking about Ally for a good two hours, but it was cleansing. The heavy weight I had been carrying on my shoulders for three weeks got a bit lighter. After a while, we started discussing other things.

"I'm going out with a few friends on Halloween," Maisy said when we were eating dessert. "You're welcome to join us if you want to go out."

I hadn't celebrated Halloween since college. Maisy, Chloe, Tyrone and I never used to do things by half. We would dress up and vote for the best costume—we always voted for ourselves, so no one ever won. Then we would go out on campus and drink all night long.

"Would I have to dress up?" I asked.

She smirked. "Of course."

"I'll think about it."

"How's Colonel?" Maisy asked.

"He's good."

She sighed. "I miss him."

"You do?" I asked in surprise.

"Of course. It was good to have him at my place for a while. I'm considering adopting a cat now."

I chuckled. "So he didn't weird you out?"

Maisy gasped in outrage. "How can you say that? He's the sweetest cat ever." She pondered, then added, "Okay, he's a bit weird, but he's adorable."

We stayed in the restaurant until we were the last guests and had no other choice than to leave. I took Maisy on my scooter and brought her home. We stayed for another hour sitting on her front steps and talking. She invited me inside a few times, but I refused and ended up going back home late, feeling a lot better.

Maisy and I texted regularly the following week. She kept reminding me about the party she had planned for Halloween. I was still hesitant and had neither confirmed nor rejected her invitation yet.

Maisy: <Can't wait to see you dressed up as Frank-N-Furter again.>

I groaned. One year back at university, Tyrone had dressed up as Eddie from the Rocky Horror Picture Show, and I had gone for Dr. Frank-N-Furter. That had been an embarrassing night. The fishnet stockings had been particularly uncomfortable.

Me: <Not gonna happen again.>

Maisy: <Too bad, I'd have loved to see you in a corset again.>

Maybe it was weird, but her winky face emoji seemed to have a flirty look.

Maisy: <Still have my old pumpkin costume if you want.>

And that had been another weird year. Maisy had worn a pumpkin costume so large that she had had trouble going through doors.

Me: <Thanks, but I'll come up with something myself.>

And that was how I accepted her invitation.

***

The following two weeks passed in a wink of time, and soon I was standing on the pier, with Maisy and her friends, eating street food. I was looking around me, not engaging in the conversation, but instead looking at the people in all kinds of costumes, laughing, eating and running around.

A warm breath grazed the shell of my ear.

"You're not having fun, are you?" Maisy whispered.

Realizing I had zoned out of the conversation—again—I snapped back to the present and turned to Maisy.

"I am." I shook my head. "Sorry, I'm a bit distracted."

I looked down at my clothes. I hadn't had much time or energy to find a costume, so I had dressed up as Harry Potter. My hair was too long, and it had been easy to mess it up and have it stick up in places. I had drawn a lightning scar on my forehead. My usual round glasses, a white shirt and a red tie completed the look. It was a lame costume, especially compared to what everyone else was wearing. They had all gone to great lengths to stand out in the crowd.

I looked around at our group of friends. We were an odd bunch of people. There were two ninja turtles, a

Buzz Lightyear, and a zombie couple. Maisy had a cowgirl costume on. She was wearing skinny jeans tucked in leather cowboy boots. Her checked flannel shirt was golden and red, which suited her fair skin tone perfectly. And it was very fitting. Since she was very small, she had to crane her neck to see other people's faces above the rim of her hat.

"I'm not the most fun to be around," I apologized.

She waved her hand dismissively. "You're fine. I like spending time with you, no matter your mood."

Her words spread warmth inside my chest, and I made a conscious effort to be more involved in the conversation.

When we were done eating, we left the pier and started going from bar to bar. The others wanted somewhere they could dance, but all the places we stopped in either had terrible music, or were so crowded we couldn't even get inside. We grabbed a few quick drinks here and there, and when we finally settled in one place, my head was already fuzzy. My cheeks were getting numb, the usual sign that I was stepping over my alcohol limit, but I didn't care. I was finally starting to have fun.

When we entered the last club, my heart started thumping faster, adjusting to the rhythm of the music. The girls went straight to the dance floor, but the other guys and I went to the bar instead and ordered a drink. And then another one. As I was emptying my third beer, Maisy joined me.

"Come and dance?" she shouted in my ear, making my eardrums vibrate painfully.

I leaned back slightly and shook my head. "I'm good," I slurred.

"But you're not having fun," she whined.

I grinned. "I am. You look funny when you dance."

I raised a hand in an attempt to give her a high five, but knocked her hat off instead. I bent down to pick it up, almost lost my balance, and caught myself just in time. As I looked up, I realized my face was right in front of Maisy's chest. She had undone the first buttons of her shirt, and her cleavage—very beautiful, full cleavage—was right in front of my face.

Heat crept up my face, and my belly tightened. I shot up straight, all flustered, but Maisy giggled and took her hat from my hands, putting it on my head. Then she took my hand and dragged me to the dance floor.

She started moving to the music, and I followed her, copying her moves. Helped on by her smiles, the alcohol and the atmosphere in the club, I started to relax and came up with my own ridiculous dance moves. I made disco fingers, making Maisy laugh. She started copying me, not caring that we were bumping into other people and getting sour looks. Our sprinkler move was top-notch, and tears of laughter spilled out of Maisy's eyes. When she tried moonwalking, she tripped on her own feet, and I caught her by the waist before she could fall onto the sticky floor. We both staggered a bit before we could find our balance again.

Maisy turned around in my arms and locked her hands behind my neck. She was so tiny that her face barely reached my shoulders. She started moving against me, and I swayed with her. Our eyes locked. The background faded around me as I fell into Maisy's beautiful brown eyes. I wasn't used to holding such a petite woman against me, and my protective instincts kicked in. I loved it.

Our moves turned languorous, and we started grinding together. Maisy's eyes fell to my lips and she bit hers. The sight of her pink, wet tongue sweeping across her lower lip made my blood boil. I leaned down and crushed my lips over hers in a passionate kiss.

After that, things became hazy and I lost track of time. One moment we were kissing on the dance floor, the next we were kissing in a taxi, then we were kissing in her living room.

And when I woke up, it was morning, and I wasn't in my bed. I jumped and sat up at the sound of soft snoring beside me. My head started pounding immediately. I groaned, holding my forehead, then looked to the side. Maisy was lying on her stomach, her head turned toward the wall. The sheets barely covered her lower body, and it was obvious that she was naked. As was I.

I got up, wincing at the feel of my sore muscles. I hadn't done that much physical activity in a while, and my body was reminding me of it. My tongue felt like sandpaper, and I had a sour taste in my mouth.

I picked up my underwear and Harry Potter clothes, and quickly put them on before leaving the room, closing the door quietly behind me. I went into the bathroom, peed and rinsed my mouth, brushing my teeth with a finger coated in toothpaste. I never looked up in the mirror, not daring to look at myself. I was afraid of what I would see.

In the kitchen, I fiddled with the coffee machine for a while before I found how to switch it on. I sat at the table, waiting for the brew to be ready, leaned my head in my hands and groaned. What had I done last night? From the snippets of memory that came to my mind—and our being naked this morning—it was obvious that Maisy and I had had sex. I cringed at the thought. We shouldn't have crossed that boundary. What if I hurt her so much she wouldn't date me, or just go out for a drink again? At the same time, what if I pushed her away only to regret it later?

"Hey," a croaky voice said, making me jump. My head gave an angry throb and I winced, lifting a hand to it.

Squinting, I looked in the doorway, where Maisy was standing, wearing a blue satin robe. Her hair was a mess and her makeup was smudged under her eyes. I was sure I didn't look any better.

"Hey," I croaked back. "Coffee's brewing. I hope you don't mind I used your coffee machine?"

"Of course not." She walked in and sat down in front of me. She handed me a Motrin. "I figured you might need this as much as I do."

"Thanks." I took it and swallowed it dry. A heavy silence fell between us. To cover my embarrassment, I stood up and opened a few cabinet doors, looking for the coffee mugs.

"Above the sink," Maisy told me.

I took two cups, filled them with coffee, and handed Maisy one.

"Do you want some breakfast?" she asked. "I have bacon and eggs."

I started shaking my head, but it pounded so hard that I stopped and put my hand to my forehead.

"Thanks, but I need to go home," I said. "I have to feed Colonel, and I've got some work to do today."

I drank my coffee in one, long gulp and went into the living room to put on my shoes. Maisy followed me. I was aware that leaving without talking to her wasn't a good idea, but since I had a hard time looking at her, I wasn't sure what I would say. My head was in all places. I was scared of saying the wrong thing since I didn't even know what I wanted.

I took a deep breath, put on my imaginary big-boy pants, and turned around to face her. Before I could open my mouth to speak, she leaned in and kissed my cheek.

"Thanks for last night," she said. "I had a great time."

I lowered my eyes and kept them on the ground. "Me too," I said quickly, losing all my frail courage. "I'll talk to you later."

And I left, feeling every bit like the coward I was.

16

OPTIMISM

Back home, I fed Colonel and gave him his morning cuddle, then went upstairs to shower. I still didn't dare look in the mirror, and could only hope that my Harry Potter lightning scar was gone with the soap. I brushed my teeth twice, trying to get rid of the lingering taste of alcohol.

I came back downstairs, gulped down two glasses of water and took another Motrin, then threw myself onto the couch. I felt like crap—hungover, regretful and ashamed of myself. Not a good combination.

I should never have slept with Maisy, not when I was drunk, and not when I was hung up on another woman. We were both wasted, and I felt like I had taken advantage of her. Using Maisy to get over Ally wasn't fair to anyone, not even me. And yet, I couldn't deny that I'd had a lot of fun last night with Maisy. And the lust I'd felt then had been real.

I groaned. I was stuck between my fantasy life with Ally and the prospect of what could happen with Maisy. But Ally was gone, wasn't she? She wasn't coming back. I couldn't even get in touch with her. Maisy, on the other hand, was here with me. She was sweet and understanding, and she seemed willing to wait for me. She was good for me. Every time I saw her, I came back home feeling energized. If Ally had been my own, private sun, Maisy was my much-needed breath of fresh air. Maybe that was exactly what I needed. Calming, cleansing breaths instead of burning passion.

In the early evening, I decided to settle things with Maisy and dialed her number.

"How are you feeling?" I asked her when she picked up.

She groaned, but she sounded more like a very cute kitten than anything else. "I'm a wreck. Next time we go out, remind me not to drink too much."

I snorted. "I would have thought you'd learned the lesson back at university." Back then, we had had our share of hangovers and nights spent with our heads in the toilet.

She groaned again. "Don't remind me of that, you'll make me barf."

I grew serious. "Look, Maisy, I need to apologize about last night. I shouldn't have taken advantage of you."

She giggled. "You didn't take advantage of me."

I frowned. Had my memories been wrong? "Didn't we... have sex?"

She laughed. "Wow, I must have made an impression, seeing how you remember it. Yes, we had sex."

I cringed. "Sorry. I was wasted last night, I don't remember much after we started dancing." I sighed. "That's why I'm apologizing. I should have kept my head straight."

"There's no need to apologize," she replied. "I was drunk too, though not so much that I couldn't have stopped you if I'd wanted to. But I didn't want to stop." I heard some shuffling over the phone, and Maisy took a deep breath. "You know how I feel about you, Steve. I wanted this to happen."

I didn't know what to say to that, so I kept my mouth shut.

"Are you still there?" she asked.

I had to say something. It was obvious Maisy wasn't angry with me. So maybe I should take the plunge and see if we could be something?

Before I could think more about it, I blurted out, "Do you want to have dinner with me sometime this week?"

I didn't mean dive in with both feet first, dumbass. Couldn't you be smoother sometimes?

There was a short silence, then Maisy said softly, "I'd love to."

I could hear the smile in her voice and started to relax. Maybe things would turn out well in the end.

I spent the next day tidying up the house. Maisy was coming over in the evening, and I said I would cook for her. She told me we could order something, but I wanted to do that for her.

I used my mother's secret recipe to make lasagna, then took a quick shower in the hope it would help me relax before Maisy arrived. It didn't. I was still feeling jittery when I got dressed. I had just uncorked a bottle of wine to let it breathe when there was a knock on the door. Maisy's smiling face greeted me when I opened the door, and only then did my nerves calm down. I went in for a hug, but she stood on tiptoes and kissed me softly on the lips.

We had a great time at dinner. Maisy kept gushing over my lasagna, insisting that she could never cook something that fantastic. I shrugged at her compliments. My mother had taught me to cook at an early age, so it was natural to me. I didn't often have the time or opportunity to cook more elaborate dishes, but I still enjoyed it.

After we ate, we settled on the couch with our glasses of wine. Things were easy between us. We kept talking, reminiscing about our time at Stanford, talking about our old friends and student jobs we had had. Every time one of us shifted on the couch, we got closer and closer. So much so, that my body started to wake up, and I felt the need to kiss her.

When Maisy leaned forward to put her glass of wine on the coffee table, her hair fell over her shoulder, hiding her face from me. She sat back, and I tucked the long strands of blond hair behind her ear. My fingers swept across her jawline and gently turned her head to me. I leaned down and brushed my lips against hers. Our kiss didn't hold the same passion as the drunken one we had shared two days before. But it was sweet and tender. I hadn't realized I needed sweet and tender.

I lay down on the couch, dragging Maisy down with me. Our kiss deepened, and Maisy started moving her body against mine. Heat spread in my lower belly as my body reacted to her touch.

I leaned back, breaking our kiss.

"Do you want to spend the night here?" I asked, panting slightly.

Maisy's mouth fell in a frown. "I'd love to, but I can't." She kissed me again, then sat up and straightened her clothes. "I'm sorry, I have to get up early tomorrow. I'm going to be out of town for a couple of days. I need to write an article about the frequent landslides along Highway 1. I'll be back on Wednesday."

I sat up too. "So I won't see you until then?"

I tried to stifle my disappointment. So what if she didn't stay here tonight? That didn't matter. We would see each other again, I was sure of it. I wanted to see where things would go between us.

Maisy wasn't fooled. She smiled softly, and leaned toward me, kissing my lips softly.

"I'll call you when I'm back, I promise."

I walked her to the door, and we shared one last kiss before she went home.

Maisy and I went out again on Wednesday night after she came back from her work mission. We went to the cinema, then back to her apartment. We had a great time together. Things were finally coming together.

We spent the night together. On Thursday morning, I woke up early and rummaged through her kitchen cabinets to find something to cook for breakfast. I made oatmeal, a fruit salad and coffee, and loaded up a tray to bring to Maisy in bed.

"How come you're up so early?" Maisy asked me, taking a bite of her oatmeal.

"I need to get going soon. I'm meeting Danny at ten, and I need to go by my house to feed Colonel first."

"You're spending the day with him?" She looked slightly put off.

"Colonel?"

She slapped my chest with humor. "No, you idiot, Danny."

"Oh, right." I shook my head, laughing. "Yeah, I'm helping him choose a wedding venue. He wants a second opinion before they make a decision."

"That sounds fun," she said, sounding unusually sarcastic. "Can't Sam do it with him?"

"She has to work."

Maisy's smile was a bit tight. "I thought we'd spend the day together."

Her reaction surprised me. I'd never seen that possessive, jealous side of her.

"I'm sorry I can't stay here, but we made plans a long time ago." I leaned forward to kiss her. "I promised I would help him."

She smiled, a bit more genuinely this time. "That's alright."

I went home, took care of Colonel, then went to Danny's place. I joined him in the kitchen.

"When's the first appointment?" I asked him.

"In an hour. There's a bit of a drive, so we have to leave in fifteen minutes." He handed me a cup of coffee. "You look good," he said, watching me closely.

"I am." I lifted my cup to hide my smile, but Danny knew me too well.

"What's going on?" he asked.

"Nothing," I said innocently.

"Don't fuck with me, mate."

He leaned toward me and looked at me with sharp eyes. He could give a very weird, penetrative stare when he wanted to. It never failed to unsettle me. My cheeks heated and I knew I was blushing. Danny's lips slowly stretched into a cocky smile.

"You hooked up with someone," he said winningly.

I put down my cup a bit forcefully and spilled coffee off the table. "For Pete's sake, could you pretend that you can't read my mind?"

He laughed. "Sorry, mate, but you can't lie for shit. Your face is an open book." He took a sip of his coffee. "So, who is it?"

Not answering, I stood up and picked up the dishcloth to wipe the coffee on the table.

Danny insisted. "Come on, I tell you everything."

I scoffed. "No, you don't."

He shrugged. "I tell you all the important stuff."

I shook my head and sat down at the table again.

"Consider this my wedding gift."

I barked out a laugh. "Damn it, I'll have to return the Ducati I bought you, then."

He gaped. "You bought me a Ducati?"

"Sure, because I have that kind of money."

He smirked. "Aren't actors supposed to be shamefully rich?"

"Not this one." I picked up my cup of coffee and drank the last drops.

He stomped his foot on the ground, like an angry toddler. "Come on, I want to know," he whined.

I sighed heavily, shaking my head. "Fine. But don't judge me, okay?"

He nodded, smiling broadly.

"It's Maisy."

He looked startled. "Maisy as in Sam's friend?"

I nodded.

"As in your former college roommate?"

"That's the one."

"The small blond?"

"I think we've established who she is."

His smile faded, and he frowned. "How did that happen?"

I told him about Halloween and our date nights—without the juicy details, of course, I wasn't one to kiss and tell. Usually.

Danny kept his eyes locked on mine. "How do you feel about her?"

I shrugged one shoulder. "I don't know. It's still new, we've only been out a few times. She's really sweet."

"Sweet?"

I cringed. That was definitely not a good word to describe the woman I was sleeping with.

"I don't know what to tell you," I said. "I feel good when I'm with her. More centered. That's what I need right now."

"Do you think you'll become serious?" Danny asked.

"How would I know? It's only been a week."

He stayed silent for a moment, then asked, "So you're happy?"

"I'm happi*er*, I guess."

"Well, that's good, then." He stood up and clapped me on the shoulder. "Come on, we have to go."

We spent the day visiting several wedding venues. After each visit, we took a moment in Danny's car to grade the place. Sam had prepared an evaluation grid, and we had to assess several aspects of the places. Was it clean? How were the restrooms? Did they offer a catering service? Was there enough room for a dance floor? What about a stage for the speeches? How were the surroundings? Would the wedding pictures look good there? The list of questions was endless.

"Do we have to do this for each place?" I asked unbelievingly, after our first visit.

"Sorry, mate." He cringed. "Sam can be a bit overbearing. She drives me crazy, sometimes."

I snorted. "Are you sure you want to marry her?"

"Absolutely," he replied very seriously. "Anyway, there's no way I could change my mind now, she would lock me up in the basement and drag me to the altar."

I laughed. Yes, Samona the stalker would definitely do that.

By five in the afternoon, we had driven a few hundred miles, had seen six different places, and had only had a quick sandwich in the car. We were starving, spent, and in much need of a cold beer.

We went to our favorite pub and sat facing each other. Danny had been acting a bit reserved all day, and even now, he still had a worried look on his face and was fiddling with his coaster in silence. I couldn't take it any longer. I put my glass down.

"Is everything alright with Sam?"

Danny bucked. "What? Of course. Why do you ask?"

"Because you're distracted, and you've had this worried look all day long. I can't figure out why, and now I'm getting worried. And you know how fragile my nerves are."

Danny shook his head. "There's nothing wrong."

He tried to sound casual. But just like he could read my mind, I too could always tell when he was lying.

I looked at him sternly, and he cringed. "Don't make that face, mate, you're giving me the same look Sam does when she's upset."

I recoiled a bit and unknit my brows slightly. "You need to stop bullshitting me, Danny."

Danny sighed. "There's something I need to tell you."

"I kind of figured that out," I huffed.

He ran a hand over his face. "You won't be happy, and I'm sorry for that." He emptied his beer in one gulp and started talking. "It's about Maisy. Sam overheard a conversation she had with Ally at my birthday party. We weren't going to tell you about it, but since you and Maisy are dating, I think you should know, before things get too serious."

My beer churned uncomfortably in my stomach. The hair on my arms raised in anticipation of the bad news I sensed coming.

"What is it?" I asked.

"It was quite late in the evening. We were in the middle of a game, and Maisy and Ally were talking."

I remembered that moment. I could still see Ally's gleaming eyes watching me in the twilight. That had been shortly before she had clammed up.

"Sam was right behind them, putting off the fire, but they didn't see her. She heard Maisy tell Ally about Nicole and the divorce. And—" He trailed off.

It was obvious that Danny didn't want to tell me about it, but I pushed. "And what, Danny?" My voice was harsher than I intended, and he flinched. "Sorry," I sighed. "Just tell me, man."

Danny took a deep breath, then spilled everything. He spoke quickly, without taking a breath, getting it all off his chest in one go. "Maisy told Ally that if she wasn't going to commit to you, she should think twice about staying longer. She said she could see that you were already in love with Ally, and it would break you the day she left. So if she wasn't going to stay, the sooner she left, the better it would be for you."

When Danny stopped talking, total silence had fallen around us. I couldn't hear a thing, except his harsh breathing and the echo of his words. I didn't see anything but the stricken look on his face.

"Maisy told Ally to leave?" I asked, my voice thick. My stomach clenched, and I felt as if I was going to be sick.

Danny nodded. "I'm really sorry."

"Why didn't you say something earlier?" I almost didn't recognize my voice. It sounded empty. "I asked you if you'd noticed something wrong. Why didn't you tell me?"

"I didn't know then. Sam only told me later."

"And you couldn't call me and explain?"

He winced. "I'm so sorry, Steve. I know I should have, but—"

"I can't believe this." I stood up in a daze, pushing the table away. Our glasses fell, spilling beer on the table, but

I barely noticed it. My brain was on a loop. *The sooner she left, the better it would be.*

"Steve?" Danny's voice seemed to come from a distance.

I walked toward the door. Danny caught up to me and grabbed my arm.

"Steve, wait."

I shrugged him off and continued walking.

"Talk to me, mate."

I whirled around and faced him. "Ally's been gone for two months, and you're only telling me now?" My voice was shaking, sounding shrill with the effort I was making not to shout at Danny.

He grimaced. "I didn't want to make you feel worse. You were a wreck when Ally left. I was so worried for you. You've only just started to get better, and I didn't want to mess you up again."

My hands were shaking. I squeezed them into fists to try and steady them. "And you thought it was better to lie to me?" I hissed.

People were staring at us, but I couldn't care less.

"I thought that was best for you." His face was ashen. "I mean, Ally was never going to stay forever, was she? So maybe Maisy's right. You guys shouldn't have reconnected."

I let out a humorless laugh. "That's rich, coming from the guy who insisted I put myself out there. I wouldn't be in this mess if it wasn't for you."

My heart was pounding in my ears. I lifted a fist to my mouth and closed my eyes, breathing deeply to stop the nausea. When I opened my eyes again, Danny was still standing in front of me.

"I'm so sorry, Steve. Please come back to our table, so we can talk it out," he said.

I shook my head and let my hand fall to my side. "I need to talk to Maisy."

Danny grabbed my elbow and tried to stir me toward the table. "I don't think now is the best time. Maybe you should sleep on it before you talk to her."

I shook him off. "Shut up. You don't know anything. I've had enough of your meddling for a while." Danny's face crumbled, but I ignored it. "I have to go."

I turned and left, ignoring his calls, and went out in the pouring rain.

17

BETRAYAL

I walked the three miles from the pub to Maisy's place in a haze. When I arrived, I was drenched. A cold wind had started to blow, freezing me to the bone. My teeth were chattering, both from the cold and the anger. I had managed to get my nerves under control and my nausea had passed, but fury was still pulsing through my veins, and my eyes were starting to burn. I took a few deep breaths before ringing her door.

"It's Steve," I said through the intercom.

Maisy buzzed me in, and I climbed the stairs two at a time. Maisy was waiting for me at the open door of her apartment, smiling happily. When she saw me, her face fell and a look of concern replaced the smile.

"My God, Steve, you're soaked."

I walked in without saying a word.

"Steve? What's wrong?"

I heard the door close behind me and whirled around to face her. "Did you tell Ally to leave?" I managed not to shout at her, but my voice was icy cold.

Maisy flinched slightly, but I saw it. Her eyebrows furrowed. "What are you talking about?" she asked in a casual voice.

"Danny's party at the beach," I growled. "Did you tell her to leave me?"

She shook her head. "Of course not."

I pointed a finger at her. "Don't lie to me," I shouted. I breathed slowly and continued in a lower voice. "Sam heard your conversation." I took one step toward her, and she stepped back. "I'll ask you again, did you tell Ally to leave?"

Maisy's face blanched. Her eyes welled up with tears. She crossed her arms, hugging herself tightly. "I was trying to protect you," she whispered.

"Bullshit!"

She flinched and took another step back. "Please, Steve, calm down. You're scaring me."

I closed my eyes. My breathing was shallow and my head was starting to spin from the lack of oxygen. I needed to calm down.

Maisy slowly stepped toward me. "Steve, please listen to me. Can we sit down?"

I made no move to leave or sit. I kept staring at her, my vision blurry, my breathing sharp. "Why did you drive her away from me?" My voice broke with the last words.

Maisy took another step forward. "Do you really think I would do that, Steve? We've been friends for a long time. How can you think I would want to hurt you?"

Maisy put a hand on my chest, but I pushed it away. She dropped her arm to her side.

"I was only looking out for you," she said in a soft voice. "I knew it would break you when she left. I was worried that the longer she stayed, the harder it would be."

Tears started rolling down her cheeks. I ran my hands over my face. I turned and flopped onto the couch. Maisy joined me, her moves measured, as if she were facing a wild animal she didn't want to scare away.

"When you first told me about her in July, I got scared for you. I know you well, Steve. I know how passionate and obsessive you can be when you care about something. How nothing else matters for you when that happens." She put her hand on mine. "I still remember when we were at Stanford, how you would get into a role and stop eating or sleeping to commit to your character. And isn't that what you did with Nicole too? You dropped everything for her. And look how that turned out."

"What's that got to do with anything?" I snarled, removing my hand from under hers.

Maisy flinched. "Sam told me how you were after Nicole cheated on you, how Danny worried you would hurt yourself."

I leaned forward, putting my elbows on my knees and burying my head in my hands. I moaned. I had been a real mess back then, and I knew Danny had been worried about me. I still didn't get where Maisy was going with this, though.

She continued softly. "When we saw each other in July, you spent the whole night talking about her. And I knew you were doing it again, obsessing over something to the point where it would hurt you. I wanted to help you. You know I care about you a lot, Steve." Maisy's voice quivered. She swallowed thickly. "I was angry at Ally, for the way she treated you. And I thought that if you could see how selfish she was, you would be able to move on. And maybe then you would start seeing me and we could get together. So I tried to make you think she was a horrible person. But when that didn't work, I—"

"Wait," I interrupted, lifting my head to look at her. "What are you talking about?"

Maisy's face froze and her eyes opened wide. She covered her mouth with her hand. "Shit."

"What do you mean, you made me think she was horrible?"

Maisy closed her eyes and tears started pouring down her cheeks again. Her shoulders slouched. My brain was spinning, trying to make sense of what she was saying. Then I got it.

"Was it you?" I asked slowly. "The texts from the fake Ally?"

A sob escaped her lips, and she covered her face with her hands.

"It was, wasn't it?" I straightened up. I grabbed her wrists and firmly lowered her hands so she would look at me.

"I'm so sorry, Steve. I didn't mean to—"

"You didn't mean to dupe me, or to tell me you did?" I growled.

She bit her lower lip. "I thought I was helping you," she whispered.

I scoffed.

"I did, I promise. And it worked." She put her hands on my cheeks. "You've been a lot better since she left. You and me, it's been good, hasn't it?" She leaned toward me and softly kissed my lips.

I jerked back and stood up abruptly.

"I can't believe I've been so stupid." My voice was shaking with rage. "How didn't I see it?" I pulled my hair by the handful, hoping the pain would help clench my emotional distress. "How could you do this to me, Maisy?"

Maisy's hands dropped to her lap. She didn't make a move.

"I need to get out of here." I turned to leave.

Maisy stood and grabbed my hand. "Steve, can't we—"

I whirled around and shook her hand off mine. "Don't ever talk to me again," I shouted. I poked her chest with my finger. She flinched, probably from the pain, but I was too far gone in my rage to care. "We're done. I'm done."

I stomped out of Maisy's apartment. I didn't turn back when she called my name, nor when she started crying. I didn't even close the door behind me.

Once I was out on the street, I walked straight ahead, not looking where I was going. The rain was falling even harder, and a chilly wind was blowing. At some point, I started running. I ran, my feet pounding the ground under me, not caring where they were taking me. I only stopped when I was out of breath. My clothes stuck to my body, soaked with rain and sweat. Only then did I realize that my face was wet, not just from the rain, but from the tears I'd been shedding while I was running.

I wiped my face and looked around me, disoriented. Where was I? I took a few more steps before realizing I was standing at the entrance of the trail leading to Marshall's Beach. To the place Ally and I had met in August. I paused, hesitating only for a second, then I walked down the path that led to the small sandy beach. I sat down in the wet sand and stayed there, looking out at the dim glow of the sun setting behind the clouds, shivering in the cold evening air, until it stopped raining and I was all cried out.

When I woke up the next day, my whole body was aching and my head was fuzzy. A dull pounding behind my eyes made me cringe, and I took a Motrin. Either I was coming down with something, or last night's revelations had taken a toll on me. Maybe both.

I went downstairs and made coffee. I looked for my phone, finding it under my drenched jeans. It had died at some point in the evening, and I hadn't cared about charging it when I had come back home. I plugged it in and switched it on. It immediately pinged with a few unread texts.

Danny: <How did it go with Maisy?>

Danny: <Call me when you can.>

Danny: <Please, talk to me.>

Danny: <I'm sorry I didn't tell you sooner.>

Danny: <I'm getting worried. Please call or text me.>

He had also tried calling me but hadn't left a voice-mail. I quickly sent him a text.

Me: <Sorry, I didn't see your texts last night.>

He replied immediately.

Danny: <Thank God, I was starting to freak out.>

Me: <Don't, I'm fine.>

Danny: <Can we talk?>

Me: <Not now.>

After a minute, I texted again.

Me: <I'm not angry. I'll call you later.>

I also had a few missed calls from Nicole. I wasn't ready to deal with her bullshit today, so I ignored them. I swallowed some cold medicine and spent the morning on the couch, curled up with Colonel in my arms, letting his purrs soothe me.

I woke up with a start a couple of hours later at the sound of my phone ringing. I jerked up and my whole body protested. I was definitely coming down with something. I picked up the phone without looking at the screen.

"Hello?" I croaked.

"Steve, it's Nicole."

Fuck. I slouched back onto the couch, groaning, eyes closed.

"This isn't a good time," I gritted through my teeth.

"I don't care, Steve. Things are getting chaotic here. I only have until the end of next week before he talks to the faculty."

I pinched the bridge of my nose. "And that's my problem why?"

"Because I need money, and you can help me with that. It is in your best interest to help. If you don't, I will leak information about you to your fans."

I opened my eyes and snorted. "I don't see what you could tell them that would matter," I said in a hoarse voice.

"I know how much you value your privacy. I will tell them everything about you, your real name, your address. I will even give them your phone number. And I will tell them about our divorce. I will give them my side of the story."

"What?" I sat up straight. I didn't care if Nicole revealed my name to Saul's fans. I had always kept both personae separated, but I didn't mind if people knew who Saul was. Giving them my home address, though—that was another matter. There were some crazy people out there, and I didn't want to find them on my doorstep. And *her* side of the story? What kind of bullshit was she going to invent? I couldn't believe this.

"Are you fucking kidding me?" I snarled. "Look who's blackmailing people now."

"I told you not to rebuff me." Her voice was icy cold.

"I can't believe you've sunk that low, Nicole."

"I will do whatever I have to do to save my career."

She never tried to fix our marriage. But her precious career, sure, she would blackmail me for it. I was so sick of her. Of everything, really. My head was pounding, my legs shaking, my eyes watery, and my heart broken. I had no room for anything else. Especially not for Nicole.

"You do you, Nicole. I don't care." And I hung up.

I went into the kitchen to get some honey and lemon infusion for my throat, took some paracetamol for the fever I felt coming in, grabbed my laptop, and sat at the table. Things had to change, starting with my relationship with Nicole. We had been dancing around each other for too long. We had been apart for two years now, and yet she still took too much room in my life. Well, if she was going to reveal my identity to the world, I might as well do it myself.

I logged on to my professional website and updated the biography, giving out my real name and date of birth. I didn't go into details about my divorce—that would be pushing it—but I did write I had lived in Seattle for a while and had moved back to San Francisco after the divorce.

Then, I opened the picture folder on my phone and searched for a while before I found a selfie Danny and I had taken exactly one year ago. We were smiling, beers in hand. Danny was holding his latest book high. We had taken the photo when Danny had published his first book after his long writer's block. We had celebrated his recovery in a bar.

I opened my Twitter account and loaded the photo, commenting, "Still going on strong a year later. Proud of you, D." I tagged Danny and his publisher and added a few hashtags for good measure—#bromance, #favoritewriter, #dontstopbelieving. I took a deep breath and posted the tweet. And I readied myself for the tsunami of comments and private messages I was sure to receive.

I knew Nicole could still find ways to hurt me if she wanted to. I had learned a lot about her in the last two years. She had cheated on me, slept with a student, made me feel guilty for her cheating, ripped me off in the divorce, and blackmailed me. Nothing could surprise me, coming from her. But at least I had removed a few ammunitions from her grasp. If she found anything else to say about me to my fans, she could go at it. I didn't care anymore.

I turned off my phone and computer, guzzled down a couple of Motrin, and spent the rest of the day cleaning the house from top to bottom. Housework often helped. It was like meditating. As if clearing up the mess in the house also cleared the one in my soul. And it worked. As I was scrubbing the fridge, I could see all the things I had messed up in the last eight months. I had neglected my friends and family. I had missed a few contracts at work because I hadn't been focused enough or hadn't replied to emails within reasonable deadlines. And now, with that cold, or flu, or whatever, affecting my throat and voice, I wouldn't be able to work for a few days, which meant possibly losing a few more contracts. Also, I hadn't eaten well, nor had done much sport in three weeks, and my body was making me pay for it.

I had thought that I was getting better this week. But looking back now as I was folding up laundry, I realized that dating Maisy had been a mistake. I had thought it would help me, but it hadn't. And it hadn't been fair to Maisy. Not that she deserved an apology from me—she had done some messed-up things herself. But I wasn't blameless in our story.

With that in mind, I went to bed at the end of the day, resolving to start fresh the next morning.

18

RECOVERY

I knew I would receive a lot of comments on my Twitter account after posting the photo of Danny and me. But I could never have anticipated the chain reaction that ensued. It was even crazier than I had imagined.

People started looking up my name on the Internet and sharing every piece of information they could find —even the most insignificant one—on social networks. Knowing my real name and what I looked like didn't seem to be enough. People had taken it upon themselves to find out everything there was to find about me. My Twitter feed was soon full of YouTube videos, extracts from the films, series and commercials I had starred in at the beginning of my career. People were posting reviews of the books I had narrated under my real name and my pseudonym. There were endless discussions about the reasons behind my revelations. Some even speculated on the nature of my relationship with Danny.

There were some mixed reactions too. A few people chastised me for ruining their auditive experience. Apparently, they now visualized my face when they listened to books I narrated, and that was unsatisfying. But in general, the comments were positive. Most fans were glad I was coming out of my shell. Their words, not mine.

By the end of the week, I had gotten over my cold, and my mind had cleared out. On Sunday, I went to my parents' house for their wedding anniversary. When I saw my father, I was shocked to see how old he looked. He seemed to have withered and aged ten years since I had last seen him. Which was, I was horrified to realize, on my birthday two months ago. We'd talked on the phone since, of course, and he'd sounded grumpy, as he always did, so I hadn't thought much of it. I never used to neglect my family the way I had lately. I had to remedy that.

So I started visiting my parents twice a week. I also started texting Danny more often. He returned it tenfold and took me out every weekend. We went for drinks, had dinner at his place, and went to the movies. We even went roller-skating like teenagers at the Church of 8 Wheels. I started going on runs or working out at home every day. With all the extra exercise and the fresh air, along with a better diet, I started feeling a lot better in just a few days. I felt younger, healthier, and more centered than I had been in a long time. My body was grateful that I was finally taking care of it again.

And weirdly, so was my cat. He had taken the habit of joining me when I was doing strength exercises, climbing onto my back during push-ups, and playing with my dumbbells. I sometimes used him instead of my weights when I was doing lunges. That is until he started chewing on my exercise mat, and I had to shoo him away.

Since Nicole had called, I hadn't heard anything from her—until the following Friday. When I checked my phone during my morning break, I had a dozen Twitter notifications. When I clicked on the first one, a video opened up, and I froze. On my screen, there was a bed in a dark room, and something moving. It only took me a few seconds to recognize my ex-wife's naked body straddling a young, dark-skinned man, equally naked. Moans and sighs resonated in my kitchen.

I watched for about a minute, mouth wide open in a silent gasp of shock, before my brain caught on. I closed the app and dropped my phone on the table. And I stood there, one hand on my eyes, the other covering my gaping mouth, for what seemed like an eternity, with the horrific images still playing behind my eyelids. The scene was similar to the one I'd witnessed when I'd walked in on them. This was like living the same nightmare again and again.

I came back to reality when my phone pinged.
Danny: <Have you seen the news?>
Me: <No. Why?>

Danny: <Check Fox.>

I picked up my phone again and opened the Fox News website. The words *Scandal at Seattle University* filled the screen. I read the first lines of the article.

"A sex tape involving a professor and a student has been released on the internal web of the University of Seattle. The faculty has launched—"

I closed the web browser and called Danny, my stomach clenching uncomfortably.

"Did you see the article?" he asked when he picked up.

"Yeah. I also saw the video on Twitter just before you texted. Someone tweeted the video and tagged me." I cringed. "I opened it before I realized what it was about."

"You saw it?"

"About a minute of it, I think."

Danny groaned sympathetically. "How was it?"

I scoffed. "What do you think?

"Sorry, mate." He sighed. "I wish I'd seen it first so I could warn you."

"It's fine. Not the first time I've seen her with that dude."

He groaned. "I can't even imagine how you're feeling."

"Like shit, to be honest."

He barked out a laugh. "I've got something that'll cheer you up. I have two tickets for the Giants on Sunday. Do you want to go?"

It was the last post-season game of the year, so of course, I wasn't going to miss it. I never refused an opportunity to watch baseball, especially since the Giants were in this year.

"What time?" I asked.

"Let's meet at the ballpark at one."

We hung up. Shortly after, my phone pinged again.

Nicole: <I'll never forgive you.>

Something snapped inside my brain and I started to laugh an unrestrained, hysterical laugh. I couldn't stop myself. It was all too much—the anger toward Nicole, mixed with the bitter sympathy for her situation, and some unwanted guilt, were all too much, and I lost it. Tears were running down my cheeks and my ribs ached, and I kept laughing. I crouched down, holding my stomach, and leaned against the wall. Slowly, the tears of laughter turned to tears of exhaustion, and I kept on crying. When I calmed down and came back to myself, I was curled up in a ball on the floor, Colonel purring on my side, my body stiff and the skin on my face crackling with dried tears. I picked up the scattered pieces of my soul and went back to work.

***

Danny was waiting for me when I arrived at Oracle Park on Sunday. We went in, making our way through the crowd. The stands were already full of people. The noise and the smell of sweat and greasy food made my head spin. I could already feel the excitement and adrenalin of the game thrumming through my veins. Danny led us to the lower box.

"These are great seats," I said when we sat down. We had a perfect view of the pitching mound and the first base. "How could you afford the tickets? Don't you have a wedding to pay for?"

Danny laughed. "Sam received them as a thank you from a client."

"I need to change jobs," I grumbled. "All I get is a lot of junk mail."

"Nah, you'd miss your fans too much."

I chuckled. "Yeah, you might be right."

I went to grab some beer for Danny and me. I joined him right when the game started.

"Thanks, mate," Danny said when I handed him a cup. "Before I forget, Sam told me to invite you for Thanksgiving. I said I'd pass along the message, but I'm guessing you're going to your parents'?"

I shook my head. "They'll be on a cruise."

"Again?"

I chuckled. My parents had never traveled much in their life, saving up as much as possible to pay for my studies. Now they were both retired, their house was paid for and I had a steady job, so they were making up for lost time and going away several times a year. They especially loved going on cruises in the Pacific Ocean.

"Where are they off to this time?" Danny asked.

"They haven't given me their itinerary yet, but I think they're going to the South Pacific islands."

"Nice. Well, good for them. I wish my parents would travel more. My dad needs to get out of his house." He shrugged. "Anyway, we're having a few people over, so you're welcome to join us if you don't have anything planned."

I didn't answer immediately. Sometimes, dinners with Sam and Danny meant that Maisy was there, since she and Sam got on well. I wasn't sure I wanted to see her just yet, let alone be cordial to her. I was still too angry.

Danny saw my hesitation and added, "It will only be us, Sam's parents and her cousin Jill."

I almost sighed in relief. "I'd love to come, thanks."

We cheered along with the crowd as the players entered the diamond.

"Not speaking of the elephant in the room, Sam went out with Maisy last night," he said in a casual tone.

I tried not to show any reaction. I could see from the corner of my eyes that he was watching me.

"How is she?" I hoped I didn't sound too bitter.

"Not well."

I stayed silent.

"I'm sorry we never got to talk about it," Danny continued. "I got distracted with wedding preparations. What happened between you?"

I shrugged. "We broke up."

"Yeah, I figured that out, thanks," he said coolly. After a beat, he asked, "Why, though?"

"You know why." I kept my eyes on the game.

He shook his head. "I don't. Is it because of what she told Ally on my birthday?"

My chest squeezed painfully at the sound of Ally's name. I didn't answer, not trusting my voice to be steady.

"Was it worth breaking up over?" Danny continued. "I mean, I understand why you would be mad, and surely she shouldn't have said anything. But Ally was going to leave anyway, wasn't she?"

I sighed. "Yeah. And honestly, if it had just been about that, I probably would have forgiven her. But you don't know the whole story."

I was reluctant to tell Danny everything. I had been so gullible and couldn't help but feel stupid. It was like I never learned from my mistakes, wasn't it? I had trusted Nicole, and that had blown up in my face. I had given my heart to Ally, and she had crushed it. Now, I had trusted Maisy, and where had that led to? Another slap in the face.

"Tell me, Steve."

I shook my head and looked down at my hands. I took a deep breath.

"Do you remember the person I chatted with in July?" I said.

"The one that pretended to be Ally?" he asked.

My stomach rolled again when he said her name. Would I ever get used to hearing it?

"Well, that was Maisy," I said.

Danny had been sipping on his cup of beer, and he choked on his mouthful at my statement. He started coughing and spluttering beer all over the seat in front of us. I patted his back and handed him a napkin.

"Thanks," he croaked, wiping his mouth and eyes. "Are you serious?"

I nodded.

"Maisy texted you pretending she was Ally?"

I nodded again.

Danny turned back toward the game. "Wow. I can't even—Why would she do that? And how did you find out?"

"She told me that night. She didn't mean to, but I was angry, and she was crying, and it slipped out."

"So, all the weird bullshit they sent about people in Louisiana, my book and all, that was Maisy messing with you?"

"Yep." I drained my beer and crushed the plastic cup in my hand.

"Shit. That's messed up, mate."

"Tell me about it."

Danny watched the game absently for a minute, before turning back to me. "What I don't get, is why she would do that."

I shrugged. "She said she was trying to make me lose interest in—you know—and fall for her instead."

He looked at me, his forehead creased. "She told you that?"

I nodded.

"Okay, I suppose that was worth breaking up over," he said. "I mean, it feels like playground drama, doesn't it?"

Danny shook his head in disbelief and turned to the game. We watched the end of the first inning in silence, and I groaned along with other Giants fans when the batter scored a home run for the Dodgers.

"By the way," Danny said after a moment. "Have you heard anything from Ally?"

My chest contracted again, even more forcefully than before, and I almost hunched over from the pain. I shook my head.

"Sam tried texting her," Danny said. "But the texts aren't going through."

"Yeah, she disconnected her phone."

Danny turned to me. "Did you know she would do that?"

I shook my head again.

"That sucks. Why would she do it?"

"I don't know." I sighed.

Danny looked at me with concern in his eyes. "How are you really doing, Steve?"

I shrugged. "I'm fine."

Danny's lips pinched into a thin line. "Fine. Sure." He turned to face the field again.

I winced. I knew what Danny wanted from me. Fine wasn't enough anymore. I had to talk to him, no matter how hard it was.

I took a deep breath. "It's been hard lately. Everything hit the fan at the same time, with Nicole, Maisy, and—" I snapped my mouth shut, biting my tongue. I could talk to Danny, but saying Ally's name was beyond me. I swallowed thickly. "But I'm better now," I continued. "Or at least, I'm getting there. I—" I tried to keep talking, but

I didn't know how. I ran my hand down my face and sighed. "I have to get better, don't I? I can't keep moping around. You wouldn't let me anyway."

I was hoping Danny would loosen up a bit, but he didn't even crack a smile. He kept watching me with pinched eyebrows.

I sighed. "I've come to realize that, for the last nine months, everything in my life revolved around her. I was obsessed with her. That's not healthy, is it?"

The batter sent a ball straight toward our box. I had to stop talking as people all around us rushed forward, pushing us around, trying to catch the ball. When things quieted down again, Danny said, "There's nothing wrong with wanting to be with someone."

"I know that." I rubbed my forehead. "But I've neglected a lot of people this year. My parents, you and Sam, and even myself. And work, too. And I've hurt Maisy. I can't go on like this. I need to move on." I closed my eyes. What I was about to say was going to hurt, but I needed to say it out loud. "I *am* moving on."

"We can set you up with someone if you want," Danny said. "Sam has a lot of single friends. Or we could go to the next drag night and try to find your old flame."

I barked out a laugh. "Thanks, I'm good."

"What about Nicole? Have you heard from her since the whole *sex-gate*?"

I scrunched up my nose at the ridiculous name the media had come up with to talk about the scandal. "Do we have to call it that?"

Danny chuckled.

"She texted me the next day, but that's all. Not a word since then."

"Is she going to get fired?" he asked.

I shrugged one shoulder. "Probably."

"You don't seem concerned."

"I'm not." My blasé tone surprised me as much as it surprised Danny. It was true, though. I wasn't concerned. "It's weird, you know. I thought I'd feel something. Relief that it's all over, anger over what she made me do, maybe some residual grief over our relationship. But I don't. I don't feel anything anymore."

"That must be a nice change."

I chuckled darkly. "Yeah, I'm not going to miss feeling like shit because of her."

"So, you really are fine?"

"I will be."

I smiled. Danny's face softened and the lines of concern on his forehead smoothened out.

We stayed and watched the entire game. When we left, despite the Giants losing, I was feeling cheerful.

It was almost six when I arrived back at my house. I parked my scooter at the back of the house. Circling back to the front door, I took out my phone and texted Danny.

Steve: <Thanks again for tonight. You're the best.>

I hit send.

"Steve?"

I jumped so hard at the sound of a small, fragile voice calling my name near my front door, that I almost dropped my phone. I looked up. And I froze. I stood speechless, staring at the person sitting on my porch.

Those light gray eyes were unmistakable. It was Ally, there was no doubt about it. Except that she looked terrible. She was extremely pale under her suntan. Her eyes had lost their spark, her cheeks were hollow, and the shadows on her face made her eyes look almost white. She wasn't smiling. Her cracked lips were stretched into a thin line. Her face held no brightness, no joy. She was but the ghost of the woman I had gotten to know and love.

Ally stood up, and I took a step back, holding up my hand as if to stop her from approaching. My heart was beating so fast that my chest hurt and my head spun. She couldn't be here. Not now, not when I was finally moving on. I was too stunned to say anything. My brain was battling too many emotions at the same time and I couldn't process what was happening. Was she really here? Was she even real, or was I hallucinating?

"I'm sorry to come by like this," she said.

I took another step back. "What are you doing here?" I asked in a low voice.

She winced. "I know I have no right to ask anything from you, but—" Her voice broke, and she looked down. "Can I stay here for a while?" she asked in a low voice.

"Why?" I asked, more sharply than I intended.

Ally didn't look at me. "I'm—I don't know. I think I—" Her face tensed. She closed her eyes and took a deep, shuddering breath. She whispered the next words so quietly that I almost didn't hear them. "I'm scared of being on my own."

Her body started shaking. Tears spilled onto her cheeks, and her knees buckled. I caught her right before she collapsed onto the ground. We both slid down and I sat on the porch, cradling her in my arms.

I had never seen anyone fall apart this badly. I'd had my share of bad days and broken hearts over the years. But this was a whole new level of breakdown.

We sat there for a few minutes. Ally let out heart-wrenching sobs and her body was shaking so hard I had to tighten my grip on her. After a while, I realized that she wasn't going to pull herself together. I stood up, lifted her, and carried her inside. I sat on the couch, still holding her. She was as limp as a rag doll. She continued crying, burying her face in my neck. I didn't say a word. I didn't know what I could say. I wasn't even sure she would hear me anyway. So I stroked her hair instead.

After about an hour of crying, she quieted down and fell asleep in my arms. And all that time, I kept hearing the last words she had said before breaking down. *I'm scared of being on my own.* Those words tore a hole in my heart and filled me with dread.

19

OVERLOAD

When I was certain that Ally was asleep, I lay her head on a cushion and grabbed a blanket from the armchair to cover her. Colonel Mustard curled up against her chest. He had come out of the laundry room at the sound of Ally's sobs, and jumped on the couch with us, patting her head softly with one of his paws, and purring in her ears.

"You keep an eye on her, right, buddy?" I scratched his head and went to bed.

I didn't sleep much that night. My brain was on a loop, trying to figure out what was best for me to do. I was afraid of having Ally back in my house. There was a high chance I would fall back into my obsession and end up losing my mental health. But could I kick her out of my house when she was in such a terrible state? *I'm scared of being on my own.* Those words haunted me all night.

At five, I gave up on sleep and got up. Ally was still asleep on the couch in the living room, Colonel still curled up with her. They didn't seem to have moved at all since last night. Colonel lifted his head when he saw me and blinked his crossed eyes before laying his head back on Ally's arm.

After a quick shower and breakfast, I decided to bring Ally's bags inside, so she could shower when she woke up. I looked around for her car key but couldn't find it. I went out to check if she had locked the car doors. Seeing how distressed she had been the night before, there was a chance she had forgotten to do it. And she had. She had actually left the key in the ignition.

When I opened the back door of her car, I froze. Ally had always been very tidy and had kept her car clean. But now, it was a mess. Clothes were thrown everywhere, there were empty bags of half-eaten food and, even more shocking, seven—no, eight—empty bottles of vodka. I had never seen Ally drunk. Tipsy, sure. But wasted, never. I couldn't believe this was the same woman as the one who had left my house a mere eight weeks ago.

I tidied up her car, threw the rubbish away, and brought in a bag of dirty clothes. I went into the laundry room and loaded up the washing machine. And during all that time, Ally never woke up. She never even stirred. I went upstairs and texted Danny.

Me: <Ally's back.>

My phone rang a few seconds later.

"What do you mean, Ally's back?" Danny asked.

"She was waiting for me when I got back home yesterday."

There was some shuffling on his side. "She was waiting for you?"

"On my doorstep."

In the short silence that ensued, I heard a door closing, and the background noise on the line disappeared. "I have to admit, I didn't see that one coming."

I chuckled humorlessly. "Yeah, me neither."

"How are you taking it?"

I could hear the concern in his voice. I almost said I was fine but stopped myself just in time. I sighed. "It's been hard." I pinched the bridge of my nose. "Honestly, I would have told her to leave if things were different."

"What do you mean, different?"

"She looks terrible, man. I don't know what happened since September, but she's a mess. She's lost some weight, she's pale as a ghost, and she spent the evening crying."

Danny whistled. "Did she tell you anything?"

"No. She's still asleep on the couch."

"You need to make her talk."

I sighed. "I know. I plan to. But right now, I think she needs the rest. She looks like she hasn't slept in weeks." I ran a hand over my face. "I'm going to get some work done, then I'll go check on her. She's going to need to eat, too."

"All right, mate. Call if you need anything."

I tried to focus on work, but it was hard. My mind was still downstairs with Ally. Every thirty minutes or so, I went to check on her, and she kept on sleeping.

At half past ten, I went downstairs again and I made myself some coffee. I sat on the armchair to drink it, watching over Ally. She slowly opened her eyes and blinked a few times. Then, her gaze focused on me. More precisely, on my cup.

"Is that coffee?" she croaked.

"Hello to you, too," I said dryly.

"Sorry." She rubbed her eyes and smiled sleepily. "Hi, handsome. Is that coffee?"

I stood up, ignoring the way my stomach flipped at the endearment.

"I'll get you a cup," I said.

I went to the kitchen without looking at her. When I came back, Ally was sitting, Colonel curled up in her lap.

"Thanks," she said when I handed her a cup of coffee. "What time is it?"

"Almost eleven."

She lifted her eyes to mine, looking confused. "What?" She frowned. "When did I arrive?"

"I don't know." I shrugged. "I came back home at around six."

Ally's eyebrows lifted.

"You slept for fifteen hours straight," I added.

Her eyes went round. "I haven't slept that much in—" She shrugged one shoulder. "Well, probably ever."

Ally took another sip of coffee, then closed her eyes and leaned back on the couch. I watched her, not breaking the silence, hoping she would start talking when she was ready. But she never did. When the silence became too heavy, I gave in.

"How are you feeling?" I asked.

"Fine." Her answer came too quickly.

I cringed. I had given that answer to Danny plenty of times in the last two years, but had never realized how it felt to hear that lie. It sucked.

Ally flinched at the look on my face and looked down at her hands.

"Have you looked in a mirror recently?" I asked sharply.

She shook her head.

"You look terrible, Ally. Don't tell me you're fine." After a short pause, I continued, "I'm going to ask you again, and I want you to tell me the truth. How are you feeling?"

She kept her eyes cast down and didn't say anything. I scoffed.

"What do you want me to say?" Ally asked, looking up. Her gray eyes seemed lifeless. They had lost the cheerful spark I had loved so much. It broke my heart a bit more.

I forced myself to keep my eyes on her. "The truth would be a good start," I said.

"I don't know what the truth is," she exclaimed forcefully.

I breathed deeply to temper my frustration. "Do you remember what you said yesterday?"

She shook her head.

"You said you were scared of being on your own."

She dropped her gaze again and looked at her half-empty cup.

"I spent all night trying to figure out what you meant, and I don't like what I came up with." I sighed. "You like honesty, right?"

She nodded.

"This morning I went through your stuff in your car."

Ally tensed and started shaking her head.

"I guess you know what I found," I continued. "I know for certain that, eight weeks ago, you didn't have any alcohol in there."

Ally's head was still going from left to right in a continuous gesture. Her jaw was tense. "You had no right to go through my stuff," she said between gritted teeth.

"You came here asking for help, Ally," I said. I managed to keep my voice calm, but my grip on my cup tightened. "So that's what I'm trying to do. Did you drink that much vodka in eight weeks?"

She closed her eyes but still didn't answer my question.

"You know what? I'm sick of this. If you need a place to stay, you can stay here, you know I won't refuse." I shook my head. "I'm sure that's why you came here. But we're going to need some ground rules." I leaned forward, putting my elbows on my knees, bracing myself for what

I was going to say. "If you want to stay here, you have to talk to me. If you don't want to, then you'll have to find somewhere else to stay. I went through you leaving twice already, and I got over it. It was not easy, but I did. I can do it once more. What I can't do, is stand here and watch you slowly kill yourself."

I stood up and walked to the couch, crouching down in front of her. She was still shaking her head. I pressed my hand against her cheek to stop her. She leaned into my hand and closed her eyes. A tear rolled down her cheek, and I wiped it out with the pad of my thumb.

I waited until she opened her eyes before I continued in a soft, soothing voice. "I always respected your need for privacy, I never pushed you, because I thought you were doing fine. But clearly, you aren't. Enough is enough, Ally. You need to talk to me. Please."

"What day is it?" she asked in a whisper.

I frowned at the sudden change of topic, but answered, "The sixteenth. Why?"

Her eyes drifted over my shoulder and a sob escaped her tightly pursed lips. "One year, six months, and nineteen days." She let out a shaky breath and closed her eyes again. "It's been one year, six months, and nineteen days."

I dropped my hand. "Since what?"

"Since he died."

A chill ran down my spine. "Who died?"

Ally's armor finally cracked open. And she started talking. She told me about her boyfriend Simon. They had been high school sweethearts, together since they were sixteen, surviving college together, and moving in as soon as they had found a job. Four years ago, they had bought an apartment near Paris together. Then, one year, six months, and nineteen days ago...

"We were driving back home from the supermarket," Ally said. "Stupid routine, you know. And we were arguing because he had bought a new video game. I hated it when he played computer games. He sometimes spent hours playing when he could have helped me with housework." She shook her head. "We always argued about that. On the way home someone ran a red light and hit his side of the car." Ally's face crumpled. Her breath became choppy, and she continued in a whisper. "Simon was in a coma for three weeks before he died."

Ally closed her eyes and swallowed thickly. Her whole body was shaking with emotion. I sat down on the coffee table, feeling numb. I'd known that Ally had gone through some ordeal. But how could I have imagined this? If my math was correct, she had been with him for almost twenty years. How could I understand what it was like to go through this kind of loss? I couldn't wrap my head around the empty space his death must have created, or the guilt she must still feel about their last conversation.

"I tried to stay in France, in our home," Ally continued, tears streaming down her cheeks. "But it was too hard. He's everywhere in that apartment. I had to run away." A sound between a sob and a chuckle came out of her. "That's my thing, running away when it gets complicated."

I didn't know what to say. I didn't know what to feel. Sadness, anger, jealousy, and above all, guilt. What Ally had gone through was heartbreaking. But I felt cheated. And I couldn't help feeling guilty for the spike of jealousy stirred by the idea that Ally had loved someone that much. The whirlwind of emotions was so overwhelming that I had to stand up and walk. I started pacing the living room.

"Why didn't you tell me about it earlier, Ally? I could have helped you."

She winced and looked down. "There's something else I haven't told you," she said in a low voice. "My name isn't Ally, it's Rosalie. I came up with Ally when I met you in New York. I wanted to reinvent myself, I think." She lifted her gaze to mine. "You're the only person who's ever called me Ally."

It was like what was left of my world crumbled down around me. Everything she and I had shared, all the time we had spent together, it had all been a fantasy, hadn't it?

"Steve?" Ally said in a soft voice.

I lifted my hands to my hair and started pulling. "So it was all a lie," I whispered. "Nothing was real, was it?"

I wanted to cry, to scream, to break something. But all I could do was stand there, legs shaking from the overload of emotions. It was all too much.

"No, Steve, it was real."

She stood up and started walking toward me, but I put my hand up to stop her.

"I need to get back to work. I've got a deadline to meet." I didn't wait for an answer. I turned around, almost running up the stairs, and locked myself in my recording booth.

Needless to say, I couldn't focus on work. Narrating romance when I was feeling like shit was beyond me. I should have been able to ignore my feelings, but the fact that I didn't understand them made it impossible.

How could I be angry at her? But also, how could I not be? I felt duped. Everything I had felt for her had been a lie. I hadn't known the real Ally—Rosalie. For Pete's sake, I didn't even know what I was supposed to call her. She had played with my feelings, just like Nicole and Maisy had. Well, not exactly in the same way, but still. Was I so gullible that everyone felt like they had the right to lie to me? Was Danny toying with me too, I wondered?

I knew I shouldn't have lost my nerves, though. She was going through a lot, and my being angry wasn't helping.

I recorded two chapters before giving up and going back downstairs, a bit calmer but still unhinged. I joined Ally on the deck. She stood up as soon as she saw me. Her face was blotchy and her eyes red, but she wasn't crying anymore.

"If you want me to go, I completely understand."

"No." I sat on the bench, leaning forward, shoulders sagging. "I'm sorry I got angry. I shouldn't have."

Ally, or Rosalie—ugh, whatever—sat at the far end of the bench, careful not to touch me. "You have every right to be angry, Steve. I messed everything up with you."

"There's one thing I need to ask you. It's going to sound insensitive, but I need to know. For my own sanity."

Ally didn't reply, so I turned to her. She was watching me with worried eyes, but she nodded.

"What are we?" I asked.

She frowned. "What?"

"You and I, what are we?"

She shook her head. "I don't—"

"I fell for you. I fell hard. You're the first person I've trusted in a long time. And I thought you had feelings for me, too. Now, you're telling me that all this time, you were grieving for someone else. So what was this for you, then?" I gestured between her and me. "A distraction? Some sort of rebound?" My voice was rising, and I tried to temper my annoyance. "I know I shouldn't be angry," I continued. "I can't even imagine what you're going through. But you lied to me. All the time we spent together, I thought there was something between us, but it wasn't real, was it?"

"Yes, it was," she whispered. She took a deep breath, then continued, her voice stronger. "I never expected I would meet someone like you. I didn't think I'd have feelings for someone so soon after it happened."

My heart clenched at her words. She had feelings for me?

"But you see, that's part of the problem, isn't it?" She let out a chuckle. "I feel even more guilty for it. My head knows that I'm allowed to move on, and that there's no time limit to do so. But I still feel guilty." She sighed. "It's so unfair, you know. Guilt and grief."

I sighed. "Yes, I suppose it is." I leaned back and closed my eyes, feeling empty. I was exhausted. "Let's not talk about it anymore. I'm tired and starving. I'm going to order pizza. Let's eat, and then we'll talk."

While we were waiting for the pizzas to be delivered, we put her clothes in the dryer, then went into the living room. There was something else I needed to clear out.

"How should I call you?" I asked. "Ally or Rosalie?"

"Do you want to call me Rosalie?"

I shrugged. "I don't know. I have no idea who Rosalie is. But you aren't really Ally, are you? I mean, you've been lying to me all this time."

She shook her head. "I haven't. I might not have told you everything, but I didn't lie."

I scoffed.

"I didn't," she said. "Even that name, Ally, isn't a lie. That's who I became when I left France. That's who I am with you. And I like Ally. I like her a lot more than Rosalie." She winced, shook her head, and mumbled, "That sounds dumb."

I sighed. "Fine, I'll keep calling you Ally, then."

I went into the kitchen and set the table. The pizzas arrived and we sat down to eat.

After a few minutes of tense silence, Ally asked, "How have you been?"

I shrugged but didn't say anything.

She winced. "Sorry, stupid question. It's just—Well, you look good, so I was wondering."

I hesitated between being flattered or insulted. I decided to go with the latter.

"Do you think that your leaving didn't make me feel terrible?" I said in a harsh tone. "That I didn't miss you at all?" I willed myself to calm down and spoke a bit more softly. "I've kept busy. Honestly, a lot of things went to hell after you left. But I've been exercising more and spending more time with my family and Danny." I pointed at her pizza. "Aren't you going to eat more?"

She had only eaten two slices and had already pushed her plate away. She shook her head.

"Why not?"

She shrugged but didn't say anything.

I sighed. "I told you, Ally, if you want to stay here, you need to talk."

She shot up straight, nostrils flaring and cheeks reddening in anger. It was good to see some color on her again. "Stop badgering me about food. I don't know why I don't eat much. I just feel sick when I do." She lifted her hand to her forehead and sighed, closing her eyes. "I want to talk to you, Steve. I really do. I know I have to make things right with you, but I don't know how. You'll need to be patient with me."

I nodded. "Sit down, please."

She complied and grabbed her glass of water. She was shaking so much that she had to hold the glass with both hands. I waited in silence for her to talk.

"It's happened before, right after the accident. I felt nauseous every time I tried to eat. But when I started planning my trip here, I got better. I was doing okay until a few months ago."

I took another slice of my pizza. "What about the night terrors?" I asked.

Ally put both her feet on the chair and curled her arms around her knees. "They've become worse," she whispered. "I haven't slept properly since I left you."

"I'm guessing they have to do with—" I stopped my-self. I didn't dare say her boyfriend's name.

"With the accident, yes." She closed her eyes and a tear rolled down her cheek. She wiped it with the back of her hand. "I keep reliving it. The fight, the crash, everything. It was—"

I waited for her to finish her sentence, but she didn't.

"Did you see someone after it happened?" I asked.

"Like a counselor?" She shook her head. "I wanted to get over it by myself." She let out a self-deprecating laugh. "That's not working too well, is it?"

I frowned. "Maybe you should consider it."

"Maybe I will, when I go back to France."

My stomach churned at her words. "You're thinking of going back to France?"

She lifted her gaze to mine. "Well, yes, I have to. My visa expires in four months." She lifted a shoulder. "I have to decide what to do with our apartment anyway. And work, too."

"I remember you said you work for a temp agency, right? And you took a leave of absence?"

She nodded. "I work in human resources."

"Do you like it?"

She shook her head. "Not really."

She took a bite of her pizza and started eating. I blinked. I guessed if talking about her job made her eat, then that was what we would do.

"Do you think you'll go back to it?"

"I don't know. I don't want to. I don't think I want to go back to France, honestly."

"What do you want to do, then?" I asked.

"I have a degree in teaching," she said. "But I've never worked as a teacher. Before I left, I'd been thinking of giving that a try." She took another bite. "Maybe I will, I don't know."

The corners of my lips curled up with the beginning of a smile. "What would you teach?" I asked.

"Foreign languages. I'm qualified to teach French, English and Spanish."

I could see it. Ally, the teacher. She could be good at it, I thought.

"Do you have family in France?" I asked.

"Just my mother. She lives in the south, so I don't see her much, but we talk on the phone occasionally. We were never really close. I was a lot closer to my dad, but he passed away eight years ago."

I couldn't imagine not being close to my family. Except when I lived in Seattle with Nicole, I had never been far away from my parents for a long time. I could always see them anytime I wanted.

"And your friends?" I asked. "There must be people you're close to back home."

She looked down at her pizza, playing with a piece of crust. "It's not my home anymore," she murmured. Then, in a much firmer voice, she said, "I have a few friends, but most people I know were Simon's friends, not mine." Her face tensed briefly. "A lot of them cut ties with me when I left. They didn't approve of my plans to travel. I guess they thought I was *moving on too fast*." She put air quotes on the last four words, then scoffed. "As if there were any rules for that."

The annoyance at her so-called friends put some color on her cheeks and she ate another slice of pizza.

We continued talking for a while until most of her pizza was gone. Little by little, her secrets unraveled. I learned more about her in an hour than I had in the weeks we had spent together.

"I have to get some work done today," I said after a while. I knew we still had a lot to discuss. I had yet a million questions that needed answering. But I also needed a break from it.

"What are you working on?" she asked.

"I just started recording a romance novel." I suddenly remembered something Ally had told me the first time we had met, in the elevator in New York. "Is all this—" I gestured broadly in her direction. "—the reason why you don't listen to romance anymore?"

She looked puzzled for a second, then it clicked. "You remember that." She brightened slightly and said, "I did listen to two of Danny's books these last few weeks. Hearing your voice was the only thing that helped me sleep for a few hours without nightmares."

My heart gave a joyful thump. I immediately smothered the spark of hope that tried to grow inside my chest.

Ally lowered her head, chewing on her bottom lip. "Do you think I can sit in a corner of your booth and listen to you while you work?" she asked. "I promise I won't make any noise."

I hesitated. No one but me—and Colonel—had ever been in my home recording booth while I was working. It was my safe space. But I could never say no to Ally. Anyway, seeing her gaunt face, I was sure she would fall asleep very quickly, so I agreed.

And I was right. A few lines in, and Ally was fast asleep in the corner of the room.

20

ACCEPTANCE

I got through three hours of work, and Ally slept the whole time. When I shut everything down for the day, Ally kept on sleeping. I carefully lifted her in my arms and carried her to the guest room. I left the door ajar when I left.

Back in the kitchen, I made myself a sandwich and sat in front of the TV to eat. I was flicking through the channels, not paying attention to what was on the screen. My mind was still spinning from everything I had learned in the last two days.

Ally joined me sometime later, Colonel Mustard trotting proudly behind her. I hadn't even noticed he had gone upstairs.

I turned the TV off as Ally sat down on the armchair facing me. Colonel promptly jumped on her lap and started kneading her legs, purring like a motorcycle.

I pointed toward him. "I'm starting to get jealous."

Ally chuckled. A soft, honest sound. Her lips stayed slightly curved up in the first real smile I had seen since her return.

"You can sit on my lap too if you want," she joked.

My cheeks started burning. "That's not what I meant," I said embarrassed.

Ally barked out a laugh. "Don't worry, Colonel loves you too."

I scoffed. "Sometimes I doubt it. After you left, I couldn't touch him for a whole week. He kept biting and scratching me. I still have a few scars to prove it."

Ally lost her smile and her eyes reddened. "I'm so sorry, Steve," she said in a low voice.

I shrugged. "It's not your fault he's a moody bastard."

She chuckled wetly and covered Colonel's ears. "Shh, you'll upset him." She dropped her hands and grew serious. "That's not why I'm apologizing. I'm saying sorry because I hurt you, and I hate myself for it." She shook her head. "I don't understand why you don't hate me too."

I didn't reply. Why didn't I hate her? Well, the answer to that was obvious, wasn't it? I'd fallen for her a long time ago.

"I made so many mistakes in the last year. I did a lot of things thinking it was going to help me get on with my life, but it all backfired, and I ended up hurting many people, including myself."

Her statement resonated with me. I knew what it felt like to mess up your life with good intentions. After all, wasn't that what I had done too after she left? Hell, even after my divorce, the way I buried myself in work and completely neglected my social life. Definitely not to the same extent, mind you, but still. I had to remind myself that I too had screwed up badly and hurt people. I couldn't blame her.

Ally was looking down at Colonel when she whispered, "You need to know that you were never just a rebound."

I closed my eyes.

"I'm not going to pretend I know what I feel for you," she continued. "Because I don't. I never expected you. I didn't think I would ever want to be close to anyone else, especially that soon. But you—"

I opened my eyes again and looked at her. Her eyes were fixated on mine, shining with unshed tears.

"You were never just a consolation prize."

My chest untied slightly.

She looked down again and continued. "I don't know how to make things better with you."

I watched her pat my cat in silence for a moment. "There's something you can do," I said finally.

Ally lifted her head and looked at me.

"Be honest. Promise me you won't lie to me again, or hide things from me. From now on, it's the whole truth and nothing but."

She watched me intensely, then slowly nodded her head. "I promise."

Ally spent the next two days resting, and I continued to live my life the way I had in the past few weeks. I went running, worked out in the living room, and spent a lot of time in the recording booth.

On Tuesday evening, I visited my parents one last time before they left on their cruise. I tried to focus on the conversation, but I didn't do a very good job. And my mother had always been good at reading me.

"That thing with Nicole hit you hard, didn't it?" she asked.

I startled. I hadn't thought about Nicole since Ally came back.

"Not really." I sighed. "No, it's about Ally."

The puzzled look on both my parents' faces told me I had never talked about her with them. After the divorce, they had been worried about me, so I never discussed my romantic life with them. But like a lot of other things in my life, this had to change. So I gave them the whole story.

When I left an hour later, I was a lot lighter, and the hug my mother gave me was a lot tighter than I was used to.

"Take care of her," she said in my ear. She leaned back and put a hand on my cheek. "It sounds as if she needs you."

"I think I need her too," I said.

That night, I was woken up by screams coming from the guest room. Ally was thrashing around in the bed, tangled in the sheets, crying. I rushed to her and woke her up. It took her a long time to come back to reality. When she did, she curled up on herself, crying silently. I lay behind her, over the comforter, and spooned her. Colonel joined us, meowing softly, and curled up in Ally's arms. We cuddled together for the rest of the night.

The following morning, I called Dr. Kwan, the psychiatrist I had seen after my divorce, and managed to get an appointment for Ally later that day. I knew Ally would give me hell for making that decision for her, but I was past caring. She knew what the deal was—if she wanted to stay, she had to accept help.

As I had anticipated, convincing her to go was no easy task. I couldn't understand her refusal.

"I'm scared of how I'll feel if I talk about it."

"Can you really be worse than you are now?" I asked.

Ally winced. "I guess not."

A few hours later, we rode to Dr. Kwan's office on my scooter. As the session lasted an hour, I waited for Ally outside the office and made a few phone calls. Tomorrow was Thanksgiving, and I was supposed to go to Danny's place, but I didn't think Ally would be well enough to spend a whole day surrounded by people, having to pretend she was fine and forcing herself to eat. And I didn't want to leave her alone the whole day. So I called Danny.

"Happy Turkey Day's Eve, mate," Danny said when he picked up. "Are you still coming tomorrow?"

"That's why I'm calling. I'm sorry to cancel last minute, but I don't think I'll be able to come."

"Is it because of Ally?"

I sighed. "Yeah, I'm sorry."

"She can come too, we'll have plenty of food," Danny said. "I'm sure Sam would be happy to see her again."

"I don't think it's a good idea. She's been sleeping a lot and not eating much. I don't think she would be comfortable meeting new people right now."

"Did she talk to you?"

"She did. She's been through some personal stuff in the last year. I can't tell you more than that, it's not my story to tell." I stood up and walked a few steps down the street. "Anyway, I don't want to leave her alone at my house tomorrow."

After another short silence, Danny asked, "Are you sure you're doing okay?" I took a bit too long to ponder, so he continued before I could answer. "It's just, in the last few weeks, I finally found the Steve I used to know. And I'd hate to see you brought down again."

I sighed. "I know. Don't worry though, I'm keeping my distance." At the sound of the door opening, I turned around. Ally stepped out of the psychiatrist's office, and my stomach flipped. "At least, I'm trying to."

Danny breathed out. "Okay. Well, take care of her, then. We'll bring you some leftover cake on Friday. Call me if you need anything."

"Sure, thanks. And tell Sam I'm sorry. I hate to cancel on you too."

"No problem, mate. You know we love you."

I smiled softly. "Love you too, man."

I hung up and took a few steps toward Ally. Her eyes were red and puffy, and there were tear tracks on her cheeks. I took her to the pier, bought two ice cream cones, and we sat down, watching the ocean in silence for an hour.

When we arrived back home, she climbed down my scooter, hugged me, and said, "Thank you for making me go."

Ally went to bed early that evening and was still asleep when I woke up the next day. I went into the kitchen and made pancakes. I loaded a tray with coffee, orange juice and a plate of pancakes, on which I had drawn a smiley face with whipped cream and blueberries, and brought her breakfast in bed. She stirred when I entered the guest room.

"Happy Thanksgiving," I said when she opened her eyes.

She blinked. "That's today?" she said in a croaky voice.

I nodded.

She sat up straight in bed, instantly awake. "I've never celebrated Thanksgiving!"

"I figured. I made you breakfast." I nodded toward the tray I was holding.

Ally smiled broadly and took the tray I handed her.

"Sit with me, we can share," Ally said.

I sat on the bed and picked a blueberry.

"Are you going to your parents' to celebrate?" Ally asked, her mouth full of pancake and cream.

I shook my head. "They're on a cruise."

She frowned. "So you don't have any plans? I thought Thanksgiving was a big deal."

I watched her. Should I have asked her opinion, before canceling on Danny? "If I did, would you come with me?" I asked.

Ally took her time to chew and swallow her mouthful before shaking her head. "I don't think I would be up for it."

My stomach untied. "Then, I don't have any plans," I said.

"Don't cancel because of me."

I shrugged. "I'm not. I mean, you're part of the reason why, but not the whole reason. Danny invited me, but I don't feel like going."

Ally looked down and took a sip of her coffee. "You can go, if you want. He's your best friend, I understand if you want to spend the day with him and Sam."

I shook my head again. "I'd rather stay here and celebrate with you. Danny understands." I kissed her forehead. "Eat your pancakes before they get cold."

We celebrated Thanksgiving in our own way, eating takeaway food and watching the parade on television. We snoozed for a while after the parade, and we both woke up at the sound of the jingle of the news broadcast. I started clearing the coffee table of all the takeout containers, but froze when Nicole's face filled in the television screen.

"The story of the scandal at the University of Seattle continues. Nicole Richmond, professor of Literature, was asked to present her resignation after a sex tape was leaked—"

I grabbed the remote control to switch the TV off, but I wasn't quick enough. Ally had seen enough.

"Was that a photo of your ex-wife?" Ally asked. "Were they talking about her?"

My stomach fell to my feet. I picked up the empty containers without answering and started walking toward the kitchen. Ally grabbed my arm to stop me.

"Steve?"

I kept my eyes down and didn't say anything.

"It was her, wasn't it?" she said, her hand on my arm tightening.

"Fuck," I breathed out. I put the tray back on the coffee table and fell on the couch. "Yes, they were talking about her."

Ally looked at the TV, then back at me. "So... what is it about? They mentioned a sex tape?"

I sighed. Keeping my eyes on my knees, I said, "Do you remember what I told you about our divorce?"

Ally nodded. "She cheated on you with a student."

"And did I tell you about the sex tape?"

"No, you didn't." Her voice was soft.

I lifted my head and looked at her. "It turned out that they had filmed themselves while they were—well, you know." I cringed. "And he was using the video for blackmail so she would give him money."

Ally grimaced.

"These last few months, Nicole has been trying to make me give her money to pay off the guy. When I refused, she blackmailed me too."

"She did what?" Ally said, her voice rising in outrage.

I nodded. "Yeah. It was really shitty. She threatened to leak personal information about me on Twitter."

Ally's expression shifted from indignation to dawning comprehension and her eyes grew. "Is that why you revealed Saul's real identity?"

"You know about that?" I asked.

She shrugged. "I might have checked your Twitter feed a few times since I left." A sly smile crossed her face. "The picture of you and Danny was sweet."

I looked at her disbelievingly. She had kept following me on social media during all this time. The news warmed my heart and my lips stretched into the beginning of a smile.

"Anyway," I continued. "I guess Nicole didn't get the money she needed, because last week the video hit the Internet. I guess by now the faculty has heard about it."

"What's going to happen to her?"

"I don't know." I shrugged. "I suppose she'll get fired from Seattle University. I don't reckon she'll ever be hired somewhere else, not with that scandal all over the Internet."

Ally sat back, looking bewildered. After a short silence, she asked, "What about you?"

I turned to her, frowning. "What about me?"

"How do you feel about all that?"

I shrugged. "I don't feel anything, really. I'm over her. There's no room for her in my life anymore."

We both stayed silent for a while. I watched Ally. She seemed lost in thought. After a minute, she turned to me.

"Is that what you meant the other day?"

"About what?"

"When you said that things went to hell in October. Was it about Nicole? Or did something else happen?" She sat up straight, seeming worried. "Did Colonel get sick again?"

I shook my head. "Colonel is fine." I sighed. "But yes, something else happened."

I pinched the bridge of my nose. I didn't want to do that now. We had had a great day, and mentioning Maisy might spoil the mood. But I had demanded that Ally be honest with me, so I had to be too.

"I dated someone for a few days," I said. "But it didn't go well."

"What happened?"

I shrugged. "She lied to me and manipulated me. That's not something I can accept, not after what happened with Nicole."

I hoped she would leave it at that, but that was wishful thinking.

"What did she lie about?"

I made a non-committal noise.

"Come on, you can talk about it, I don't mind." Ally chuckled. "I want to know."

Ally's soft laugh threw me off balance and I looked at her. I couldn't read her face, but her eyes were shining. I cleared my throat. "Do you remember Maisy, at Danny's birthday party?"

Ally's face contracted slightly. "Yes. What about her?"

I gave her a look.

She narrowed her eyes. "You dated *her*?"

I nodded. "But then Danny told me about the conversation you and she had on the beach, so I broke it off."

Ally frowned. "You dumped her because of that?"

"I didn't dump her," I said indignantly. "Well, I did, but not in a mean way. Kind of." I cringed. "You know what I mean, right?" I sighed. "Anyway, we only dated for a few days, and I had perfectly good reasons to be angry."

"Because she told me not to stick around too long?"

I could feel my cheeks grow pink, and tried to keep a straight face, looking anywhere but at Ally.

"First, that was out of line," I said firmly. "She had no right to tell you anything. Second, that's not the only reason. She had already started playing mind games with me even before you came to San Francisco. I didn't want to be with someone who would lie to me, I've had enough of that with Nicole."

As soon as the words left my mouth, I realized how they must sound to Ally's ears, with all the secrets she had kept from me. So I hurried to explain.

"Back in July, I chatted with someone who I thought was you. That was before I received your email. That person and I texted for a while, but then they became obnoxious and started insulting Danny, and the messages became full of prejudiced bullshit. Anyway, I learned in October that it had been Maisy pretending to be you."

Ally was gaping, her eyes wide open. She closed her mouth and shook her head, frowning. "Why would she do that?"

"She said she was trying to protect me. She wanted to push me away from you. And it almost worked. If you hadn't sent me an email, I would have told you—well, her, but I didn't know that—to fuck off. And I would never have agreed to see you again."

I stopped talking. Ally was speechless, staring into space. Her face was crisp and pink. My heart started beating faster as panic rose inside me. Before I could say or do anything, Ally started laughing. Earnest, genuine laughter.

I gaped at her. "It's not funny."

She shook her head, still laughing. "I'm sorry. It's just that it sounds like high school drama."

I started laughing too. "That's exactly what Danny said."

"I can't believe you dated her."

"I didn't know about it," I defended myself. "She didn't use to be like that when we were at university. Not that I remember, at least. And after you left, she was very supportive."

Ally's laughter quieted, and she wiped her eyes. "I bet she was."

I sighed. "Anyway, that's over now. She screwed up."

Ally leaned toward me and put a hand on my cheek. "Well, I'm glad I sent you an email, if only to spare you a failed relationship with another manipulative bitch."

I chuckled. "Me too. That's the only reason I'm grateful that you emailed me."

She smiled the cheeky smile she used to give me in August. We stared into each other's eyes for a few seconds, then my eyes dropped to her lips. I cleared my throat and turned my head.

"I'm going to clear this up," I said in a strained voice.

I stood up, picked up the tray, and went to the kitchen. Ally joined me after a few minutes, and we tidied up together in a comfortable silence.

21

TRUST

As time went by, Ally slowly started getting better. She had appointments with Dr. Kwan twice a week, had come running with me a few times, and had started eating more. She was looking better day after day. No alcohol, a few good nights' sleep and a few square meals worked wonders.

Three weeks after Thanksgiving, I received a surprise visit from my parents, who had just come back from their cruise. I had planned on visiting them during the weekend, but they decided they couldn't wait to see me.

I opened the door and froze when I saw them standing there, huge grins on their tanned faces, and paper bags in hand.

"What are you doing here?" I said as a way of hello.

"That's a nice way to greet us," my father grunted. The grin on his face belittled his reprimand, though.

My mother hugged me and walked past me, not waiting for me to invite her in.

"Colonel," she called. "Come here, baby. Come give Nana a kiss."

I hurried behind my mother, just as Ally was coming out of the kitchen.

"Oh," my mother said. "Hello, dear. You must be Ally."

To Ally's and my surprise, my mother rushed forward and took Ally in her arms, hugging her tight. Ally looked at me over my mother's shoulder, looking every bit like a rabbit caught in headlights. She raised her arms hesitantly and hugged my mother back.

"Hi," she said, her voice shaking slightly.

My mother held Ally at arm's length to look at her. "It's so nice to finally meet you. Steve has told us a lot about you."

Ally's eyes darted to me. I winced and discreetly shook my head, trying to silently tell her I hadn't said that much.

"You look lovely," my mother added, with her very maternal spontaneity that never failed to unease me. "I can see why Steve cares so much about you."

Ally smiled softly. "Thank you. It's a pleasure to meet you." Two pink spots appeared on her cheeks. "And I care about him a lot, too," she added softly.

We all sat in the living room, my parents sharing the couch while Ally and I squeezed onto the armchair.

Colonel darted out of the laundry room and jumped onto my mother's lap, purring and throwing my dad challenging glares.

"There you are, baby boy," my mother cooed.

I elbowed Ally gently. "You have competition."

She chuckled, but she sounded strained. I stood up, taking her hand. "We'll go and make some coffee."

I walked out of the living room, not letting go of Ally. Once in the kitchen, I turned to her. Her face was a bit tense, and her eyes were wide. She still looked like a rabbit ready to flee.

"I'll go for a walk so you can talk to your parents," she said in a low voice.

I gently tucked her hair behind her left ear.

"Please, stay," I said quietly. "They might leave sooner if they think they're intruding. Or they might not." I shrugged. "You never know with my mother."

"They won't mind my presence?" she asked.

I shook my head, smiling. "I think my mother already loves you."

She smiled a bit hesitantly.

"What did you tell them about me?" she whispered.

"Nothing much, I promise. Please, stay. I'm sure they want to get to know you."

She breathed out, puffing her cheeks, then nodded.

Without thinking, I leaned down and pressed my lips to hers in a soft kiss. Then I froze. I took a step back. "I'm sorry. I don't know what came over me."

Ally's face was pink. She seemed to melt on the spot. From what, I wasn't sure—until she stepped toward me and kissed me back. Another quick peck on the lips.

She smiled. "Nothing to be sorry for."

I started the coffee machine and prepared a tray with the muffins that Ally and I had made the day before, and we went back to the living room, both still a bit pink in the face.

My parents had taken about a million pictures on their trip, and had also bought souvenirs for Colonel and me. They even gave Ally a thin bracelet they had bought on the Samoan Islands. How had they known Ally would still be here, I had no idea. Knowing my mother, she bought it on impulse and would have given it to someone else if Ally had left. When Ally opened her gift, her eyes became watery and she hugged both my parents.

They left about an hour later, but not before inviting Ally to our Christmas dinner two weeks later.

"I'll try to make it," Ally promised.

That had me wondering. When my parents were gone, I asked her, "Will you still be here for Christmas?"

Ally looked embarrassed. "I don't know. I don't want to overstay my welcome, so it's up to you to decide."

I looked at her, feeling strangely warm inside. "I'd love for you to be there. That is, if you want to."

She nodded. "I'd like that." She paused and bit her lip. "I want you to know, I don't want to leave, but at some point, I'll have to. My visa expires in March. And there are a lot of things I need to take care of in France. My job, my apartment, all my stuff." She winced and lifted a hand to her forehead. "I have no idea how I'm going to deal with everything." She huffed out a strained laugh and dropped her hand.

My stomach clenched. "What's going to happen to us when you go back home?"

She shrugged. "You tell me. What do you want?"

I had to swallow past the ball of nerves that had lodged in my throat.

"You," I breathed out. I cleared my throat. "I want to keep seeing you. I know you still have a lot to deal with, I get that. I'm not asking you to move in, or even to come and live in the States. I know your life is in France. But maybe you can promise me that we'll see each other again?"

Ally put her arms around my neck.

"I'll promise you more than that," she whispered.

She stepped on tiptoes and kissed me. A volcano erupted in my chest. I held her tight against me. I think she intended the kiss to be soft and short, but I deepened it immediately, not releasing my grip on her. When we broke the kiss, we were both a bit breathless.

"What does that mean?" I asked.

"I promise I'll come back as soon as I can to be with you."

***

"You know you don't need to buy presents for anyone," I told Ally.

We were at the mall, shopping for Christmas presents, and Ally was starting to freak out completely because she couldn't find any good ideas for gifts.

"I can't show up empty-handed, that's rude," she said.

We were spending Christmas with my parents in two days. Ally insisted she wanted to get a present for everyone. Everyone meant my parents, my grandmother and my cousin. Also, Danny and Sam, since we would see them in the evening on Christmas Day.

"I've got presents," I said. "We can say it's from both of us."

She looked at me with an outraged look that made me burst out laughing.

Ally had been back for a month now, and she was looking better and better. She still had weekly sessions with Dr. Kwan and still had night terrors, but they were coming further and further apart. We had also gotten a lot closer. Not in the passionate way we had known before. This thing that was now between us—I was reluctant to call it a relationship—was tender. We still slept in separate rooms, and I was fine with that, even though my body was craving her touch. But she clearly needed things to go slow. For my part, I wanted to be sure of her feelings for me before getting my heart more involved.

"Will you stop making fun of me and help me?" she said in a slightly angry voice.

"Sorry." I leaned down and kissed her forehead. "I'm not making fun of you, I promise."

"So, gifts?"

"Do you still have the pictures you took at Danny's birthday party?" I asked.

Ally frowned. "I think so. They should still be on my phone."

"Do you have a nice one of Danny and Sam together?"

Ally mused. "I can remember taking a nice photo of them near the fire." She rummaged through her bag and fished out her phone. "Let's see." She scrolled down her gallery for a while. "Aha!"

She turned her phone to me. On the screen was a photo of Danny and Sam, standing in front of each other, smiling. They weren't hugging, but their bodies were touching. They were standing behind the fire, and the gold light of the flames illuminated their faces in a soft, orange light contrasting with the pink glow of the setting sun behind them. It was a gorgeous picture.

"It's perfect," I said. "You can have it printed and framed. I think they would love that."

Ally nodded. "That's a great idea. Okay, that's one. What about your grandmother?"

"Chocolate," I said with no hesitation.

"Great. And your parents?"

"My dad loves whiskey, he's always keen to try new brands. And I know my mother would love a new aloe vera plant since Colonel killed her last one recently."

Ally was staring at me, her face scrunched up in a look of disgust.

"What's wrong?" I asked.

"First," she lifted one finger in the air. "Your cat killed a plant?"

"Yes. More than one, frankly."

Ally nodded, her brows still furrowed. "Second," she lifted a second finger. "You've had good ideas for gifts all this time?"

I grinned. "I did."

Ally's nose scrunched up even more. She lifted a third finger. "Third, you let me freak out all day long for nothing."

I nodded. "That's correct."

Ally lowered two fingers, keeping the middle one in the air. "You see that? That's how much I hate you right now."

I burst out laughing. I put an arm around her shoulder and pulled her to me for a quick kiss. "I know you do."

Ally leaned into me and kissed me again.

"But I don't, really," she said. "I kind of like you, actually."

Warm, fuzzy tingles ran down my arms.

"You kind of like me?" I asked casually, trying to play it cool.

Ally smiled softly. "I really kind of do."

I leaned down and kissed her deeply. I didn't care that we were in the middle of an alley in a shopping mall. I didn't care that people were walking briskly all around us, under pressure from gift-hunting, sometimes bumping into us. I didn't care that Mariah Carey's Christmas song was getting on my nerves. All I cared about was this wonderful woman in my arms, who had just told me she liked me.

I broke the kiss and looked down at her. "I kind of like you, too."

She smiled. "I know you do." She stepped back and sighed. "Let's go, the gifts won't buy themselves."

***

Ally and I celebrated Christmas Eve at home. We didn't make a big deal out of it. I hadn't planned on putting up a tree, especially since I knew Colonel would make a mess of it, but I asked Ally whether she wanted us to buy one or not. She said she was fine with no tree and no gifts—just us, Colonel and food. I had already gotten her a gift, but she didn't need to know that.

We bought a lot of snacks and champagne, and blueberries for the monster. At five in the evening, we showered, put on our pajamas, and settled on the couch. The coffee table was full of things to eat, and *Home Alone* was playing on TV.

Colonel was curled up on his brand-new cushion, wearing a stupid Christmas pullover Ally had bought him. When I'd seen it, I had laughed so loud the cat had gotten scared and run away. I'd been sure that Ally wouldn't be able to put it on Colonel, since he didn't allow me to brush his fur without giving me a few scratches. But I'd been wrong. I should have known. Ally could do anything she wanted to my cat, and he would let her. So she had squeezed him into his cat sweater —well, dog sweater actually, there was nothing made

282

for cats that fitted him, he was so massive—and had rewarded his good behavior with a few blueberries and kisses on the nose.

When *Home Alone* was over, and we had eaten all the snacks, I opened the drawer on the coffee table and took out a small, square box wrapped in Christmas paper, and handed it to Ally.

She looked at it, then at my face. "I thought we said no gifts," she said.

I shook my head. "*You* said no gifts. I didn't say anything. And I had already bought this." I put the box on her leg. "I promise it's not much."

Ally took the box and unwrapped it one corner at a time. She carefully took out the thin silver chain and stared at the small sun pendant. She lifted her gaze to mine.

"Not much?" she said in a strained voice.

I smiled. "When I saw it, I knew I had to get it for you."

"Why?"

I pointed at the pendant. "You're like sunshine, Ally. You shine so brightly that the world around you seems more beautiful. And you've brought so much light into my life." I touched her cheek with the tips of my fingers. "I've always thought of you as my own, private sun."

Ally's lower lip started trembling and her eyes filled with tears. I took the chain out of the box, put it around her neck, and clasped it. Ally's hand immediately went to her chest, and she touched the pendant.

"Do you like it?" I asked anxiously, using the pad of my thumb to wipe the tear that was rolling down her cheek.

She nodded. "I love it," she said in a whisper.

She leaned toward me and kissed me. When we broke the kiss, she leaned back.

"I'm sorry I didn't get you anything," she said, her voice still strained.

I put my arms around her. "You're still here, that's all I need."

We spent the night playing games, eating and drinking, and occasionally throwing blueberries for Colonel to catch. When *Kiss Kiss Bang Bang* started on TV, we settled on the couch to watch it. Ten minutes after the film had started, I leaned sideways on the couch and dragged Ally down with me, taking her in my arms and spooning her.

I wanted to be close to her again. I was craving her touch, longing for the passion we'd had during the summer. I loved how things were going between us. We were building the foundation for an actual relationship. But I wanted more.

I started kissing Ally's skin. Gentle, feather-like kisses on her most sensitive spots; on her neck, behind her ear, in the curve of her shoulder.

"Steve," she whispered.

I could feel her body tensing against mine. I stopped kissing her and leaned back. "Sorry," I whispered.

She turned around in my arms and looked at me. Her eyes were darker than usual and her pupils dilated.

"Kiss me," she said softly.

So I did.

We didn't get to see the end of the film. But I didn't mind one bit.

When I woke up the next morning, Ally was still lying in my arms, our naked bodies pressed together.

"Best Christmas ever," I murmured, making her giggle.

***

I spent the holidays floating on a cloud of happiness. Christmas at my parents' and at Danny's had gone great, and everyone had loved her gifts. Ally had been nervous before going to Danny's, worrying about how they would act toward her. But they had welcomed her back into their life without batting an eyelid. We spent New Year's Eve at Danny's again, and had lunch with my parents the next day. Ally got along with everyone, and everyone seemed to love her in return. It all felt too perfect to be true.

My bubble of happiness burst a few days after New Year. Ally and I were lying in bed, facing each other, when her face suddenly grew serious.

"I'm thinking of going back to France in a few days," she said.

I tensed. "I thought your visa expired in March."

She nodded. "It does. But I have a lot to sort out, and the sooner I do it, the better. I think I'm ready to move on with my life."

"When do you think you'll go?" I tried to keep my tone casual, but my heart was hammering in my chest.

"I don't know yet. I need to book a plane ticket." She propped up on her elbow to look at me. "I promise we'll keep in touch, Steve."

A heavy weight fell on my chest, and I had to close my eyes at the pain. "I know," I whispered.

Her hand touched my cheek softly. "I don't know if I'll be able to get a new visa soon, but I'll try. You know I want to come back." Her lips fell onto mine. "I'll always want to come back to you."

I opened my eyes and looked at her, falling into the depths of her light gray eyes.

"Come on, let's shower," she said.

She got up and dragged me to my feet, and I followed her into the bathroom.

***

One short week later, I helped Ally pack her bags and load them in her car. I drove her to the airport, and would drive back home without her. We had agreed I would keep her car at my house until she came back.

Once out of the car, I took her hand and interlocked our fingers. I didn't let go of her until she had to go through security and I could go no further. I tried to keep my eyes dry when we kissed goodbye, but I couldn't. A tear rolled down my cheek, and Ally wiped it away.

"I'll text you when I land," she said.

"Can you call me instead?" I asked.

She shook her head. "I think I'll need some time before I can talk to anyone. It's going to be hard, going back to France."

I nodded. I understood where she came from, but it was hard to hear anyway.

"I'll keep having video sessions with Dr. Kwan every other week, and I promise I'll text you regularly."

I had to trust her. As hard as it was after everything we'd been through, after her leaving me twice already, I had to try. I had to give us a chance.

I watched her go through security, turn back, and wave one last time before she was out of sight.

22

FULFILLMENT

My hands were shaking with nerves. I was sitting in a coffee shop at the airport, waiting for Ally's plane to land. I couldn't stop my leg from jumping up and down, which got me some annoyed glares from the people around me. I knew it was still too early for Ally's plane, but I couldn't help looking at the people coming out of Customs to see if she was among them.

The last three months had been hard. For three weeks after Ally had gone back to France, I hadn't heard much from her. A quick text every few days saying she was alright, but that was it. She never gave me any details on what she was doing, or when she was planning to come back, and I didn't ask. She needed to grieve on her own terms, and I got that. But I was getting more and more anxious.

Until she finally called me in February. She told me she had emptied her apartment and sold most of the things she had shared with Simon, and was now trying to sell the apartment itself. After that, we talked on the phone almost every day, when our schedules and the time difference allowed it. Again, she never mentioned coming back, and I still didn't ask.

During all that time, I kept busy. I went to Los Angeles to work on the second season of the cartoon I had worked on in July, received an Audie award for my narration work, started collaborating with a new up-and-coming author, and gained the exclusivity for the narration of her series of fantasy novels. I also helped Danny and Sam plan the wedding, which would take place on April 4, and organized the best bachelor's party ever—not that I was bragging, but Sam did point out that I was the best best man ever, after all.

I hadn't heard anything from Nicole. I knew she had been fired from the university, and I had expected some retribution from her, but none had come. Not a peep. It was like she had vanished into thin air. Maybe she was finally out of my life for good.

At long last, at the end of March, Ally had told me that she would be flying back to San Francisco the day before the wedding.

One hour and two disgusting coffees later, Ally's plane finally landed. She arrived very shortly afterward, trailing a huge suitcase behind her. Her hair had grown out and now reached her armpits. Her dyed strands weren't green anymore, but a deep blue.

I stood up as soon as I saw her. Her eyes were scanning the crowd, looking for me. I raised my arm to wave at her. When she saw me, her face split into a huge grin and she rushed toward me, as fast as she could go with the weight of her suitcase. I did the same, not caring about the people I shoved away. When we stood facing each other, we stopped and stared at each other for a long minute, without saying a word. My whole body was shaking with the need to touch her.

Then, we started laughing. I cradled her face with my hands and crushed my lips to hers in a searing kiss. I didn't care that we were in the middle of the airport terminal. Nor that we were surrounded by people and families. I only cared about her.

When we broke apart, I leaned my forehead against hers, closed my eyes, and breathed deeply, inhaling her earthy, spring-like smell. And I knew I was home again.

"I missed you," she whispered.

I opened my eyes and looked at her. Her eyes were bright, shining with tears.

"I missed you too, beautiful." I kissed her softly. "Let's go home."

On our way out, I kept my eyes on Ally. She looked a lot younger than she had before she left. Her skin was glowing and there were no bags under her eyes. She had put on a few much-needed pounds, making her face less gaunt and her cheeks almost chubby.

"You look good," I said.

"You, too." She pinched my bicep. "You're ripped," she said.

"Well, yeah," I said, trying not to sound proud. "I've been exercising a lot."

She kissed me again. I saw the thin silver chain around her neck and touched the pendant.

"You're still wearing it," I said, my throat tightening with emotion.

She put her hand on mine. "I'm always wearing it. It helped me a lot in France. When things got too hard, I touched it."

I stared into her eyes, my stomach flip-flopping wildly.

Ally smiled. "So, what time do we have to leave tomorrow?" she asked.

I cleared my throat. "The ceremony is at ten, but we need to pick up Danny and drive him to the wedding location, so we have to get up at five.

Ally groaned.

"Yeah, sorry, I know it's early. But I'm the best man. I have to be there to support Danny."

"In case he's having cold feet?"

I scoffed. "That's never going to happen. But he might need help to do his bowtie."

When we arrived home, I barely had time to open the door when a flash of yellow fur passed in front of me, and Colonel crashed into Ally's legs. She almost fell to the ground, but caught herself and grabbed Colonel to hug him. He kept meowing and purring, trying to knead her chest and lick her face all at once. He was so overwhelmed with emotion at seeing her again that he seemed not to know what to do. I understood his feelings perfectly well.

We didn't have much time to speak that night. Ally was jet-lagged, and went to bed early, wanting to be in good shape for the wedding. I followed her and cradled her in my arms. We fell asleep spooning, and she slept through the night. No nightmares, no screaming, no waking up early.

When my alarm woke us up the next morning at an ungodly hour, we were both too sleepy to do much talking either. There were so many questions I wanted to ask her. What happened in France? How was she feeling? How long was she going to stay here? But the grumpy look on her face shut me up and I put up with waiting for the right time.

The right time never seemed to come, though. After a quick shower and breakfast—and a gallon of coffee each—we packed our clothes for the wedding, and went to Danny's house. Sam wasn't there, having stayed with her cousin for the night. Danny was jittery with nerves. I made him and Ally some coffee, and sat behind the wheel of Danny's car. The hour-long drive to the wedding location seemed to last forever. Danny kept wiggling in his seat and rambling about the day to come, and I kept glancing at a giggling Ally in the rearview mirror.

When we arrived, Ally joined Sam and Jill in the bridal suite, while I took care of Danny. Sam and he had agreed to respect tradition and not see each other before the ceremony. But Danny couldn't keep still. He pretended to have to pee, to need a drink, even to faint, to try and escape my watchful eye and sneak into Sam's room. He was so annoying that I considered tying him down.

"You're a real child, Danny," I said exasperatedly. "Don't act like you didn't see her yesterday. You can wait for another hour, can't you?"

He grinned broadly and tackled me to the ground.

We got dressed, and he did indeed need help with the bowtie. We took a couple of selfies to post on social media. Both he and I were more and more visible on Twitter and Instagram, and the readers loved our bromance story.

When we had both dressed up, Danny's father entered the room and I left, giving them some private time. I wanted to see Ally, anyway. I knocked on the door of the bridal suite, and heard some shuffling before the door cracked open and Jill's face appeared.

"It's just me," I said.

Jill opened the door, and I walked in.

Sam turned around to face me. She was wearing a long, vintage dress in a soft gold color, and her long wavy red hair was decorated with golden pearls.

"Sam, you look gorgeous." I went to her and kissed her on the cheek.

"How's Danny?" she asked.

"He's a pain in my ass," I said.

She chuckled.

"He's fine. He's with his dad, so I thought I'd leave them alone."

I turned around then and saw Ally. She was wearing a knee-length silk dress, in a deep blue that matched the strands in her hair. The light gray of her eyes was enhanced by the dark makeup she had put on. She was wearing no other jewelry than the necklace I had given her. I took in the sight of her and she smiled shyly.

I jumped slightly when Sam cleared her throat, and suddenly remembered we weren't alone.

"Maybe you two need to talk outside," Sam said. "The sexual tension between you is making me horny."

We left the room, ignoring the women's peals of laughter. As soon as the door closed behind her, I pushed Ally back until her back hit the wall. I ran my nose along her neck and nibbled her earlobe.

"You look hot as hell," I murmured in a low, husky voice.

We kissed passionately. We jumped apart when a door slammed close by, and Danny's voice came from the end of the corridor, calling my name.

I sighed and took a step back.

"I have to go." I winced, resisting the urge to readjust myself. "That hard-on is not going to be embarrassing at all during the ceremony."

Ally smiled slyly. "I promise I'll take care of it later."

I groaned and closed my eyes. "Thanks for the image."

Ally shrugged. "You're welcome. Just something to think about at the chapel."

I rolled my eyes, smiling. "That's not inappropriate at all."

I went back to Danny's room. Half an hour later, it was finally time for the ceremony.

Danny and I took our places at the front and waved at the people sitting in the chapel. It was a small, intimate ceremony. There were Danny's and Sam's families and close friends, and a few work friends. I noticed Maisy sitting at the back, next to a brown-haired man I had never seen. When Maisy looked at me, her cheeks grew slightly pink, and she smiled shyly. We hadn't spoken since the whole debacle in November. I knew I would have to face her at some point, but that didn't have to be now. I was glad she seemed to have moved on, though.

My eyes landed on Ally then, and stayed there. She was so radiant I couldn't look away.

I spent most of the ceremony looking at Ally talking with the people around her, smiling and crying during the vows. Sam made the crowd laugh during her vows, finally telling Danny about the fanfictions she wrote as a teenager. He laughed and cried, and had her promise to let him read them. When the ceremony was over, we gathered outside for wedding pictures. Ally tried to stay away, but she finally gave in to Sam's insisting demand and joined us for a few photos. I took her hand and didn't let go until we were seated at the head table.

After a few hours of speeches, eating and drinking, music started, and Danny and Sam stood up for their first dance as a married couple. As expected by anyone who knew Sam, they didn't slow dance. Instead, they got into a wild rock and roll, until the music segued into a country song and everyone joined for a line dance.

I leaned down and whispered to Ally, "Do you want to dance or go for a walk?"

"We can dance later," she whispered back. "Let's go out for a bit."

I took her hand and led her toward the small lake in the garden. We sat on the wooden bench, looking at the sun setting over the water. The soft thumping of the music in the reception hall, and the rippling of the water were soothing.

"Now that we're finally alone, will you tell me what happened in France?" I asked.

Ally turned to me. "I told you already when we talked on the phone, didn't I?"

I shrugged. "You didn't say much. You're trying to sell your apartment, that's all I know."

Her eyes opened wide. "Oh, I forgot to tell you, I've sold it already."

I raised my eyebrows. "That fast?"

"Yeah. There's still some paperwork to do, I'll have to go back during the summer to sign the deed of sale, but basically, it's done."

"That's good news," I said. After a few seconds of silence, I asked, "What about work?"

Ally's smile grew wider. "I found a job here in San Francisco."

My heart all but exploded in my chest. "You did?"

She nodded vigorously. "I applied to all the schools in the area, and I've been hired as a substitute teacher at Stuart Hall High School. Their French teacher has just retired, and they need someone to fill in. I start on Monday. It's only for a few weeks, until the end of the school year, but that's a start. Maybe they'll hire me again next year."

I shook my head, trying to clear my head. "So you're staying?"

"Yes, I'm on a work visa for now."

"And where will you live?"

She looked at me and said in a soft voice, "I was hoping I could stay with you."

That was so much better than anything I had imagined. Even with the school year ending in two months, that still meant two months with her living at my place. That was what I would focus on—the silver lining, right?

"And after that?" I asked.

She smiled the brightest, liveliest smile I had ever seen. "I have no fucking idea."

ABOUT THE AUTHOR

As far back as she can remember, Rory has been making up stories in her head at night. It started as a way to help her fall asleep – sometimes it worked, and sometimes the stories invaded her dreams. With time, those stories took up too much space, so she decided to write them down. By giving a voice to her fictional characters, she makes these stories real, and her mind can be at peace again... until the next story pops up and fills in the empty space.

Rory lives in Belgium with her lop-ear rabbit Lulu, and a brood of hens. She works as a teacher, runs a local market gardening business, writes all kinds of stories, and creates jewelry – she might have a touch of hyperactivity. She still manages to find some time to do what she loves: reading, cooking, working out, photography, and weirdly, ironing.